WILD KIDS

Modern Chinese Literature from Taiwan

wild kids

Two Novels About Growing Up

CHANG TA-CHUN

Translated from the Chinese

by Michael Berry

COLUMBIA UNIVERSITY PRESS   NEW YORK

Columbia University Press wishes to express its appreciation for assistance given by the Chiang
Ching-kuo Foundation for International Scholarly Exchange, the Council for Cultural Affairs, and
the Himalaya Foundation in the preparation of the translation and in the publication of this series.

Quotations on pages 122 and 123 are from *The Book of Common Prayer* (New RSV)
(London: Oxford University Press, 1990).

Quotation on page 12 from *The Songs of the South: An Anthology of Ancient Chinese Poems
by Qu Yuan and Other Poets*, translated, annotated, and introduced by David Hawkes
(New York: Penguin Classics, 1985).

Quotation on page 20 from Jean-Paul Sartre, *Nausea*, trans. Lloyd Alexander,
introduction by Hayden Carruth. (New York: New Directions, 1964).

Interior art reproduced from the Taiwanese editions published by UNITAS,
Wo meimei (1993) and *Ye haizi* (1996).

Columbia University Press
Publishers Since 1893
New York   Chichester, West Sussex

Library of Congress Cataloging-in-Publication Data
Chang, Ta-ch'un, 1957–
   [Yeh hai tzu. English]
   Wild kids : two novels about growing up / Chang Ta-chun ; translated from the
Chinese by Michael Berry.
        p.   cm. — (Modern Chinese literature from Taiwan)
   Contents: My kid sister — Wild child.
   ISBN 0–231–12096–6
   1. Chang, Ta-ch'un, 1957– —Translations into English. I. Chang, Ta-ch'un, 1957–
Wo mei mei. English. II. Berry, Michael. III. Title. IV. Series.
PL2837.T3 Y4413 2000
895.1'352—dc21   99–088264

Contents

Chang Ta-chun[1] is not just a writer; in his native Taiwan he is a cultural phenomenon. He is one of the rare literary figures on the island to have crossed the bridge from popular writer to pop culture icon. During the eighties and nineties Chang's image moved from the jackets of his books to the sides of public buses, life-size cardboard bookstore displays, and ultimately every television set in Taiwan. Chang Ta-chun hosted and produced two popular television shows in the nineties, *Navigating the Sea of Literature* (*Zhongheng shuhai*) and *Super Traveler* (*Chaoji lüxingjia*). A press conference held in 1996 to announce the publication of *Wild Child* even made it into the entertainment section of Chinese-language newspapers, placing Chang's image right alongside those of Chow Yun-fat and Jackie Chan.

Although seemingly comfortable in the spotlight, Chang is by training a literary critic and by profession a writer. Born in 1957, Chang Ta-chun attended Fu Jen Catholic University where he pursued both undergraduate and graduate degrees in Chinese literature. A voracious reader, he has been influenced by Nobel laureate Gabriel García Márquez and the acclaimed author of *The Name of the Rose*, Umberto Eco. Chang Ta-chun began to win acclaim as a writer with his very first short story, "Suspended" (*Xuandang*), published in 1976 when he was just nineteen years old. Following two years of compulsory military service, Chang worked as a reporter and editor at one of Taiwan's leading newspapers, *China Times*, and eventually returned to his alma mater as a lecturer. Meanwhile, his writing career flourished, and by the mid to late eighties he had firmly established himself as Taiwan's most inventive and creative writer.[2]

Chang's major, breakthrough success came in 1986 with his second collection of short stories, *Apartment Building Tour Guide* (*Gongyu daoyou*). The thirteen stories included were a rare display of literary creativity by an increasingly productive writer. The title story of the collection is an intricately woven portrait of how a group of seemingly alienated and disconnected urbanites living in an apartment complex in contemporary Taipei unknowingly affect one another's lives. Fellow writer and critic Yang Chao (Yang Zhao) notes that it was with the publication of this book that "Chang Ta-chun ceased to cover up his impatience with traditional narrative conventions"[3] and embarked upon a new linguistic and literary voyage.

Two years later, Chang produced a follow-up collection of stories hailed by critics. *Lucky Worries About His Country* (*Sixi youguo*) features the award-winning story "The General's Monument" (*Jiangjun bei*), a historical parable of sorts about a retired general who can travel through time. First published on the eve of the lifting of martial law in Taiwan,[4] "The General's Monument" not only struck a sensitive chord in readers but also foreshadowed Chang's later politically and current event-inspired literary experiments.

Chang's literary field of vision expanded even further when he produced a volume of stories written in the spirit of the knight-errant or *wuxia* novels of Jin Yong, *Happy Thieves* (*Huanxi zei*), in early 1989 and a collection of science fiction stories, *Pathological Changes* (*Bingbian*), in February 1990. Chang's arguably most inventive effort, however, was begun in late 1988. Hailed as the world's first "spontaneous news novel," *The Grand Liar* (*Da shuohuang jia*) was part hard-boiled detective fiction, part political satire, part fact, part fiction. From December 12, 1988 until June 13, 1989 Chang went to his office at the *China Times* each morning and wrote the morning's news directly into that day's segment of his novel, which would be published in the evening edition of the newspaper. The result was a spontaneous mixture of news, politics, history, and literature that served to challenge and deconstruct traditional narrative and literary structures.

What *The Grand Liar* lacks in plot it recovers in ingenuity and form, making it one of the decade's crowning works of Chinese fiction.

Chang followed *The Grand Liar* with two additional full-length political novels, *No One Wrote a Letter to the Colonel* (*Meiren xiezin gei shangxiao*) (1994) and *Disciples of the Liar* (*Sahuang de xintu*) (1996). The latter work, marketed as the "Taiwanese *Satanic Verses*," was published to coincide with the first-ever free presidential election in Chinese history in 1996. The novel is a highly satiric journey into the mind of Li Zhengnan, a clearly recognizable literary incarnation of Taiwanese president Lee Teng-hui. It was Chang's most heavily marketed and overtly commercial literary venture.

In between his politically inspired novels of the early to mid-nineties, the ever-productive Chang still found time to give birth to a literary alter ego. In 1992 he published his first novel under the pen name Big Head Spring (Datou Chun). In both structure and voice, *The Weekly Journal of Young Big Head Spring* (*Shaonian Datou Chun de shenghuo zhouji*) was yet another major turn for Chang Ta-chun. The novel is a fictitious collection of mandatory weekly journal entries written in the tone and style of a middle school student. The utter frankness and tell-it-as-it-is nature of the narrative are also a stark and refreshing contrast to the world of fictions and lies Chang constructed in *The Grand Liar* and *Disciples of the Liar*. Upon the work's publication, noted critic Pang-yuan Chi (Qi Banyuan) even went so far as to state, "Chang Ta-chun's speed in inventing new writing tactics can be compared with America's current speed at which it produces high-tech products."[5] *The Weekly Journal of Young Big Head Spring* not only went on to become Chang Ta-chun's best-selling work to date,[6] but also inaugurated a series of novels by Big Head Spring. The second and third installments of Chang's Big Head Spring trilogy, *My Kid Sister* and *Wild Child*, both postmodern versions of the "formation novel" (*Bildungsroman*), are the focus of this volume.

Published in 1993, *My Kid Sister* was a stylistic reinvention of Big Head Spring. Although thematically it still dealt with the frustrations and woes of youth, the journal format and Chang's sarcastic teenage narrative voice were gone. The Big Head Spring of *My Kid Sister* is a mature twenty-seven-year-old writer delivering an unforgettable document of growing up in

Taiwan in the eighties. Ingeniously crafted, the novel is temporally complex, meticulously interweaving the events between the birth of the narrator's younger sister and her abortion at the age of nineteen. *My Kid Sister* is a portrait of both the sorrows and the hysterics of youth.

"Compared with the way in which *The Weekly Journal* serves as a direct mouthpiece [for the youth], the narrative style of *My Kid Sister* is clearly much more intricate," writes Yang Chao. "In weekly installments, *The Weekly Journal* writes reality and records the present. *My Kid Sister*, on the other hand, is continually chasing after the past, summoning up memories, and amid the repetitive voices of yesterday, carries an ever-present confessional overtone of varying subtleties."[7] The result of this narrative maturity is, ironically, an enhanced feeling of uncertainty, not just of memory but of meaning. No longer does the narrator seem to know what went wrong, or why. This feeling of powerlessness is further enhanced by playful discussions about fate, psychology, existentialism, and genetics. Chang Ta-chun creates a wave of sarcasm, wit, and humor that inundates *My Kid Sister*; however, beneath the laughter lies a somber portrait documenting the loss of innocence and the deconstruction of a family.

Wild Child is the darkest chapter in the trilogy; it intimately traces the protagonist, Big Head Spring, as he drops out of school, runs away from home, and seeks out a new life in the Taiwanese underworld. Although all the works in the trilogy are written in the first person, thematically similar, and feature the character Big Head, readers will be hard pressed to identify this "wild child" with his beloved counterpart in *The Weekly Journal*. We would perhaps better view Big Head as an allegorical symbol (or sociological phenomenon) than as a recurring character.

In *Wild Child*, an unbridled, rebellious, and at times surprisingly mature fourteen-year-old Big Head Spring embarks upon an adventure that will forever change his life. In both style and content, *Wild Child* will inevitably invite comparisons with the modern American classic *The Catcher in the Rye*. Both protagonists are teenage school dropouts who run away from home to explore the decadent side of big city life. However, unlike Holden Caulfield, who is continually given second chances, Big Head gets none. In this entertaining yet heavy-handed portrayal of Big Head and other members of his gang, the author ultimately testifies to a new form of spiritual and cultural bankruptcy.

According to Chang Ta-chun, the central theme of the work is "escaping," from society and from oneself. "As Annie, the débutante of *Wild Child*, says, just as 'all the cars in the junkyard were wasted before they were even delivered there,'"[8] so Big Head was also wasted before he ever ran away from home. From the beginning, the characters are not simply delinquent but more broadly, spiritually dead (thus the mention of ghosts from the onset of the novel). *Wild Child* is as much a portrait of death and wandering ghosts as it is of wasted youth. "Death," says Chang Ta-chun, "is what starts everything, as long as one keeps 'escape' in mind."[9]

The literary mindscape of Chang Ta-chun is a unique and complex collage of news, history, politics, literature, personal experience, and, sometimes, irony. In 1999 both of the "wild kids" followed in the footsteps of their creator and successfully made the leap into pop culture— *My Kid Sister* was transformed into a major stage production in Taipei, while *Wild Child* was adapted into a made-for-TV movie. The tales of the "wild kids" have continued to captivate and to evolve, even beyond the realm of the written word. *Wild Kids* humorously and insightfully captures not only a slice of Taiwanese life, but also what it means to grow up.

This work began with a handshake just before the subway doors closed between the author and myself beneath the streets of Manhattan in May 1998. Thus began my one-year period of cohabitation with Chang Ta-chun's "wild kids." Since that time, a number of individuals have aided in making this project a reality. My sincere thanks to Chen Lai-hsing, Chang Ta-chun, and Push for generously allowing their artwork to be reproduced. Thanks to Steve Bradbury for suggesting the jacket art and taking the time to secure the rights from the artist. Lois Tai and Grace Sun provided valuable assistance with Taiwanese phrases that appeared in the novels. Thanks to Carlos Rojas, Joshua Tanzer, the two anonymous readers for Columbia University Press, and especially Leslie Kriesel, my editor at Columbia University Press, for their careful reading and invaluable editorial and stylistic comments. I would also like to thank the faculty and students at the Department of East Asian Languages and Cultures at Columbia University for their encouragement, and Jennifer Crewe at Columbia University Press for her interest and support. Special thanks go to Professor David Der-wei Wang, who was instrumental in guiding this project to fruition, and my heartfelt appreciation to the author for his enthusiasm and his unwavering support of this translation.

NOTES

1. "Chang Ta-chun" is the spelling preferred by the author and has been used throughout. His name is rendered "Zhang Dachun" according to pinyin and "Chang Ta-ch'un" according to the Wade-Giles system.

2. Besides his fiction, Chang Ta-chun has produced several volumes of essays and literary criticism, including a 1998 book hailed as the first Chinese work on creative writing theory.

3. Yang Zhao, "Just What Are the Sorrows of Youth?—Reading Chang Ta-chun's *My Kid Sister*" (Qingchun de aichou shi zenme yihuishi?—du Datou Chun's *Wo meimei*) in *My Kid Sister* (*Wo meimei*) (Taipei: Unitas Publishing, 1993), 182.

4. The R.O.C. on Taiwan existed in a state of martial law from 1949 until 1987, when ailing president Chiang Ching-kuo lifted the decree shortly before his death.

5. "A Critical Introduction to *The Weekly Journal of Young Big Head Spring*" (Pingjie Shaonian Datou Chun de shenghuo zhouji) in *The Weekly Journal of Young Big Head Spring*, 3rd ed. (Taipei: Unitas Publishing, 1993), 174.

6. *The Weekly Journal of Young Big Head Spring* was number one on the Taiwan best-seller list for almost an entire year from its date of publication. It broke virtually every book sales record in Taiwan's publishing history.

7. Yang Zhao, "Just What Are the Sorrows of Youth?" in *My Kid Sister* (*Wo meimei*), 177.

8. Interview with the author, February 1999.

9. Ibid.

WILD KIDS

my kid sister

For my sister

It was her courage in facing the viciousness of reality that provided the abundance of precious material used in the writing of this book. As for my grandparents, parents, and everyone else, they don't necessarily have either the interest or the ability to understand this rather unsubstantial work; they would prefer to confront the other disturbances and anxieties of life.

我的禮物

A Present Just for Me

I was eight years old the year my kid sister was born. You know, when you are just around the age of eight, you get hit by virtually every stroke of bad luck out there. I ended up with a case of German measles that later turned into pneumonia—I was laid up for, must have been what, six months? During that time my parents ditched me at the run-down *juancun*[*] where my grandpa lived. Grandma made me hot chicken soup and rice with pig liver. After five meals a day of that it got to the point where even in my dreams I was coughing up chicken necks. I will always remember the strange sight of Grandma's gold-plated front teeth as she blew on the hot soup and lectured me. Puffing on the soup, she would tell me, "A bowl of soup before you eat is even better than prescription medicine. Once you're all better and get your strength back, you can go home and see your little

---

[*] Makeshift housing communities occupied by Guomindang (Nationalist Party) military personnel and their families from mainland China who came to Taiwan in 1947–49. Though they were initially intended to be temporary, thousands continued to live in the deplorable conditions of the *juancun* for several decades thereafter.

sister." (At the time my sister had yet to be born, but Grandma was already quite sure about her sex.) She made it seem as if my little sister were my present for being such a good patient.

In the beginning I really thought that if I was good and had my shots, took my medicine, ate my chicken soup and pig liver, stayed away from the window so I wouldn't get a draft—as long as I did everything that I didn't want to do and didn't do anything that I wanted to do—I would get a baby sister as a present. And then one day when my father came over to Grandpa's place with a couple jars of beef cubes, powdered milk, and all kinds of other worthless garbage, I told him that I wanted to go home. He glared back at me, saying, "Go home? Your little sister hasn't even been born yet and already you want to kill her with your pneumonia?"

Last year I went with my sister when she had her abortion, and in that gynecology ward, which reeked with the irritating fishy stench of disinfectant, I shared our father's bullshit comment with my sister for the very first time. She opened her pale cracked lips and said, "You must have fucking hated me back then." Pulling her slender hand out from underneath the sheet, she first wiped the tears from the corners of her eyes and then grabbed hold of my wrist. "I must be hateful," she said, laughing. "I've always been nothing but a despicable *wang ba dan*, haven't I?"

I have absolutely no idea where I learned the term *wang ba dan*, or just how I taught it to my sister. All I know is that the first time I used this expression it was directed at my father. Hearing that word sneak out of my mouth, my grandpa and grandma instantly screamed out in unison, "What did you say?"

"Dad's a *wang ba dan*," I repeated.

Grandpa and Grandma must have been shocked out of their wits. They immediately jumped out of their rattan chairs and came over to me. One of them glared at me with light-bulb eyes while the other squatted down to rub my forehead. They spent the entire afternoon cross-examining me on how *wang ba dan* had escaped from my mouth and explaining the origin of the term.

Grandma believed that *wang ba* referred to a turtle. Now this turtle represents any one of those johns who, after going for his share of romps in the whorehouse, starts to really hit it off with one particular prostitute. So *wang ba dan*, under normal circumstances, refers to the illegitimate child of the prostitute and the turtle. Now if I curse my father as a *wang ba dan*, that will make me a turtle grandson, and if we follow this logical progression, it will make my grandparents a turtle and a hooker. This explanation truly enriched my knowledge of the world—at least I learned "romp," "turtle grandson," and other new vocabulary words that I would later make frequent use of. What broadened my horizons even further was the fact that Grandpa disagreed—he insisted that that *wang ba* did not mean the turtle in the whorehouse, but the turtle in the ocean! He said that after sea turtles breed, the male runs off, leaving the female to lay and incubate the eggs. But the female can't do everything herself, so she gets another nearby male turtle to help out. This male turtle, who obviously has absolutely zero common sense, keeps believing that all those baby turtles are his, so he faithfully carries out all fatherly responsibilities with the utmost care. Looking at it like this, the male turtle is a worthless idiot while the female is nothing better than a prostitute; this is why, in so many people's minds, *wang ba dan* is tied to the term "bastard."

It seemed as if my grandparents had come to a bit of a disagreement as to the origin of the term *wang ba dan*. This apparently stemmed from the fact that Grandma felt that the first male turtle was truly the most despicable figure in the story. She thought that he took advantage of the mother turtle, leaving her to take care of all those baby turtles; so how could she be compared to a prostitute? Moreover, that second male who came to help out wasn't bad; at least he knew what loyalty was. And that little *wang ba* in the egg, what did he do wrong? How can you compare him to a bastard? It's not like he doesn't have a father, his father is that first male turtle, so just what is so illegitimate about him? The more Grandma spoke, the more furious she became. In the end I couldn't figure out if she was annoyed at that male turtle, at the whole origin of the expression *wang ba dan*, or at Grandpa, who was sitting beside her violently shaking his head. In any case, she declared that she wasn't cooking dinner that night.

"It is totally unnecessary for you to get so pissed off over a bastard *wang ba!*" Grandpa exclaimed.

That was the last sentence uttered for the evening in our tattered room in the run-down *juancun*. Even today I still haven't forgotten that scene and the stunning impression that it left. As time goes by, I feel more and more that the whole thing stemmed from the simple fact that Grandma didn't know just whom she should be angry at, and all the while it was, as Grandpa said, "totally unnecessary."

During the last period of my sick stay at the dingy *juancun*, I had all but given up hope of returning home. Just like the chicken soup and pig liver, my father's temper had lost its flavor. I had even forgotten about my baby sister—the prize I was to get for coming home. Even after Grandpa ran home excitedly all the way from the hospital and confirmed Grandma's conjecture about my kid sister's sex, I still didn't think there was anything the least bit odd about it. That day was the fourteenth of April, a date my little sister would remind me of for many years to come. According to those who are experts in being thankful, birthdays are a "day of suffering" for the mother. April fourteenth was also my grandpa's day of suffering. While he was sprinting home from the hospital, he fell down, and from that day onward he needed a cane to help him walk. He also knocked out one of his front teeth, so that whenever he would speak, curse people, sing opera, or recite the holy verses in church he would always appear a bit ridiculous.

As for those elements of the comic and ridiculous that often manifested themselves in Grandpa's overly serious life, I needn't go into them. But the reason people felt he was funny while being so solemn was simply that he wanted so badly to prove that he really was an extremely earnest person. Yet every time he got close to proving just how serious he was, some comical aspect of his nature would rear its ugly head. You can imagine what it was like to see him with his missing tooth (the other front tooth was also half crooked), shouting out, "Hallelujah!" In high school, while reading through some awkward-sounding and abstruse books on existentialism, I picked up some new vocabulary words that were both peculiar and attractive. One of them was "absurd" (this term was extremely easy to adapt to daily life circumstances, much less complicated than "nothingness" and "existential"). That's right, "absurd," and it was that grandpa of mine, whose ridiculousness seemed to increase with his attempted seriousness, that enabled me to understand absurdity on an incomparable level.

As for my kid sister, she was eight years old when she first learned the term "absurd"—she used it in class to describe that little peckerhead who was using a cigarette lighter to burn the girls' ponytails in class. She and my grandfather are so different and yet so very similar. It was as if she was trying so hard to prove how funny she could be, but every time she tried to be the clown, I realized just what a serious character she really was.

Putting it like that is perhaps a bit too abstract. Here, let me give you a more concrete example: The night my sister was lying on the bed in the gynecology ward telling me how much of a *wang ba dan* she was, her eyes suddenly popped open and she said, "Did you notice? That doctor who was just here was cross-eyed." I shook my head; of course he wasn't cross-eyed. "He definitely is!" She focused her eyes on the bridge of her nose so that they would cross and continued, "Just now as he was beginning, he kept going like this, didn't you see? After doing this operation so many times, you end up crosseyed."

"Stop playing around, I'm not in a laughing mood."

"Humph!" She continued to cross her black eyes. "Don't tell me you're crosseyed too?"

Has my sister ever been sad? This is such a childish question. Back when I was even more childish—that was just about nineteen years ago—and had just come home from my grandparents', I saw my mother lying in bed. In her arms was this little thing that wouldn't stop crying. The baby's eyes, nose, and mouth were completely squished together in the center of her face, her swollen red cheeks were full of wrinkles, and on top of her head there was a piece of skin that kept twitching up and down. "Your baby sister," my mother announced.

She was a sad baby sister.

But that's not what Grandpa thought. After spending several days digging through countless books, he chose an upbeat name for my kid sister: Junxin, or "merry god." Grandpa mysteriously pulled the small piece of paper bearing my sister's name from the pocket of his white shirt. With his fingers shaking, Grandpa opened the folded paper and laid it flat on the coffee table. Immediately, Grandma, Dad, Mom, my kid sister in Mom's arms, and I practically bumped heads as we leaned forward to read aloud in unison, "Junxin."

"Junxin." My Grandpa still wasn't quite used to the impediment in his speech caused by his missing tooth, so he did the best he could to cover the gap with his upper lip. When he spoke he looked like a kissing fish. "It's a literary quotation," he said through his puckered lips. "Where did I get the allusion? It's from *The Songs of the South*. The first section of chapter 1, *The Nine Songs*, is titled *The Great Unity, God of the Eastern Sky*. Just who is this God of the Eastern Sky? He is the god of the gods! To the gods he's this!" Grandpa said, flashing us a thumbs-up sign. "So they say, 'On a lucky day with an auspicious name, / Reverently we come to delight the Lord on High.' Now what this means is that this is a good day, so we have to be extremely serious—no goofing around—to make the Lord on High happy—that means make God happy—this . . ."

"So she's called Junxin." With a satisfied look on her face, Grandma cut him off and provided the conclusion.

"What's your rush?" Grandpa asked as his upper lip quickly pouted up. Covering his lone front tooth again with his lip, Grandpa continued, "So the section ends with these two lines: 'The fine notes mingle in rich harmony, / And the god is merry and takes his pleasure.' "

"So she's called Junxin," Grandma once again added.

"Junxin," said Grandpa.

It was just at that moment that Junxin started sneezing. It was not until after I had become comfortable holding a baby that I learned the reason. It was because she had wet herself. Normally if she sneezed for a while and still no knowledgeable adults came to change her diaper, she would start to cry sadly.

Just before the weather began to turn cold, I went back to school and entered the third grade. My classroom also moved to the campus one street over. Just under our classroom was the music room, which was haunted by those rich whiz kids. Below the music room were the kindergarten and the nursery school. That's also where they had the swing set, merry-go-round, slide, miniature jungle gym, and the small spherical iron cage that we called the *S.S. Earth*. For us "normal third-grade boys," who were neither wealthy nor brilliant and had already lost the special right of little kids to be spoiled, *S.S. Earth* became our secret weapon. We would often keep watch from the grassy field behind the swings; if not there, we would be hiding under the water fountain beside the hallway. As soon as those little geniuses were finished performing their Bach, Mendelssohn, or Mozart, or those chirping little devils from the kindergarten entered the metal cage, we would emerge like a swarm of hornets. As we closed in, we would shout: "*S.S. Earth*, preparing for takeoff!"

We used every bit of strength we had to spin the *S.S. Earth* as fast as we could, not stopping for even a second. As we began, the kids inside would laugh and have a good time, but before long they would discover that something was wrong. We were a group of Herculean alien warriors with a never-ending supply of magic powers. We could propel the world, making it turn faster than the speed of sound, faster than the speed of light— we could spin the planet a hundred, a thousand, ten thousand, a billion times faster than anything else. With sweat dripping from our pores, we mischievously propelled the Earth to the edge of the universe. And that was when we heard the sound of screams, curses, and crying. It was the echo of their crying that was most pleasing to our ears. The weak earthlings on board stretched out their arms to hit us; they spit at us and cursed our families and several generations of our ancestors—but this only increased our ecstasy. When the school bell rang, we would summon up the last vestiges of our strength to propel the *S.S. Earth* even faster. It was also under the safety of the bell that we would chant our anthem: "*S.S. Earth! S.S. Earth!* Take your daddy to get banged, take your mommy to get hanged! *S.S. Earth! S.S. Earth!* Take your daddy to get banged, take your mommy to get hanged. . . ."

In the midst of this mischief, there wasn't a single one of us who took that perverted song seriously. But just as winter was arriving, Family Morals Shen, who sat in the back row in class, suddenly left the ranks of the alien warriors. Afterward, he would always wear a wool turtleneck sweater, at least until the end of the next semester when he transferred to a new school and disappeared. It was not until we were in the fifth grade (it may have been a bit later than that), after a parent-teacher conference, that we heard what had happened: Family Morals Shen's father really did end up banging some other woman. Then during the winter we were in the third grade, Family Morals's mother hanged herself and her two children—Family Morals was the sole survivor.

During that last winter we spent together, I remember taking my kid sister to the school playground and seeing Family Morals Shen sitting all alone in the *S.S. Earth*. He was trying so hard to spin the iron cage, but the *S.S. Earth* just gently rocked back and forth with no intention of taking off.

"Give me a spin," said Family Morals as he pulled my sister inside.

At the time my sister was wearing a wool hat, blouse, pants, and a pair of wool socks. On the outside she was wearing a cotton-padded jacket and was wrapped up in a cotton blanket. In Shen's arms she looked like a big cloth bundle, especially once the *S.S. Earth* began to pick up some speed—from the outside it looked like Family Morals Shen was holding on to a bunch of luggage preparing for a distant journey.

"How old is your kid sister?" Family Morals asked in mid-flight.

"Almost ten months," I responded as, hand over hand, I spun the equatorial bar. My feet left the ground and we began to fly.

"She's much younger than my sister."

"How old is your sister?"

"On Earth she is six, but she has been on Neptune three months now. One day on Neptune is equal to one year on Earth, so my sister is almost one hundred. Faster! We are about to pass Mars! Next stop is Jupiter. Be careful of the asteroids. And don't screw up the direction! Veer starboard .75 degrees!"

Just as the *S.S. Earth* was speeding by Saturn, my kid sister began to wail. I jumped back to ground to let the *S.S. Earth* automatically reduce its speed. Then I even grabbed hold of the Mediterranean line to stop it completely.

"Don't you realize that we were almost there?"

I ignored him and grabbed hold of my sister to console her.

"Doesn't your sister look like a meat dumpling?" he asked with indignation.

"Your sister is the meat dumpling!" I responded. I kicked the *S.S. Earth* and set it spinning. I kicked it a few more times and it began to pick up speed. Family Morals Shen was about to squeeze his way out, but he was so scared that he had to curl back inside.

"You're a *wang ba dan!*"

"Well, you're a turtle grandson!" I yelled, and dashed out of the schoolyard and ran all the way home. I'm not sure when my sister stopped crying and began concentrating on studying my face, but as we got close to home and I slowed down, I saw her smile. As far as I can remember, that is the first time I saw her smile. I will never forget her smiling face, for it enabled me to rediscover the happiness of having a living person as a present. Right after that, my present cruelly vomited milk all over my face and head.

Nausea

My little sister didn't learn to how to talk until quite late. As far back as I can remember, Grandma would always be mumbling between her sighs, "How come she still doesn't speak?" Indeed, during the first two years after my sister came into this world, all she did was eat, drink, piss, shit, cry, laugh, and vomit.

At the time when I began high school, the greatest person in the world was Reagan and my father's idol, Grace Kelly, had just kicked the bucket in a car accident. Grandpa had just had his cataracts removed and would often take out the soybean-sized crystal cataracts, which he had asked the nurse to save for him, in order to show them off to his friends and relatives. As for me, I met my very first girlfriend and she in turn introduced me to Sartre and his *Nausea*. Actually, this is how it all started:

"Have you heard of Camus? How about Sartre?"

"Do you mean that U.S. president that used to sell peanuts?"

If that chick had really wanted to get acquainted with somebody who could talk philosophy with her, she should have dropped me and walked.

But she didn't. Not only that, but she patiently explained that Camus and Sartre together do not add up to Carter.

Then she even read me a portion of *Nausea*. It was only later, after I began to seriously study (actually, it's more likely that it wasn't until I had finished graduate school and was serving my required time in the military), when I saw that chick appear in an educational film giving a general lecture on military law, that I finally realized: way back when, she didn't really want to have any kind of a conversation with me; she just wanted me as a guinea pig to test out her educational methods.

"'Everything is meaningless,'" she read, "'this park, this city, and myself. When you realize that, it turns your heart upside down and everything begins to float . . . here is "Nausea."'" After that, she closed both the book and her eyes and became lost in her thoughts. Sitting less than half an inch away from her on that stone chair, I gazed at the lotus flowers that were dancing in the wind and bathing in the sun. Not bad at all, I thought, this botanical garden, this whole city is completely without meaning. Not even I had any meaning; probably the only thing of meaning was this chick. Beneath her eyes she was covered with freckles and fine gold hairs had sprouted up all over her face and neck—just one look was enough to make your head start to spin.

"Do you understand the meaning of 'Nausea'?" she asked me.

At the time I was only a freshman. I still hadn't experienced getting drunk, I hadn't yet picked up that nasty smoking habit, nor had I begun to suffer from sinus infections. Other than Grandma forcing those disgustingly bitter antibiotics and liquid medicines down my throat when I was little, I must admit I really had no clue just what was "Nausea" and what wasn't.

"Of course I understand—what I mean is, I get the gist of it," I replied.

Memory can be such a frustrating ability, for I have absolutely no recollection of what happened after that. But from that point on, anytime I laid my eyes on lotus flowers dancing in the wind, stone benches, peach fuzz on the face or neck of my little sister or any other young girl; or even if I came in contact with anyone drunk, carsick, or suffering from morning sickness, I would always be reminded of Sartre.

Then during one of our weekly political-education days, I awakened from a heavy slumber to see an educational film featuring the babe who had enlightened me with existential thought. However, as she was presenting an unbiased account of the relationship between law and ethics, it wasn't Sartre *Nausea* and his early theories that I was reminded of—it was my sister.

Not long after my kid sister began middle school, the Department of Education lifted its restriction on hair length. From that point on, my sister could fix her gleaming black hair in any way her heart desired. It was also during this time that my sister began to present her opinions on my "ex-girlfriends."

"Didn't you once go out with this really ugly chick? She had freckles all over her face, her hair just went up to here"—she drew a line right above her ear—"and she couldn't keep her mouth shut."

I said I didn't recall, but she insisted that she remembered quite clearly. That chick once told my sister a story: There once was a king who made a bet with one hundred concubines. The king would tell each concubine a story. He would continue until the concubine fell asleep and then go right on to the next one. If any one of them was able to get through the story and not fall asleep, the king would give her the throne. But if all of them fell asleep, then the king would attain immortality and rule his country forever.

"So what happened?" I asked.

"I don't know, afterward I fell asleep."

When I was awakened in the army assembly hall by that film, I wasn't in the least drawn in by the topic of law and ethics. Half-stupefied, having just come out of a deep slumber, all I could do was collect myself enough to recollect the somewhat disdainful eyes of my little sister. With that scornful look, she began a new game—sizing up my girlfriends. She would criticize them and explore all aspects of my relationships with them. What she said was more sharp and incisive than what anyone would have anticipated—it was almost impossible to think of her as that same little baby whom we treated like a virtual mute for almost two years.

During the days when my kid sister had yet to learn to speak, just what exactly was she thinking? What was she feeling, observing, and understanding? I'm afraid the answers to these questions will forever remain a secret. Actually, her silence was extremely powerful. She didn't speak, but we had no way of knowing if she really couldn't or she just didn't want to. As for us big people—that's right, big people, at the time I was nine or ten— we could often sense that her reason for not speaking grew from a kind of contempt she had for us. She did not speak, but during what we big people took to be the most critical of moments, she would always belch, giggle, cry, fall asleep, or, of course, display her most shocking reaction: vomit.

It was also at that time that she would often repeat the same action of putting something small into some other larger vessel. She would put her pacifier into her mouth, her bottle into the garbage can, her slippers into the fish tank, or a set of keys in the slippers. Even more common was to find her gold-plated bracelet in a coffee mug, to discover Grandpa's dentures in the ashtray, or to fish Donald Duck out of the toilet. In any jar, can, or bucket, we could always find some long-lost object that we had been searching for.

In regard to these trivial matters, that old pervert Freud had quite an explanation. It was a coincidence that the management at my father's newspaper just then transferred him to what was said to be a most insignificant job—covering medical and health news. This enabled my father to make the acquaintance of several doctors (among them a certain Dr. Chen, who would very soon proclaim my sister autistic), and it allowed my whole family—including Grandpa and Grandma—to make the acquaintance of Sigmund Freud.

When Freud first came to our house he really caused quite a commotion. My father had to teach both my grandpa and me a bunch of strange theories that he barely even understood himself. For example, he told us about a guy named Oedipus who, without even knowing it, knocked off his old man and then went on to marry his own mother. Grandpa felt that anyone who could make up such a story had to have been under the influence of Satan. I thought it was pretty cool, although I did not dare show just how delighted I really was. Grandma said that it was natural for fools to do evil deeds. (That is not always true.) My mother, on the other hand, had absolutely no interest in the story; she was too busy looking for some object lost within another. As for my kid sister, if I remember correctly, she was casting sidelong glances at us with her normally large and radiant eyes as she sat off to one side, belching.

My father's infatuation with Freudian theory led him to take an intellectual interest in my sister. He spent long hours observing (I should say spying on) her every action. Then he would take the simplest of movements and give an interpretation that was both complex and enchanting. The best example is the time when my little sister ate feces.

When I was serving in the military I wrote a few letters to my sister. One of them touched upon an incident that occurred while on a military outing: I went to take a shit in the woods, but forgot the toilet paper and was forced to use leaves. This led me to reminisce about the time my father and I witnessed my baby sister using her finger to wipe up a piece of feces oozing out of the side of her diaper, then popping it into her mouth. In the letter, I joyfully made fun of her—climaxing with the un- bridled paragraph which follows: "That very moment when the shit entered your mouth, the heavens collapsed and the earth was shattered. The wind rushed and the clouds rolled. The demons wailed and the gods howled. In the next day's paper came the news of Chiang Kai-shek's death. Oh, what sorrow!"

I'm not making this up—that is exactly what the scene was like on that day. I was practically scared to death as Mom burst out of her bedroom screaming, "The weather is just too strange. It seems to be the work of the devil!" My father remained extremely focused on my kid sister. He gazed at her as she sucked the feces off her fingertips, and he proclaimed slowly, one word at a time, "Freud was right on the money! She is going through her oral pleasure receptor to rediscover the enjoyment of her anal pleasure receptor."

Unfortunately, the army security officer in charge of inspecting letters did not find anything funny about my sister eating feces. He paid even less attention to how my father, a man repressed by his own will to power, could direct his attention to the observation and research of the manifestations of a baby's sexual urge. The security officer cared about only one thing: why I mentioned the death of Chiang Kai-shek and a disgusting incident like eating feces IN THE SAME SENTENCE.

"I didn't," I retorted. "That's exactly what really happened."

"Do you realize that I could have you court-martialed and sentenced for defiling our national leader?"

My little sister never learned that I almost didn't make it out of the army; she also never received that confiscated letter. It was during my three subsequent weeks in solitary confinement that I finally understood not only that people can go without speaking, but that not speaking can also create an incredibly powerful state of mind.

During my period of confinement, Dr. Chen, who had once proclaimed my kid sister an autistic, often appeared in my daydreams. He hadn't changed one bit since the time I first met him when I was eight or nine years old; not his moral integrity, fair-skinned complexion, white hands, or even his pale nose, which gave people a feeling of transparency. My daydreams would sometimes occur in the middle of the night; periodically, he would whirl in from the window, muttering, "You are going insane."

"I feel perfectly fine, how could I be going insane?" I asked him, and myself—then I began to sweat. After all the sweat from my pores was released, I would even sometimes cry. I cried because I knew that I would never forget—I was also terribly afraid that I would never forget—what saved me from being court-martialed.

The only reason the army officer saved my ass was because I got down on my knees for him. Without the least bit of hesitation, my knees hit the ground, just like those of every truly repentant son in almost every low-budget soap opera. While on the ground, inching forward on my knees, I let the officer outstretch his loving and protecting hands to touch my shoulders that were begging for forgiveness. "Up we go, be good now. Come on, get up," he said. Although on my knees, deep down I was thinking, fuck him—and fuck me.

It was then that I curled up in my cell and began to vomit.

Suppose Freud had had his own take on Nausea—I wonder what that would have been. What I remember doing next was picking up the disgusting items I had puked up and throwing them in the toilet, whose pump was already kind of screwed up. As I flushed the toilet it emitted a loud grumbling noise. A short while later we were both silent.

Subconsciously, what was I trying to wash away? Was this penance? Was I using the irresistible power of an ethical rite, which human nature makes us susceptible to, in order to deceive an old fool who deeply loved our country's leader? Was I so weak that I could not even admit just how much of a coward I really was? Was I going insane?

Long before I even realized that I had the potential to go insane, my kid sister began middle school and began to grow her long, beautiful hair. One time—actually it was a whole bunch of times—she asked me, "You've dated so many girls. Is it always you who does the love talk, or is it them?"

"What do you mean?"

My sister almost didn't finish her line of questioning, but at the last minute she burst out with: "Do you talk and they listen or do they talk and you listen?"

"What are you talking about?"

Actually, I already understood what she was trying to say. She was bringing up a concern that she still did not really comprehend yet already knew existed: Does the king have to keep telling story after story while the concubines just listen, listen, listen until they fall asleep? Does the speaker have to continuously talk to guarantee his right to the throne?

It was not until I was on the brink of madness that I finally began to know something about this principle. I had already thrown up everything in my stomach, yet it was only then that I felt the filth within myself. That was also when I realized that everything was pointless.

"What's the point?" This is the peculiar sentence that my kid sister began using just around October 1976—at the time she was two and a half. Everyone in the family has long since forgotten the context of this sentence, but just the fact that she could speak left a deep impression on all of us. From then on we could all rest easy. I had a normal sister who could both listen and speak—moreover, for a long, long time afterward, she could use these two abilities to help her learn just how very crazy and unfair this world is.

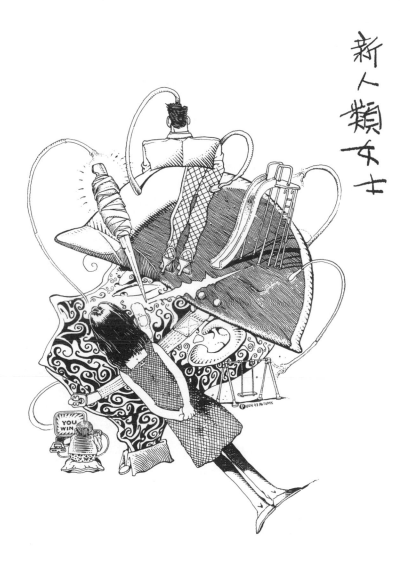

新人類女士

A New Breed of Woman

After my kid sister began middle school she suddenly developed an interest in issues such as whether or not there was any true equality between the sexes. Each time she wrote a letter to me in the military, she couldn't help offering a profound analysis of the wording and phrasing of my last letter. On top of that, she would spare no effort in digging up any hidden ideological problem that she could find (actually, "problem" is a rather gracious term; "error" or "evil" is a bit more like it). From then on, I would often look back upon every aspect of my little sister's early childhood with a feeling of nostalgia. I missed her expressions, tone of voice, attitude, features, and even the way she used to dress.

A long, long time before that, just after she had begun nursery school, she loved to wear a certain kind of checkered cloth skirt. She liked yellow and white, red and white, pink and white, blue and white . . . in short, as long as there were two alternating colors and the checks were no larger than a fingernail, she would wear it. Mom also liked to wear checks, and the two of them together looked like a couple of perfume bottles from the same factory—one big, one little, but other than the size difference, all the other specifications were identical. The big one would usually be carrying the little one or holding her hand as they strolled under the covered sidewalk to every place imaginable: the supermarket, the park, or the recreation center. Even on rainy days, the balcony behind our apartment could always serve as a most ideal extension of their stage. Mom liked to hear people say, "Look at how adorable that mother and daughter are!" Even if they didn't say it out loud, you could see the admiration in their eyes; to Mom, this was all music to her ears. "So cute!" That is what Dad would usually say. Who could have guessed that at the time he was already screwing that woman painter with the black silk fishnet stockings?

"So cute!" Dad said. "You really look just like Renoir's painting *The Swing*. So cute." As he pronounced the first syllable of Renoir's name, it sounded like there was phlegm stuck in his throat. Later I learned that that was French and the technical name for the place where that special sound comes from is the uvula. Afterward, while in graduate school, my precise pronunciation of this sound would leave a deep impression upon a language instructor—I never bothered to explain to her how my father taught me to make uvular sounds as a child.

My kid sister going with Mom to the small park to play on the swings was truly a regular activity. Every afternoon after Mom got off work she would pick up my sister at nursery school; first they would go to the supermarket and then to the park. Looking out over the school wall from my third-floor classroom, I could regularly catch sight of them. Often that wouldn't be until dusk—I would still be at school studying abacus calculation, mental arithmetic, and composition.

For one of my homework essays, I wrote about my little sister. In my composition I characterized her as stunningly beautiful and extremely obedient, just like a little princess. Aside from my description of my sister barely even coming close to reality, I also fabricated a few aspects of the plot (that was simply to fulfill the teacher's requirement that the composition be "no less than three pages"). I wrote that my sister had once fallen off the swing set and ended up with a cerebral concussion. Thanks to the devoted care of my father, mother, and me, she was slowly able to regain her health. God only knows if I ever really took good care of my sister. However, at the same time, the extreme joy I felt when in the position of caring for my sister was second not even to my mother's delight in dressing my sister exactly like her.

What was the implication of having to look after my sister? Naturally, it meant that I had already grown up. At first I must have hated it. Growing up and going to the third grade meant that I had to move to a new classroom—and that meant that I had to climb three flights of stairs and endure the periodic noise of those whiz kids practicing in the second-floor music room. Growing up and starting fifth grade implied that I would have to stay after school to take part in voluntary night cram school—while in class I had to bear watching those little bastards from the lower grades playing and laughing in the schoolyard. Growing up and going into middle school was a definite nightmare—at the time, I never believed that I would live long enough to see that day. Most distressing of all was the fact that even though I had grown up only a bit more than my little sister, everyone in the family would never fail to remind me: "You're her big brother. You have to start acting like a big brother."

What does it mean to act like a big brother? My answer was quite simple: to recognize that fact that I could no longer act like a child and blame others for what I did. It was almost precisely at the moment I was accepting this reality that I became conscious of my sexual orientation. It was my sex that determined that I *must* take care of my kid sister. Sometimes, in order to assert this, I would specially seek out some things to do in order to protect my sister.

For example, fighting. (It is okay if you want to take the term "fighting" in the broad sense.) When my sister was a sophomore in high school she once used her class time to write me a letter. At the time I was taking part in a divisional-level defensive military exercise. She wrote, "I'm not sure if by the time you receive this you and the blue army will have already finished fighting with the red?"

Actually, I laughed when I read that letter, but hidden in my laugh was a sadness. When we got back to the barracks, it was pouring outside. Inside there were over one hundred men who for seven days and seven nights had had not a single opportunity to wash away the stench of mud, grime, and sweat from their bodies. In order to make out my little sister's handwriting, which was practically dancing off the page, I needed to constantly wipe away the steam from my eyeglass lenses. It was at that moment I truly had the desire to go back in time; how I genuinely cherished the days of remote antiquity when my kid sister would still offer her heartfelt appreciation when I fought for her.

Back then she had her hair tied back in a checkered scarf and was wearing a long checkered skirt. She held my hand as we walked home—she had already begun kindergarten. During my elementary-school years the kindergarten was just beneath where those whiz kids would practice Bach's half-step dance music. And just outside the kindergarten classroom, in the small playground, was where the spherical cage we called *S.S. Earth* was preserved. Just beside the *S.S. Earth*, near the slide, was where my little sister would usually be waiting for me to pick her up as I walked two blocks over from my middle school. During that short two-block journey I would often fantasize that there was someone who dared to bully my kid sister (for example, pushing her down the slide or forcing her into the *S.S. Earth* and then spinning her at high speed). That fantasy one day actually became a reality when I delivered a wicked blow to a little bastard fifth-grader who had stayed after to study his abacus calculation. The reason for my attack was that as he went down the slide he rammed into my sister's butt.

Afterward, not only would my little sister raise strong inquiries about male fighting, the launching of wars, and other issues, but she would also completely forget that I had hit more than one guy for her and, in one battle, even chipped off half of one of my bicuspids.

Then again, possibly I'm mistaken. A chick named Little Chess should perhaps get the credit for that broken bicuspid. I think the place of battle was the movie theater at Ximending;[*] my opponents were a couple of ticket scalpers who had taken over the ticket window. I learned many lessons from the Battle of Ximending; first was the fact that I really didn't

---

[*] *Ximending* (Hsimenting) is a busy district in central Taipei famous for its movie theaters, pubs, and nightlife.

deserve those two stripes in Tae Kwon Do. It was obvious that my strength was only sufficient to deal with opponents that didn't hit back, such as pieces of wood or tile (or my class partners, who were restricted under set rules). The second thing I learned stemmed from Little Chess's renunciation of my use of violence—which was because during the chaos of battle I knocked her in the back of the head with a circle kick. Besides this, I also had a deep realization of the taste of fear. Just before the fight broke out, my veins pulsated and my mind went blank; then, after the battle was over, I had too much time to recollect. As for my recollection of violence—I believe it will forever remain much more terrifying than violence itself. Several years later, as I drove past Ximending, I suddenly realized just how close that young me, full of energy and vitality, had come to biting the dust. I couldn't help but begin to shudder all over. No wonder my sister stated in her letter: "War can only prove that men are animals capable of fear."

My kid sister's feminist period did not last too long (I am afraid it was even shorter than my martial-arts phase). That day, after the military exercise, while in the disgusting and chaotic barracks, I read yet another letter—it was an official document from the Ministry of Defense. The document stated that I had passed the military instructor examination and would be able to leave my division for a post as an instructor at an officer school. Before assuming my new post, I had a five-day vacation. I used the first three days to go down to Xitou** with this chick I had just met, and we screwed like crazy for a few days. On the fourth day, when I arrived back in Taipei, I heard the news from Grandma and Grandpa that my parents were getting divorced.

Sitting alone in the living room, I hung up the phone and imagined the scene of my mother and father busy with their separate chores. Night had already fallen and he was probably in the brightly lit newspaper office going through a stack of written or printed material. She was most likely at the nearby supermarket going through the fish, meat, and vegetables,

---

** *Xitou* (Hsitou) is a scenic mountain park in central Taiwan popular among honeymooners.

trying to figure out which were fresh and which were even fresher. I imagined it very probable that their physical movements and expressions were almost identical. After thinking about them for a long time, I couldn't come up with any more suitable term to describe them than "absurd." Just then, my whistling kid sister swaggered in. She still had her backpack on. She didn't turn on the light, but I suspect that, from the half-closed door and the silhouette of my army helmet, she had already discovered I had returned. She was so wrapped up in whistling her song that she didn't even bother saying hello.

"They're still splitting up?" I asked.

She grunted, "Uh," and then continued to whistle.

"Absurd," I muttered.

Only after my sister finished that song did she answer me. In the darkness, she responded with a single sentence: "It's better for Mom."

"Give me a break from your feminist theory!" I forcefully whipped off my helmet, but my scalp instantly felt a chill and I had no choice but to put it back on.

"From this week on, I'm not going to talk anymore about that feminism stuff." She smiled and turned on the lamp, continuing, "It is a waste of time, it just makes me an anxious mess."

For a while she really made *me* an anxious mess. Not long before, during that military outing, my brothers in arms would occasionally sing that song, "I've got two pistols, their sizes are different, use the long one for the commies, use the short one for the girlies." Each time I heard that tune I would feel an uncomfortable quiver all the way down to my bones as if the lyrics were a kind of blasphemy. But less than a year later—just when Dad had forsaken Mom—my sister suddenly became graceful and merry, as if feminism was an outfit that had already gone out of style. Before I had a chance to ponder the implications of this change, she had jumped into my arms. She wrapped her arms around my neck, and reflected in each of her sparkling eyes was the distorted image of my face. "So, tell me about that chick you've been seeing," she said.

It had already been quite some time since she had used the term "chick." I thought that she had already been completely awakened to the fact that "concealed within this term were the evils and faults of the male ideology." And so I softly pulled her hands away and explained to her what I thought. What happened to all of those evils and faults?

"What's the point?" Her retort was the same pet phrase that she had become fluent with when just two and a half years old. Then she abruptly jumped up as if she had suddenly thought of something and went back to whistling that same tune from before. As she whistled, her four limbs twisted up and down in a kind of dance that looked like an automated crank trying fruitlessly to produce oil. She looked like a puppet dangling from strings. Finally she assumed a pose that looked like a cross between a stiff corpse and the Hunchback of Notre Dame and said, "Moreover, I like to say whatever is on my mind."

I should have taken that as a cause for celebration, so how come I didn't? My sister took a detour through the devil's gate of feminism, the ideology that is like thorns scraping on the back of every man, and was then brought back to life. A pedantic nitpicker no more, she became cute and witty again and I had my normal sister back. Who could ask for anything better? However, instead of rejoicing, I had the same feeling as I did when I drove back to the scene of that fight at Ximending. I felt myself on the brink of being crushed—I suddenly became scared. A thought instinctively flashed through my brain: my sister was growing ever farther away from me. For me this was even more terrifying than my parents' ruined marriage.

It was during that time that my father formally moved out to live with that woman artist. I guess that after ten-odd years of secretly sleeping together their relationship was probably already exhausted and tasteless as well. However, the event that truly took me by surprise did not occur until after I had left the military. Trying to make me laugh, my sister, lying on the filthy sheet in the foul gynecological ward, hit me with a "tragically realistic and hilariously ridiculous" news flash: "That father of ours is having an art exhibition!"

This news indeed was enough to make you laugh your guts out. Dad also sent an invitation to my sister—that was the first time in her life she had been addressed as "Miss." She was but eighteen at the time, yet already had three months' experience as a single pregnant woman. Just over a year before she was called "Miss," she still believed that this extremely traditional title was quite suspicious. But her attitude changed, just like so many other events, beliefs, actions, people, dreams, and feelings in her life that stayed for a while and then disappeared. Before she had the ability to grab hold of something, she already didn't want it. "What's the point?" she would say.

That evening, wearing my army helmet, I discussed feminism and our parents' divorce with my kid sister. We had dinner with Mom—we ate a fresh fast-food hot pot that Mom had brought home from the grocery. After supper I went for a walk with my sister. Just like so long ago, I held her hand as we walked past the small park and cut through the schoolyard, which looked no larger than the palms of our hands. We kept going until

we got to the old run-down *juancun*, which still hadn't been torn down. That was the place where our grandparents had screamed and fought for several decades—neither of us wanted to go there. On the way, I asked her if she remembered wearing a scarf and dress of the same color and style as Mom's. She shook her head. I asked if she remembered playing on the swings in the small park. She shook her head again. I asked her if she remembered waiting by the slide for me to take her home when she was in kindergarten. Again, she shook her head. At first I thought that she would be ashamed for not remembering those events—who knows, it is possible that subconsciously, I just wanted to force her to feel shame for so easily forgetting. For one short second she dropped her head and stared at the ground, and her head bobbed like a rattle; I thought she was so ashamed that she was going to cry. But in the end she quickly straightened her neck, exposing a beaming smile. "Grandma's really something," she said. "Do you know that she bought a Mah-jongg Mate cartridge for her Nintendo and stays up playing until after midnight? She won't stop until all four of the women inside have stripped butt naked!"

Grandma really did have quite a way with that electronic mah-jongg, and that day she displayed her prowess to her heart's content. Later she even cooked us some noodles. No one mentioned Dad. Grandpa shouted out a few names in his sleep; from what I could tell, they were all people who had absolutely no connection to our family. After I finished my noodles, I rested my elbows on the edge of the balcony, which had been declared off-limits to me when I was eight years old, and for a long, long time not a single thing passed through my mind. It was only then that I realized that my kid sister's forgetfulness was a kind of boundary; she was a part of a different breed of humanity. I'm afraid that I will never understand much more about her than that—even though she herself shared with me all kinds of forgotten secrets.

First Love

The most obvious characteristic that my little sister inherited from my father was her unflagging enthusiasm for trivial knowledge. It was so easy for her to be moved by the most insignificant of theories—and because of this, she was that much more prone to fall in love with someone who knew more about these principles than her. When she was six years old she fell in love first with Huang Anbang, then Brave Tree Lü, Grandpa, and finally Chen Peifen. Even after she had begun middle school, she would still occasionally bring up Chen Peifen, referring to her as "the woman who almost made a lesbian out of me."

In my estimation, it is more than probable that it was just this kind of a strange—bordering on perverted—thirst for knowledge that facilitated my parents' union in wedlock. That was approximately twenty-eight years ago. At the time my dad was an intern reporter at a small newspaper office and Mom, who was studying medicine at a state university, had her heart set on becoming an amateur photographer. During one weekend in the middle of March, Mom brought her brand-new Canon camera to Yangming Mountain to shoot the cherry blossoms. It was during that trip that she witnessed a tour bus loaded with passengers drive off a cliff. It is unclear why, but at the time Mom aimed her lens at the completely flattened body of the bus and snapped a photo. Of the two rolls of film she had brought with her, she took only two photos of cherry blossoms—the rest were of twisted and broken metal and glass, rising smoke, and crushed and burned bodies. Squeezed into that bus were ninety-one elementary school students and five chaperons who were on a class field trip. During the height of their terror and pain, the majority of both the survivors and the deceased were captured by my mother's lens. It was at the time of that accident that my father met my mother. Once he got his hands on her negatives, he had them developed and printed them in the Sunday edition of his small paper. Afterward my mother refused to pick up her camera again, and she also lost the ability to calmly face the clammy, stiff cadavers on the dissection table. Yet it was obvious that the knowledge of the human body and physiology she had acquired was already more than enough to satisfy my father's demand. Every morning Dad would be chasing stories; in the afternoon he would have a date with Mom; then in the evening he would weave together all the information he had gathered up for the day and write some decent articles. Mom collected every story or article of Dad's that made it to print. She used the exquisite craftsmanship that could have come only from a surgeon's training to cut, paste, mount, and bind those cutouts—leaving behind a rich record of how my father tapped into the secrets of the common people. When I would occasionally thumb through those essays, I would always be able to instantaneously pick out those articles whose content touched upon specialized knowledge relating to the natural sciences, all of which were the result of my mother's enlightenment.

These dates on which my mother would instruct my father continued for a few months. Then, during a date sometime in August, sexual desire, impassioned by my father's lust for knowledge, inspired a multitude of sperm to ejaculate into my mother's body. Of those sperm taking part in the excursion, I was the sole survivor.

In 1980, as I began my third year of middle school, my body also had its own supply of self-produced sperm. A triangular area of thin and sparse pubic hair began to appear around *laoer*,* and I also learned from my health textbook that the reason for *laoer* getting hard was that my sponge filled up with blood. Actually, my sponge would often get hard even back in grammar school. The reason for this expansion, however, was not, as it said in the textbook, "owing to sexual stimulation"; it would frequently and secretly get larger as I rode my bicycle or skateboard or jumped rope. During my second year of middle school something as seemingly unstimulating as my history textbook's description of the "Communist bandits seizing the opportunity to expand" during the war of Japanese resistance would cause my *laoer* to seize the opportunity to expand as well. It wasn't necessarily only sex that could stimulate it.

Sex—as both an instinct and a kind of knowledge—is indeed enough to cause a fourteen-year-old youngster to be lost in both indulgence and insecurity. My classmate Brave Tree Lü was the one who enlightened me about this mysterious pleasure and anxiety.

"If you can piss farther than your height, then that's normal," Brave Tree Lü told me. "Do you know what 'normal' means?" Brave Tree was half a head taller than I was, and when he pissed he proved that he was much more "normal" than I was. Later he taught me a method of "rectification"—while in the cleaning area, he wrapped his five fingers around a broomstick handle and stroked up and down. As he rubbed, he told me, "Just practice when you get home and you'll be fine."

I don't quite remember what came first: did I learn to drill *laoer*, or did I become Chen Peifen's private student? Whichever, in the period just before all this, you could hear the name "Huang Anbang" mentioned all the time. Huang Anbang was the genius in my class. It was said that even during elementary school he was already brilliant. He would get a hundred on every exam, he could play the violin and represent the class in speech, calligraphy, and essay competitions; of course, he would also beat us when it

---

* *Laoer* literally refers to a little brother or a second child.

came to the number of times he went up to the podium to receive awards. How are you supposed to deal with someone like this? The only thing you can do is pretend that he is a Superman secretly sent to Earth from outer space. After you have acknowledged this, you invite this Superman over to wish you a happy birthday.

At the end of June after all our exams, just before my third year of middle school, my mom arranged for my classmates to come over for my birthday party. "Invite all your good friends over for a good time," Mom told me. As she spoke, she took out the prior month's class report card and proceeded to circle the names of the twenty students with the highest grades. It was a good thing that Brave Tree was ranked nineteen that month.

After showing up at my birthday party, Huang Anbang, who was ranked first, went on to destroy my kid sister and some other idiot whose name I can't even remember in Chinese checkers. In Chinese chess he beat Zhu Youhua and my father. Zhu Youhua was so pissed that he left early and took with him the present he originally had intended to give me. Huang Anbang even recommended we play a round of Go, but not even my grandpa knew how to play that kind of chess. Thus Huang Anbang had had no choice but to give us a private violin concert and a brush-calligraphy demonstration. The unforgettable performance was of *The Nutcracker* and the large characters written in the *Dakai* style were *shou bi nan shan* (may your longevity surpass that of the southern mountains)! Finally he delivered a lecture to all the adults and children on "Classification of the Dinosaurs and the Reason for Their Extinction." That day, not only did my kid sister cut Huang Anbang the biggest piece of cake, but she even wished *him* a happy birthday! Just before he left, Huang Anbang said to my sister, "Bye-bye, Little Xinxin!" Turning to hide her head in Mom's arms, she felt the sadness of departure and began to cry aloud in sorrow.

In light of the omnipotence of Huang Anbang, my mother came up with the idea of hiring a private home tutor for me. And so, from that point on, Chen Peifen and her ponytail, pure white skin, and short skirts, and the shape of her breasts, which would be occasionally be slightly exposed, entered into my exercise and rectification fantasy for *laoer*.

According to Brave Tree Lü's estimation, Chen Peifen was definitely no virgin. A few short fair hairs always sprout up between the eyebrows of a virgin. The cartilage in a virgin's nose will be completely intact, and when her heels are raised her calf muscles shouldn't have any stretch marks— "moreover, the first time you screw a virgin, she'll clamp you so tight it will hurt like hell." The day Brave Tree told me all this, he also encouraged me to rub Chen Peifen's nose. At first I did not dare. I put it off until the end of the year and then, after an exam where I had made more than twenty points' improvement in English, I finally made my request.

Her nose cartilage was broken. Probably as I was caressing Chen Peifen's nose she became conscious of the fact that I was just a naughty little devil (and the term "naughty" is extremely easy for people to misinterpret as solely belonging to immature, undeveloped children). The very second that I became convinced that Chen Peifen was not a virgin, she let out a deep sigh and muttered, "Oh! You kids!" "You kids" was directed at both my kid sister and me. Following that, Chen Peifen expressed how good kids had it, not understanding the sorrow of adults. Just what exactly had happened to make her so sad? I wondered. As Chen Peifen declared the answer, her eyes shone and sparkled, emitting a ray of brilliance. "John Lennon is dead," she announced.

John Lennon being shot dead by some maniac shouldn't have had the least effect upon my little sister and me. Even when he was alive, we never heard of this guy or his rock band, The Beatles. The strange thing is that Chen Peifen seemed to infect my little sister with her depression. My kid sister started to continually interrupt Chen Peifen's lessons with a bunch of stupid questions. "Then—was the head of the Beetle really scary?" "Then—afterward did the Beetle get murdered too?" or "Then—what happens after you die?"

Ever since kindergarten, when I first heard the theory that people become ghosts after death, I had not only believed it but also never gained the courage to repudiate this explanation. But during the summer just before John Lennon died, Brave Tree Lü offered a new theory. He told my sister and me that after a person dies, they become the "opposite" thing. Men become women, old people become children, fat people become skinny, white people become black, long tongues turn into short ones, people with all of their facial features intact come back missing some, things that walk with feet come back walking without their feet ever touching the ground. . . . When you put all of these "opposite things" together, they naturally look like a bunch of ghosts.

From that point on my kid sister had the utmost interest in this notion of "opposite." From the end of summer all the way until winter when her scarf and jacket came out of the closet, it was all as if she were repeatedly practicing the same game. It didn't matter who it was or what they said, she would always answer with the same phrase: "The opposite." When Dad yelled for her to shower, she would say, "The opposite." When Mom called her to dinner, her response would be, "The opposite." When I screamed at her to "Shut up!" she'd say, "The opposite." Sometimes she would invent some mind twisters, such as "What is the opposite of a refrigerator?" "What is the opposite of Garfield?" or "What is the opposite of Brave Tree Lü?" Then one day she was standing beside the sofa and, without even realizing it, she began to rub against the armrest with the part of her body that we saw pictures of in the health book. Smiling, she told Brave Tree Lü, "I hate you." Without even laying an eye on her, Brave Tree responded, "I'm gonna give you a whipping." At the time, Brave Tree was busy going through the *Dictionary of Human Anatomy* that was on my mom's bookshelf.

If my mother's understanding of people went beyond the physiological, she might have taken precautions to prevent Dad's enthusiasm and demand for intellectual stimulation being so intimately tied together. I deeply believe that had my father not been restricted to being a little reporter at a small newspaper in a tiny island country, there is an extremely high probability that he would have run all over the world searching for the women with the greatest knowledge. Once my sister's class and spiritual advisor, Xu Hua, recommended she read a book titled *On Chinese Women.* I remember the author had this long foreign name so I played a joke on Dad, telling him that she was as beautiful as a goddess, like a carbon copy of Catherine Deneuve. I noticed that Dad's eyes lit up as I spoke. One year later, when he left the family to move in with that woman artist, he took the book that Mrs. Xu had lent my kid sister. It is possible that the woman artist did not know the whole story behind *On Chinese Women*, but I secretly believe that when my father took that book with him, he also brought with him a secret lover (or rather, an imaginary sexual partner).

My kid sister's crush on Huang Anbang lasted only a week or two. However, during that time Mom or Dad had only to mention his name in comparison with their inferior son and my sister would begin whining about wanting to study the violin or calligraphy. And I still believe that it was Brave Tree Lü who shortly thereafter overtook Huang Anbang's multitude of knowledge and abilities with his skill at speaking bullshit. Although Brave Tree ignored my sister, she still reserved the highest admiration for him. Just as before, she would periodically remind me, "Why don't you invite Brave Tree Lü over to play?" The next time Brave Tree came over he told her that when boys get to be thirteen or fourteen they grow an Adam's apple. He went on to tell her that this Adam's apple is a poisonous growth and that if it breaks, black hair will grow all over the body of the victim and he will suffer death by poison. Not even I doubted this theory, and my kid sister went as far as seeking proof from Grandpa. She pinched the skin on Grandpa's flabby, wrinkled neck and asked, "If this is punctured, will you die?"

"Of course!" Grandpa answered. "If you don't die how are you supposed to become a celestial being?"

It was during that most spiritual autumn that my little sister became by far the most heretical elementary school student in her class. Her advisor called home almost every other day saying she was overindulging her imagination. Moreover, she was constantly transferring these corrupted thoughts to her classmates. One of her most ridiculous thoughts was the belief that within the virtually restricted area of the principal's office was a secret treasure. Buried there were a chest of gold, ten corpses, and several dozen wigs. The principal would regularly change his wig and put on the skin of one of the dead bodies. He would then transform the gold into clothing and jewelry and go around giving lessons to each class. Sometimes it would take extra time to change clothes and jewelry, and that was why teachers would be late. Afterward, there really was one incident in which a female teacher, decked out in a very gaudy black dress, came in late and one third of the kids in class were so terrified that they began to cry hysterically.

This was when Grandpa decided to undertake the mission of "establishing a spiritual life" for my kid sister. Every Sunday my sister would go to Catholic school. Bible study was on Wednesdays and Fridays, and Tuesdays and Thursdays were reserved for violin lessons. Mondays were fairly free, so she had ample time to interrupt my lessons with my tutor, Chen Peifen.

Not long after John Lennon died, Christmas arrived. Grandpa initiated a family get-together; all three generations were present, but Grandpa fell asleep. Later, after he had recovered his energy, he stayed up half the night telling stories from the Bible. When he got to the sufferings endured by Job, the part that goes on forever, a tear fell from my sister's eye as she muttered, "It's so sad!" At the time my intuition told me that Job was an idiot. But my sister pitied him, proving that Grandpa was an even better storyteller than Brave Tree Lü.

It was as if my sister were suddenly no longer under the spell of Brave Tree Lü's style of nonsense. As the whole family had hoped for so long, she began to take the path of the fair maiden. After each Chinese New Year, she would count up all the money she had received. As she handed the money over to Mom, she would say firmly, "Save it for me."

Mom acted as if she were surprised, asking, "What are you saving it for?"

"For my dowry! After a long, long time, when I grow up I am going to marry Grandpa."

At the time, all three generations of our family couldn't stop laughing. This was the first time I experienced the disconcerted anger of my sister. She took the money back and ripped it up into tiny pieces without saying a word, all the while staring blankly at Grandpa. Grandpa's way of smoothing things over was the following excuse: by the time my little sister was of marrying age, he would already be dead. What was she supposed to do then?

"Then I'll look for you in heaven," my sister answered decisively.

"And supposing I go to hell?" Grandpa asked. His missing front tooth was once again exposed, and he still hadn't realized the severity of breaking a young girl's heart.

"If you don't want to marry me, then just forget it!" my kid sister resolutely declared. "But stop with all these excuses!"

First Love

Many, many years later, Grandpa was still healthy as an ox. Except for being tactfully denied life insurance by Huang Anbang, he was fine. Nothing could shake our confidence in Grandpa living a long life, his longevity surpassing that of the southern mountains. He himself, however, would often raise that one lingering doubt: "After I die, it's still up in the air as to whether I'll be able to get into heaven or not." But one thing is certain: if my kid sister wants to go to heaven to look for somebody, it definitely isn't going to be Grandpa.

In the spring just before my sister's seventh birthday, she placed her yearning for heaven, love, and knowledge all in the hands of Chen Peifen. That year I wasn't even fifteen, yet in my head there was nothing but lust, fantasies, and a bunch of odd theories on how to satisfy these fantasies and desires. The cause of this variety of desires and fantasies was, of course, the opposite sex. From this perspective, my kid sister was at the time spiritually much more pure and noble than I, who was a full eight years her senior.

You could say that the questions she put to Chen Peifen were extremely childish. Some of them included, "Why do foreigners talk like that?" "How come you can speak a foreign language?" and "How come when foreigners sing they always go 'oh, oh,' 'yeah, yeah'?"* Aside from answering all of the above questions reflecting my sister's curiosity about a foreign country—which is required of all English tutors—Chen Peifen occasionally had to address questions like, "How many languages does God know?" "Then—how about the devil?" "Then—after people go to heaven what language do they speak?" "How come you don't wear pants?" "How come you keep talking to my brother?" And, of course, "Do you like me?"

---

* "yeah, yeah" (*yeye*) is a pun on "grandpa" (*yeye*). Junxin wants to know why they are singing, "Oh, oh, Grandpa."

The fact that my kid sister had an affinity for Chen Peifen was obvious from the way she expressed it. Each time Chen Peifen came over, my sister would want a hug, and when she left, my sister wanted another. She would always be drawing Chen Peifen little cards in hopes of hearing, "Oh, how cute!" or receiving a kiss in exchange. When cards were not enough, she would take my satin handkerchief, Mom's lipstick, or Grandpa's Bible to win her affection. Chen Peifen would usually secretly return any gift she sensed to be too expensive, but there was one thing she never knew. Each time she answered one of my sister's little questions or provided her with some tidbit of information, she was allowing my kid sister to fall even deeper into the snare of love.

"Can girls fall in love with other girls?" This time, I was the target of my sister's question.

50

"Of course not," I answered.

"Then—can they get married?"

"Give it a rest," I said as I glared back at her.

Owing to the above conversation, my kid sister was depressed because I had crushed her fervent desire (or you might say she was embarrassed because I had exposed her hidden anxiety). She bit her lip and her chin trembled. It was some time before she screamed out: "It's—Not—True!"

That spring, my kid sister's violin playing advanced by leaps and bounds. Before summer, she had already transferred to the private elementary school where I had wormed my way through six years. As she entered music class, she diligently practiced Mendelssohn's *A Midsummer Night's Dream* and *Violin Concerto in E Minor*. It was obvious that properly handling and interpreting these pieces was far more than she could manage. Yet as long as she was playing her violin, no one would laugh at her, discourage her, or attempt to stop her because her endeavors had gone beyond what was appropriate for her age.

As for sex and love, we of slight age are not in the least interested in seeing other people experience them in a premature fashion. This is perhaps the fundamental reason why for many people their first love is so very bitter.

她
的
禁
忌

Her Taboo

My sister's performance career began when she was eight, and by the time she was twelve it was already over. Later, after she had studied some historical anecdotes, her explanation was that just as Boya had smashed his zither, having lost his musical soul mate Zhong Ziqi, she too lacked a musical soul mate. However noble this explanation may have been, it was only partly true.

Even today, that broken violin remains locked away in a black leather violin case with red lining; that case may be in a closet, or perhaps it is under some bed somewhere. No one in the family (including Grandma and Grandpa, who rarely come by anymore, and Dad, who ran away and divorced Mom) ever suspected that the violin had left the house, but at the same time not one of them ever looked for it. Seriously thinking about this violin and its curious characteristic of "disappearing while still existing" brings to mind such terms as "taboo."

That's right, taboo. An object that clearly exists yet cannot be touched. Just as my kid sister had begun to use the term "absurd," which she had learned directly from me (or indirectly from that chick with the freckles), the word "taboo" was already beginning to pop out of my mouth without notice. I must have been inspired to use the term after reading the book *Totem and Taboo*. That was during an age when it was particularly easy to get caught up in popular vocabulary, terminology, accents, or fashionable clothing and dance steps. I used all kinds of newly learned terms and phases, most of which I was still only half-familiar with, to describe the multitude of objects in our apartment. Take for instance the photo of my great-grandfather and the portrait of Jesus. Without even the slightest show of sentimentality, I naturally pointed out how they were both totems of a sort. Even supposing that my mother and grandpa didn't truly understand the meaning of "totem," they could still sense that my comments were a product of the resentment that marks a rebellious youth.

That year I was a sophomore and my face was covered with pimples.

The chicks I had dated all either went to college or ended up screwing some other punk—one of them was even burned to death in an arcade fire of unknown origin. How could I not be in a towering rage? In my eyes, that photograph of Great-grandfather; the image of Jesus in the frame; our president, who continued to suffer from diabetes even after having had his prostate removed; the profusion of Hong Kong superstars who, following in the footsteps of Chu Liuxiang,[*] assaulted Taiwan; Michael Jackson, who had just begun his journey to whitehood through plastic surgery; and any other character who was worshipped in some corner somewhere were all totems that needed to be disposed of before anyone could be happy. I'm not pulling your leg; when you are that age there are a fucking lot of things around from which you have to free yourself before you can begin to lighten up. The most infuriating is when you can't even squeeze all the pus out of your pimples.

Why the hell would a sixteen-year-old punk filled with pent-up anger care about the anthropological or psychological definition of the term

[*] Chu Liuxiang is the hero in a series of *wuxia* or knight-errant novels by the author Gu Long. In 1983 *Chu Liuxiang da jieju* (*The Denouncement of Chu Liu Hsiang*) written by Gu Long and starring Zheng Shaoqiu (Adam Cheng), became the first major Hong Kong film to win over Taiwanese audiences.

"totem"? Knowing that it implied a kind of taboo was enough; for me to feel myself from head to foot being tabooed was about all I could bear.

I was sixteen years old. My kid sister was eight. She transferred to my old private school, becoming one of the little whiz kids in the music class. Every morning I would spend at least a half an hour playing with my zits, while she would spend more than four hours every day sawing away at her violin before she went to sleep. It was truly a situation wherein we practically never saw each other. Little did I know that she had gotten into the habit of eavesdropping on my phone calls with a bunch of babes during her practice time. And it was from those conversations that my kid sister learned more than a few idiomatic expressions used by kids my age.

The use of one of these expressions was closely connected with my sister transferring schools. It was during May or June in arts and crafts class when a little peckerhead named Ji Kaiming was lighting up the ponytail of a girl in class with a cigarette lighter. My sister probably couldn't take the sight of it anymore and, grabbing a broomstick, lunged at Ji Kaiming's face while screaming out: "You are just too absurd!" The bridge of Ji Kaiming's nose was broken on the spot. Afterward my sister's advisor paid a personal visit to our house, providing us with a detailed description of the cause and progression of the event. She even tried to reassure my parents that my sister should not receive excessive punishment for her actions. However, Ji Kaiming's parents did not want their only son to have to face the continual threat of disability or even death for the remaining years of his elementary-school career. That advisor recommended that my little sister move to a different class or transfer schools; and so, on account of this incident of violence, my sister became a outstanding violinist at another school. My father indeed did not adopt the same blunt tactics to lecture my sister as he had used in the past for me. He just squatted down beside her, smiled, and softly asked her, "Where did you learn to say 'absurd'?" Like lightning, my sister's eyes flashed over toward me, but in the end she didn't expose me. What was really absurd was my father, who continued squatting there for an unnervingly long time, repeating, "Oh, I see. I see."

Dad always believed that my little sister's outstanding qualities were all inherited from him, and of these qualities, the one that Dad relished most was her "artistic" talent. This gift was displayed during her time studying the violin—actually, her time spent playing it was much too short to prove anything. The violin incident was something my father never expected, and that is why that dust-covered violin case and violin were just as taboo for him as some unmentionable disease.

Moreover, this is only the most superficial aspect of the whole affair. My father would not even consider the possibility that my kid sister's fiercely violent actions were a result of her seeing him set me straight one too many times. He preferred to believe that every last breath of obstreperousness in both my sister and me was a definite inheritance of Mom's nervous disposition.

My mother's compulsiveness was often manifested in the most trivial details of her life. Every day she would empty the trash a dozen or more times. Any area visible to the naked eye she would be forced to wipe clean of even the finest dust. While chatting with guests over tea in the living room, from time to time she would rub the grimy spots from the coffee table with her finger. It is possible that when my sister's advisor and my father's friends came over, they all thought it was a bit strange that during their conversation my mother felt the need to continually resituate their teacups. Actually, by placing each teacup in the center of the coaster she was maintaining a pattern of concentric beauty. This is how things were early on. Then on a clear and cool March day during the second semester of my sister's senior year the evening news reported the story of a painter who disemboweled himself after spraying a tub of sulfuric acid in the faces of several dozen elementary-school children. Mom suddenly began to tremble all over; she curled up in a ball on the sofa and started to roll about. Then she began shaking her head, continuously shaking, as if there were hundreds of ants or some other kind of insect crawling in her ears and she had to get them out. Dad was at the office and my sister was in her room practicing the violin, so only I witnessed this peculiar scene. A few minutes later, Mom returned to normal and rushed into the kitchen to wash her hands and face; she continued washing until the start of the nightly miniseries. As she came back into the living room, she asked me, "What do you want for dinner?"

"Didn't we just eat?" I asked.

"Oh," she responded. And I realized that in the midst of our family there had appeared a genuine lunatic. Afterward I said to myself: You're now a university student and there are some pretty heavy things that you are going to have to start facing up to. Your dad is having an affair, except for playing her violin your sister doesn't understand shit, and your mother is insane.

My mother's insanity was extremely reserved. She never once screamed out to the heavens, knocked her head on the ground, or grimaced in pain. For the most part she remained tranquil, gentle, and lost in her addiction of maintaining perfect cleanliness in the house. The most obvious symptom was the increased time spent washing her hands, scrubbing her face, and bathing. In addition, she was almost constantly thirsty. Every day she would have to drink several dozen glasses of distilled water that she had dragged home from the pharmacy. Because of this, she began to gain weight, and often when she listened to my sister practicing the violin she would doze off and a long string of saliva would dribble out of her mouth.

It was also just about this time that my sister's body started to go through some changes. The first signs are always quite unexpected. For example, one morning after getting out of bed I knocked on the bathroom door. Suddenly the door opened and my sister was standing there in her pajamas. Perhaps she was brushing her teeth and still had toothpaste bubbles dripping from the edge of her mouth, or maybe she was drying the curly ends of her soaked hair. In any case, all of this is unimportant—what's of significance is the fact that I discovered she had curves. This was unsettling. You can't not look because you have already seen it. Since you have already seen it there are some things you have to admit: just like you, she will develop and mature, and eventually she will be just like those chicks you used to fantasize about. There is no way you can treat them equally, but at the same time they are so very similar. If you don't instantly admit this, you will be tempted to take a second glimpse, which would prove their similarity. Also, wait until you take that second peek and the other party will also start to feel uncomfortable. It is my guess that my sister and I (perhaps also my father) were led on a cycle of discovery, uneasiness, rediscovery, and more awkwardness, which eventually brought us to the acceptance of the proverb: "Among our family there is a young girl coming of age." The most vulgar part of all of this must have been the way my sister and the males in the house looked upon those curves, which could not have been any more natural, as a kind of taboo. That's right, a taboo—an object that clearly exists yet cannot be touched.

One day as my developing sister was going on eleven, she asked me: "Is Dad having an affair?" She wasn't looking for an answer; I knew this because when I was her age I already had come to this same conclusion. My father is the kind of person who just can't keep a secret to himself, especially one that makes him excited and joyous. Back when my sister was in kindergarten and was still wearing the same checkered outfits as Mom, Dad bought his first painting by that woman artist—he hung it on the wall next to the front entrance. Every morning after Mom had gone to work at the pharmacy, I suspect that Dad was doing one of two things before he headed out the door running after some story. If he wasn't squeezing in some time to sweet-talk that woman artist on the phone, then he was standing before her painting, whistling that song "I Love to Whistle"—by chance, I had witnessed both of these actions. I owe this discovery to the aftereffects of my bout with pneumonia. I would often stay home sick with a cold, and because of this I also ended up getting sick of that father of mine, who was indefatigably whistling behind Mom's back.

I don't dare comment on that woman artist's skill as a painter because I don't even understand her work. But when my little sister was still very small she pointed out the following: in the center of the painting is a leaf; beside the leaf is the hair of the princess. Inside the hair are a whole bunch of little suns; outside the hair is a black forest, and within this forest lives an old witch. The old witch must have been a spontaneous fabrication on the part of my sister. Dad, however, seemed to praise her art review. Holding my sister, he used to rock back and forth before the painting, asking, "Where is the old witch?"

During the later years of my childhood, my response was that the old witch was in Dad's heart. After I got a little older, I would say the old witch was in Dad's arms. By the time I began college and my sister asked me, "Is Dad having an affair?" our home already had a second work by that woman artist. The painting was of a spotlessly transparent blue sky, only in the left-hand corner was an object that looked like a cross between a spaghetti noodle and a roundworm. The painting hung in the hallway between my sister's bedroom and mine. Taking one look at that painting, I answered my sister, "It's none of your damn business."

This was my sister's first lesson in recognizing what a taboo was. She was a really quick learner. One day one of her friends from her ensemble came over to spend the day hanging out. When, out of the blue, he asked, "Isn't your mom a little weird?" my sister's instant reply was, "It's none of your damn business." Originally that little bastard was supposed to perform a pair of duets with my sister during their graduation ceremony. However, during practice one day he started relaying the story of Mom's water addiction and other strange habits to some of the other whiz kids. My sister's method of dealing with him was not unlike the way she handled that peckerhead Ji Kaiming—she smashed her violin over his head. Then she put her fiddle back in its case, carried it home, and stashed it away in a closet or under a bed somewhere. No longer would she await her musical soul mate.

This incident of violence had yet another irrefutable official version. My sister asserted that as the conflict was unfolding, the other party poked her with his violin bow; moreover, the class pianist and score turner were able to verify my sister's accusation. During the graduation ceremony, that little bastard with his head wrapped in gauze bandages successfully completed his violin solo, winning thunderous applause from the audience. My sister was hiding far away in the balcony of the assembly hall. As she tore up her corsage petal by petal, she quietly told me the secret of why she raised her hand to harm another. She asked me, "Could I also have some kind of disease mental (*shenjing bing*)?" I found it difficult to restrain myself. I couldn't bring myself to correct her: she should have said "mental disease (*jingshen bing*)." I also didn't believe that she could have some kind of strange illness. I reached out to hold her, but she instantly pulled away. She had grown up, already.

關於治療

On Treatment

After my sister started middle school, she began to endlessly ask me, "Why do you want to write?" Her expression was extremely sincere, as if crouching over my desk with my atrocious posture—which from childhood had never been properly corrected—and writing line after line of poetry, essays, and novels were among the most inconceivable of careers. She never once mocked my dream of "one day becoming a writer," she simply didn't understand just what there was about this career worth dreaming about. There was at least one argument that provided a reason good enough to support her suspicion. That was because each time she asked, "Why do you write?" I never failed to give a different response. Author—what an indeterminate career.

I simply don't recall if I ever confessed to my kid sister that when I was younger I once fabricated a story of her falling off the swing set and ending up with a cerebral concussion in order to fulfill an essay assignment. This type of event, however, would actually often occur in my day-to-day life. What I mean is that everyday life frequently puts people in a position where they have no choice but to tell a small untruth. I don't like to do it, but sometimes that's how things go. And so, I became a writer.

As far as I can remember, I wrote my first novel when I was a junior in high school, and my first reader was my sister. She had just gotten her braces and was able to perform the soothingly sweet A and D scales both fluidly and gracefully—at times her performance could even be delightfully witty. That winter, after finishing her nightly practice, she would often push open my door and collapse face-down on my bed. In a muffled voice, she would ask, "How come you don't have to practice the violin?" My usual response would be, "But I have to study for the college entrance exams." After continuing this completely insincere dialogue for several days—it was probably more like several weeks—I had the inspiration for a story. It was about a four-person family. The reporter father suddenly lost his job and yet was not in the least bit depressed; in fact, he used every last penny of his severance pay to buy gifts for the whole family. Mom got a pearl necklace, his son got a cross-country motorcycle, his daughter got a set of braces, and he bought himself a computer—which was in preparation for his working at home. Unfortunately, their home was robbed and the thief made off with the pearl necklace. Then the son and daughter got into an accident while chasing after the robber on the motorcycle, completely smashing the daughter's new set of braces. Good fortune, however, came from this sad news: the father turned this tragedy into a novel. His novel was published and it shook the literary scene. He became a famous writer.

I read the finished story to my kid sister, who sat on the bed hugging a pillow. Right afterward, she asked me several questions: "Why do you have to write about me?" "Why do I have to have such bad luck?" and, of course, the question she would later continuously bring up: "Why do you have to write?"

"It's fun!" I said.

By the time my sister had begun to suspect that she had inherited some kind of mental disease from Mom, my answers to questions like "Why do you write?" had become relatively serious and depressing—no longer was it very fun. Barely even taking the time to think about it, I would respond, "Writing is my form of self-treatment."

In real, everyday life, my sister had already had her braces removed, exposing her white, straight, beautiful teeth. It had been seven years since she had touched a violin or any other musical instrument. Dad had successfully attained the position of assistant editor-in-chief, a job in which he barely had to lift a finger, and thanks to praise and flattery from his connections, his art exhibition was an overwhelming success. As always, Mom would take her daily walk to the pharmacy three blocks away to fill prescriptions for cold and diarrhea medicine, skin creams, health tonics, and other medication for the middle-class families in the neighborhood. Not one of her patients knew that she had divorced and for some unknown reason had been stricken with a kind of manic depression. I had been living in a neighborhood no larger than three square kilometers for twenty-seven years, but using a few figments of my imagination, a handful of little white lies, and a bit of exaggeration, I became "the new comet that the literary scene had been awaiting."

Occasionally, this new comet's kid sister would scribble down a few sentences that fell somewhere between a joke and a pop-song lyric—for example: "My feelings are a faded blue, my tears are invisible, moreover they do not flow." Aside from this, she would write only when she wanted to make me laugh, composing all her notes on those little yellow Post-it notepads. During the last winter vacation before I graduated from college, I received my first literary award. In a little note she drew up an acceptance speech for me: "I would like to thank God for creating the world, my parents for creating me, and myself for creating this novel. I would also like to thank my little sister for not creating anything. It is her lack of creation that has provided hope for both me and the world."

I suppose that all those years of suffering through violin practice probably had a subtle influence on my sister. Brewing in her subconscious was a compulsion for structure, order, and precision; however, because of the torture brought on by this array of needs, she also developed a thirst for freedom. I read between the lines of the notes and handful of letters she gave me, and my analysis told me that she never underwent any kind of training whatsoever (she never even learned how to write an essay), yet she was still able to pick up the profound intricacies of manipulating language. And so time after time, she carefully read through my writings, offering conjectures about each work's origin in real life. She compared every aspect of the content of my works with the content of my life. Every now and then she would praise my work, but I felt like a diseased specimen of mangled flesh and blood stripped naked in a glass display case for examination.

My prize-winning story, "The Invisible Man," was for me the beginning. I wrote about a university student who is possibly suffering from paranoia and how he is used by Uncle Tang, a character whom I don't know whether to classify as real or fictional. The main character eventually becomes a career student who develops underground intelligence on campus for the ruling political party. Toward the end of the story, the university student is sent to a sanatorium to live out the rest of his life in confinement. In my opinion, the most clever aspect of the novel is the fact that no one can figure out if the student is truly insane or if he is society's victim, his deranged values and inability to distinguish right from wrong, truth from falsehood, all a result of intense political persecution. The book got excellent reviews, and the prize money I received for the first award allowed me to become the first on campus to own a high-performance cross-country motorcycle. During the lunar holiday, my sister went with me to test out the motorcycle. While we were riding, she asked, "Didn't you incorporate some real people into your novel?"

She couldn't remember clearly, but that is indeed what I did. It was June of the previous year. One day during final exams, as I dragged myself out of the deal with the Faustian Lucifer, I was left with a lingering fear. The only thought in my head was: "I'm screwed! I have to rewrite the fucking thing again!" With that also came an extreme anger, even hatred toward Goethe. I rushed out of the examination hall cursing every one of those old bastards responsible for writing the literary classics. And then someone across the tree-shaded avenue shouted my name. He called out two or three times.

It was that weirdo whom everyone on campus called "Zombie." All year round he would wear turtleneck shirts; he was over six feet tall, and even when he was directly under the noon sun, his shadow seemed to stretch over the entire street. His body was like the pole holding up a basketball net and his head was like the rim, with his chin dangling high above me. I had heard that Zombie was a student in the philosophy department. He usually did-n't have much to do with his classmates and was a rather shady character. Occasionally he would spend long periods of time chatting with one of the most unpopular instructors, which is why someone started the rumor that he was a mole sent to campus by the Guomindang.

"Do you remember me?" he asked. Lowering his head, he sneered at me with the hint of a smile appearing at the edges of his mouth. His expression lasted for about ten seconds, maybe a bit longer, and then he waved his hands, saying, "Forget it."

"Excuse me . . ." I continued to think about all those basketball superstars whom his tall frame had reminded me of.

"Forget it." As he turned his head and walked away, he said, "Your essays aren't bad. Keep up the good work." It was hard to tell if he was talking to me or to himself.

Later I remembered that during the previous spring I had an essay or story published in the campus magazine. I wrote about my kid sister when she was still a baby, and I mentioned a certain person. Who would have guessed that "Zombie" was this very person, Family Morals Shen—my primary-school classmate who came a hair away from meeting an ugly demise by hanging with his mother and little sister.

When I told my kid sister about my chance encounter with Zombie, I couldn't help but also share with her the widely known stories that were flying around campus about the spy's multitude of activities. What she couldn't understand, however, was why I later wrote Family Morals Shen into "The Invisible Man." She leaned on my back, her hands wrapped around my waist. My cross-country bike hit sixty miles an hour as we flew past Clear Water Reservoir on that lonely scenic roadway. Over the howling wind, she asked me, "Didn't you incorporate some real people into your story?"

"Family Morals Shen?" I asked. "Are you talking about Family Morals Shen?"

How are you supposed to clearly explain issues such as literary creation, the drawing of materials, fabrication, and realism to a little devil who has just begun her sophomore year of high school? I could barely even explain it to myself—and I was almost finished with college. "Of course not," I said, contradicting myself.

"But unconsciously you were," my sister said.

"What the hell do you know!" I shouted, and slowed the motorcycle down to a stop.

"You're the one who doesn't know anything! Not only did you stick him in your book, you wrote Mom in too! You know, you're really lame!"

My mother never once resorted to writing as a means of dealing with her trivial fantasies. For her, the voices she heard, the images she saw, the feelings she felt, and all the items she became conscious of were alive. The nature of reality bloodily forced its way into her daily life. That kind of thing is too real—so real that it cannot endure translation into written words. I, however, having already grown accustomed to translating life and other items that did not even exist into language, could not endure the intent gaze of my kid sister.

"Well, your writing is brilliant anyway," my kid sister admitted in a whisper.

My self-treatment was brilliant. A doctor from the psychiatric ward who once declared my sister autistic and my mother as healthy as an ox (God only knows how much my mother hated this analogy) once relayed to me a conversation he and my father had had about my novel. At the time, I was busy trying to cope with the weeding-out stage of my first year of graduate school. It must have started when Dr. Chen came over the house to talk to my mom about something. He took advantage of the free time while my mother was getting herself a glass of distilled water to tell me that he was extremely interested in my writings. He also told me that my father felt his interpretation of my novel was quite sound. What was his sound analysis about?

"You never expose yourself in your writings. Actually, it is just the opposite: your novels are a kind of tool to protect yourself." His mouth emitted the stench of garlic, and from time to time he would honk through his nostrils as he attempted to clear his stuffed nose. "You are running away and your novel is your vehicle for escape. What I want to get to the bottom of is, what are you running away from?"

I repeated his last sentence: "What am I running away from?"

Because of this he assumed that I agreed with his analysis. "You probably understand what I mean. You are a very interesting **case**.* Let's look at this problem together—I want to know your true fear." Saying this, he began to move closer to me.

On Treatment

Perhaps, like Dr. Chen said, so-called true fear does indeed exist in this world. But just then the healthy ox came back to her seat, interrupting the single instance of close interaction with psychology in my life. Afterward, I never again laid eyes on Dr. Chen. Apparently he said something that offended some gang boss (or a friend of some gang boss), because they found him two or three months later frozen stark naked in an eleven-square-foot cement block.

I am afraid, however, that the deep rift created by his words was extremely difficult to recover from. At the least, I had deep, unswerving faith in the view that I was running away from something. Even though several times afterward I went to great lengths to expose those aspects of the world that I found most difficult to face, my readers were still not gullible enough to believe that the painful disclosure of those unbearable characteristics was actually a result of self-dissection. On the contrary, they would prefer to believe that it was owing to my "sharp observances of the subtleties of human nature."

Did I say "my readers"? Indeed, when I was twenty-three I became conscious of the fact that I had readers—they were on the street, beside the noodle stands, at the entrance to the pharmacy, at university club meetings, and in my mailbox. My sister at the time had her own share of school stress to deal with, yet she never once abandoned her responsibility of dissecting the relationship between my novels and my life. She was sharper than all of those strangers who made up "my readers" put together; her responsibility included pointing out all elements of untruth in my books, as well as the degree of these lies.

For example, she believed that the short story that established my reputation as a writer, "The General's Monument," took Grandpa as a

---

* Boldface words are in English in the original edition.

model. But Grandpa was never a general, he never lived in a mountain re-treat, he didn't have the ability to travel through time, nor was he men-tally deranged. Moreover, not only did I transpose my mother's mental disorder onto Grandpa, I also presented the general's son as a homosex-ual who loved wearing white windbreakers (just like the ones Dad liked to wear). "What's the point?" she blurted out. "You should have de-scribed him as a playboy, a real skirt-chaser like our dad really is." And then came her habitual judgment: "I really don't get it, why do you have to write?"

It is possible that she had a point. Haven't I been talking about liter-ary "creation"? During the past several years, just what have I actually "cre-ated"? All I do is take those little details of life that are lacking and add a little of something else; I take D event that occurred during A time at B

place to C person, and rewrite it in E time at F place to G person. Then I add a bit of material H or remove a tad of K—did I forget I and J? Oh, I'm saving them so critics and readers will have space to exercise their imagination. In that space, the critics and readers will believe that enclos-ing a living person in an eleven-square-foot cement coffin is a stroke of originality, full of symbolism and hidden meaning. The night after my sis-ter had her abortion, I indignantly composed a five-thousand-character short story. The story described how a big brother burning with revenge located this asshole guy who forced his sister to get pregnant, and then buried him alive in a tub of cement. No one knew that was the last actu-al scene that Dr. Chen experienced before he died. Critics just felt that the story's conclusion was extremely inventive, full of symbolism and hidden meaning. My sister, however, with tears dripping from her eyes, said, "How can you have so much hate for someone?"

Did I hate that little bastard who got my sister pregnant? I examined my conscience for more than a year, and even today I just seem to become more and more confused. Perhaps it is because hatred cannot endure the passage of time, or maybe hatred cannot withstand contemplation and recollection. Moreover, lately I have been spending even more time won-dering: Do I hate my grandpa? Do I hate my father? Do I hate my moth-er? What about my sister? Dr. Chen? Family Morals Shen? Those characters whom I had cut apart and woven together, dishing them up in new forms in so many stories—did I despise them? I dismembered them, tearing their bodies apart and then putting them back together; could this be the full meaning of my self-treatment?

Perhaps my mother, who never once received any type of treatment, was much better off. Early in 1985, someone suddenly put up over a dozen identical posters outside Mom's pharmacy. On the top of each poster were three horizontally written characters: DRINK BREAST MILK. In the center was a portrait of a young mother breast-feeding. Toward the bottom of the poster were two smaller lines that read something like: BABIES WHO DRINK BREAST MILK ARE THE HEALTHIEST. SMART MOTHERS BREAST-FEED. The line on the very bottom read: PRINTED BY THE EXECUTIVE YUAN DEPARTMENT OF HEALTH. I will never forget that poster; I also learned from it that our country had a poster-printing organ in the Department of Health. At the time, my kid sister was in the sixth grade and already had the developed chest and hips of a young woman. Emerging from the pharmacy, she would wave her violin case before my eyes, not allowing me to see that poster. As she waved her case, she would yell, "Pervert! Pervert! You're not allowed to look!" This game of my sister's violin case blocking my eyes lasted until we got two blocks away, ending when we arrived at the entrance to the small park. Then she stopped laughing and playing and suddenly widened her eyes. With her mouth half-gaping, she began to stare at the same scene I had caught sight of—sitting in the white French-style easy chair next to the swings was Mom. She had her thumbs covered by her other fingers just like she used to when we were little and she would pretend to be holding a camera. She aimed at some of the children playing by the swing set and "click, click" pressed her index finger down. That "click" sound was to provide audio support for her two empty hands. Not one of those little kids paid any attention to her.

That was the first time my kid sister saw that Mom's behavior was oddly different from that of other people. She cowered up close to me and, grabbing hold of my arm, she called out, "Ma!"

My mother looked over as if she had just woken up. She unclenched her ten fingers, fixed the strands of hair coming out of her bun, and then, turning around, quickly walked toward home.

For many years afterward, that encounter in the little park led me to a whole series of different opinions when pondering creative writing. Each time Mom whispered she had heard a child speaking in the kitchen or a car honking downstairs or had smelled a burning odor coming from the bathroom, I would always carefully ask her, "What happened next?"

What happened next? It's the question that every reader or writer is continually asking. The instant we ask, "What happened next?" what we are actually concerned with is time. We express our feelings through the little bits of rescue, satisfaction, and hope that time brings us. But my mother never answers this question. She is enclosed in one specific temporal space, like a block of solid, hardened cement.

Comparatively speaking, having gradually transformed into a writer, must I be both superficial and common? I follow the story's axis of time until the end, running away from those aspects of myself that I do not understand, imagining that this is all a form of treatment. My little sister thoroughly understood this, she just never stated it clearly—that is because she didn't want to hurt me.

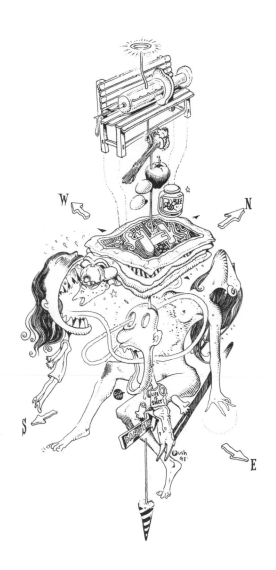

我們剩下軀殼

All That Remains Is Our Shell of Flesh

During the autumn six months before my sister was born I came down with pneumonia. I was forced to spend twenty-four hours a day locked up in my grandparents' dingy room in that run-down *juancun* with a never-ending high fever. In my half-comatose condition, I often had the delusion that I was a tiny ant forced to carry a cotton blanket as thick and heavy as a bed down a long corridor. The floor of the hallway was exactly like the ceiling in the *juancun*, made up of three-square-foot plates with yellow water stains. Carrying that blanket, I had been crawling for God knows how long when a woman came over. She removed the cumbersome burden from my back, but just as I was enjoying the happiness of freedom from the blanket, she stuck out her index finger, snatched me up, and popped me into her mouth. I never felt that this scene was a dream—the same dream cannot recur every single day. Yet my cotton blanket, the long corridor composed of ceiling panels, that woman, and I would tangle almost every day. Each time Dr. Zhong (who I later learned was an unlicensed veterinarian) examined me, I knew that after he declared my temperature above 101.3 and I had my shots and went home and had my medicine and Grandma tucked me in, it would be time to return to my life as an ant.

In all probability, my grandparents had been hiding the severity of my illness from the beginning. When they occasionally telephoned my parents, I would hear them say that I had bronchitis and that Dr. Zhong was a doctor sent by God who could work miracles. Dr. Zhong did indeed believe in God—he also had cured my father's case of childhood dysentery—thus I had no choice but to accept my fate as a feverish ant. Amid the misery of sickness I did not, however, abandon my search for entertainment. For example, when I was awake I would look for the way to the side street medical clinic in the images that appeared on the television screen and in the newspapers and magazines . . . searching for traces of the woman who gulped me down with one bite.

Dr. Zhong's wife was a beautiful and reserved Japanese woman. She had several daughters, all of whom looked almost exactly like her; each had almond-white skin, large wide eyes, long eyelashes, and delicate fingers that they used to wrap up the prescriptions. These features were enough to make the eight-year-old me want to take one of these lovely daughters home to be my wife—the only problem was, I had to first figure out how many of them there were and which one was which.

After I had fully recovered from my bout with pneumonia, I went back home. Upon arrival I found that I now had a kid sister. From that point on, I almost never again saw that woman who swallowed me up in one gulp. I also slowly began to forget about the medicine posters, that long wooden chair, and the needles of the clinic. When Grandma brought me the message that "Dr. Zhong's daughters asked how the little handsome man in the family was feeling. You little devil, the women really love you," I couldn't even remember anything about Dr. Zhong or his daughters.

Only several years later, when my kid sister began to ask me, "When was the first time you had feelings for a woman?" did I slowly recall some of those incidents from the past and tell my sister about my days of illness at the run-down *juancun*. I concluded that the first woman I had "feelings" for was the giant woman with the blurry face who gulped me down—my feeling at that time was the most extreme terror. My little sister continued her line of questioning: "What I mean is a *real* woman." And so I answered with, "A couple of girls who used to wrap up medicine."

Were they *real* women? Are those people who appear once during a certain time in your life, later disappear, and are finally forgotten (perhaps you will later remember them), or the people who forget you—are they *real*? My sister said they didn't count. I think the reason my kid sister continued to pester me was that she already had in mind what she wanted to hear. "Are you telling me that Little Chess isn't the one?" she asked, her eyes blazing at me.

Actually, Little Chess once used the exact same question to grill me. Every chick in this world has asked this of her father, big brother, or boyfriend—I'm so sure about this that I'm willing to bet. They always start by asking the roundabout question, "When was the first time you had feelings for a woman?" If you diligently rack your brains searching through the past, it isn't that difficult to find some hazy scene from your childhood that makes you blush—but the interrogator instantly declares, "That doesn't count."

Little Chess was playing with a fish bone when she told me in one breath that neither the woman who swallowed me whole nor Dr. Zhong's daughters counted. Then she threw away the fish bone, turned over, and pushed me to the floor. She ruthlessly shoved her breast into my mouth and made known her instructions: "Let me tell you, only I count! Got it?" This girl with whom I had my first sexual experience led me to the hazy understanding that chicks will always inextricably combine love with the concepts of *the first time*, *the only one*, and *forever*; moreover, these concepts all imply an extreme exclusiveness.

After I began to write, I never once touched the topic of love. But every editor from papers, magazines, and book publishers that I came in contact with invariably encouraged me. "What do you think? How about an essay on feelings?" they suggested. What they meant by so-called "feelings" was love, because that is what today's readers are interested in. If, however, they hire an author to write specifically on love, it comes off a bit cheap and superficial, so they must attack the matter through innuendo, asking you to "talk about feelings."

And then I would proceed to think about the multitude of women with whom I "talked about feelings," as well as Brave Tree Lü. It is possible that my middle-school classmate Brave Tree Lü is currently doing almost anything to scrape by. He was a salesman, an engineer for a television program, a substitute elementary-school teacher, even a cab driver for a while, and then he eventually became the assembly advisor to one of the members of the Legislative Yuan. When I was fourteen years old he taught me how to whack my pistol and told me that virgins will squeeze you to death between their legs. He also entrusted me with the secret method of how to make your penis larger: take some celery, one apple, a spoonful of honey, and one raw egg, mix them together in a blender, and drink up. What happens after you drink it?

"After you drink up, you'll feel so damn good you'll be in ecstasy!" said Brave Tree Lü. "She'll be in ecstasy too!" he added, and then pointed to my crotch, instructing me: "If you can make this strong, in the future you won't have any troubles in the love department." On top of that, he gave me another peculiar prescription: eat a whole silver carp cooked in garlic two hours before you do it, and the girl will love you for the rest of her life.

As for the secret recipe of celery, apple, honey, and raw egg, I needn't go into too much detail; in short, after two or three glasses I started to get an upset stomach. My diarrhea was so bad that it was as if the world were engulfed in a total darkness; life had lost its glimmer. As I was on the brink of total collapse, I promised myself that I would never fall in love, love presumably being an emotion imbued with pain and suffering.

After my sister had her braces removed, she became quite a stunning young girl; she had a set of legs that were slender and shapely, a tiny little waist, and breasts that were firm and round. She was going into middle school and I was a junior in college when Little Chess became one of our topics of conversation. Those conversations gave me the opportunity to ask myself: Are you truly in love? My kid sister seemed much more eager to learn about the array of events and emotions associated with love than I was. She would endlessly repeat the same questions: "Do you love her or not?" "Do you think about her?" "In what ways do you think of her?"

Sometimes I would spit out some answer just to end the matter, but other times I would fall into a solemn, confused daze. (That's because these rotten old questions can only lead to rotten old answers, and I refused to believe that I had truly become rotten and old.) The worst was one day when my sister asked me if Little Chess and I "did it." I instantly replied, "How could we?" as if doing it would defile my love.

In actuality, how could we not do it? The Saturday afternoon Little Chess said she wanted to take me up to her granddad's mountain retreat, I knew that the time had come. Her grandfather was a retired general with a touch of senility. Every spring and autumn, just as the seasons were changing, he would use his military telescope to scan the activities of the birds in the mountains, and from time to time he would issue tactical orders to be followed by the old housekeeper who took care of him.

The day Little Chess brought me up there, the old housekeeper asked us what we wanted to eat. Little Chess said anything was fine. I asked if there was any silver carp cooked in garlic. The housekeeper said they had some grass carp, how about grass carp? I said grass carp would be okay. Afterward I ate a grass carp reeking with an earthen stench and even though I got a fish bone stuck in my throat I had to continually praise the housekeeper's cooking. The housekeeper said, "No, no, it's really not that good," and then she told me that I could sleep upstairs in the room facing west. An hour later Little Chess emerged from her downstairs room, which faced south, and tiptoed upstairs. She softly pushed open the door to my room and called out my name. We quickly undressed each other and, under the cover of darkness, did it.

That is one activity that can make you feel completely free and liberated. I had heard this from Brave Tree Lü, and read about it in some foreign novel with a handsome man and beautiful woman on the cover, but I am completely at a loss to describe just what it is. All I know is that the words other people use don't even come close. Just as we were at that crucial moment that is most difficult to describe, I suddenly coughed, spitting up that fish bone into Little Chess's face. A moment later Little Chess turned on the bedside lamp and began to inquire into everything related to such concepts as *the first time*, *the only one*, and *forever*—this went on until just before dawn, when the general issued his senile order for all fronts to begin their assault.

A few months later, during a tangled street fight with ticket scalpers outside the movie theater, I accidentally kicked Little Chess in the back of the head. Wearing a neck brace, she came to tell me that she could not love an advocate of violence. With that, she handed me a package; I didn't have to look to know what was inside. It was a framed picture, a photo taken just after I had been promoted from the beginner level in Tae Kwon Do class. Besides this were a few letters, two books of poetry, and a box of worthless jewelry. As she turned to leave, I thought I was finished! That was because I didn't feel even the slightest hint of sadness. When I confessed this to my sister, she was in complete disbelief. "You had to feel something," she said. Okay, I did have a feeling. I truly felt that Little Chess's neck looked quite long in that neck brace, longer than you can even imagine.

Subsequent to that, I went out with over a dozen other chicks, and each time, my kid sister would hit me with the same few questions. One of the required questions was: "Did you and her do it?" I always said no; she always said she didn't believe me. This way at least she didn't have an opportunity to get into the nitty-gritty, and I never took the time to ponder why I felt it necessary to hide this true and natural act from her.

During May of last year, after I had completed my military service and published my first collection of short stories, I was awarded a national art and literature award, which included a hefty monetary prize. The day I received the award I took my kid sister out to a restaurant renowned for its Jiangsu and Zhejiang cuisine. After drinking two glasses of beer and smoking one of my cigarettes, she told me, "I'm pregnant."

She wasn't willing to tell me the details, including who the father was, how it happened, what was the other party's response, or what she planned to do.

"You haven't even graduated from high school. . . ."

As I got to this point, she raised her head and looked me straight in the eye as if I were in the midst of saying the most rotten and despicable sentence in the world. I shut my mouth and began to meditate on the mess that constituted my own so-called love life.

I referred to them as "chicks," my "babes," or my "old ladies," and deep down, I meant what I said. As I met them, I used my intuition to judge if I could get them into bed or not. Then I got to know them a bit better, just enough to figure out approximately how long it would take to get them to do you-know-what. Actually, most of them were pretty close to what I had imagined, and a few times I had them figured out so well that when we did it there wasn't even a bit of excitement. Afterward I would just have to patiently wait until each of our bodies wore out that feeling of excitement and novelty. It was that simple. That's me: a simple guy. Moreover, I always seemed to run into girlfriends who also looked at things quite simply.

Sitting in that clamorous restaurant, I would from time to time glance over at my kid sister (for most of the time she was grinning with her lips closed while rearranging the empty beer mugs on the table, which were dripping with the remnants of foam), and then look over at the patrons at the next table. Most of them were old-timers—the men were bald and the women were fat. Their voices bore thick accents as they went on with their old-fogey greetings and gossip. Their conversation was helpless in stirring up any recollection of their waning bodies or the lost excitement of their mundane lives.

If at that moment my sister had asked me what I was thinking, I wouldn't have hesitated for a second to tell her. I would have told her that the reason I had always concealed the fact that I really did do it with all those girls was because for me sex was too simple, too easy, too commonplace. It was like nothing. But I could not accept the fact that I was a completely uncomplicated person who faced no difficulties, was not in the least bit serious, and worried about nothing. I was unwilling to 'fess up about my sexual experience, not because I was afraid it would defile my love but because I didn't even have anything to defile in the first place. Although this is what I was thinking, what I finally blurted out had nothing to do with me, but my sister: "Whatever you do, don't mistake this for love."

Just as before, my sister continued to move the mugs around; she barely paid any attention to me. After a few minutes—perhaps it was a bit longer—she finally said, "Do you think it's possible I would have a kid as screwed up as me?"

All of my ex-girlfriends had said similar things to me. Pressing on top of me at her granddad's retreat on Yangming Mountain, Little Chess, right after telling me that only she counted as "the first woman whom I had feelings for," heaved a deep sigh and said, "But I'm so afraid of one day having a child. If I have one, do you think the kid will be as screwed up as you?"

"As screwed up as *me?*" I asked.

"No, I'm talking about me." Little Chess turned, lying on the side of the bed facing the window. The shadow of my head cast by the bedside lamp projected onto Little Chess's face. This made her appear much darker, and only the beads of sweat on her face glimmered in the light. "I don't want my child to be like me," she said. "It's too dreadful!"

From that point on, every time we did it, she would babble on like that for a while. Just like the prayer that my grandparents offered before every meal, this was a kind of orthodox ritual. Each aspect of the whole affair, from our dinner with the senile old general to her getting dressed and sneaking back downstairs to her room; every step, every move, even every thought was like a routine ceremony. We tried to spice things up as much as we could—we'd change rooms, turn on a different light, change our clothing, or switch positions. We would try to change everything we could, but we couldn't change our bodies. At the same time we were desperately trying to change everything around us, we discovered a stagnant feeling hidden within our unchangeable bodies. That feeling was terror. We were both terrified that we would too easily become sick of our partner's shell of flesh, and that our partner would become sick of ours.

Growing weary of someone and having someone grow weary of you, fear of growing weary and fear of being the object of weariness; it is the difference between the movers and the shakers and those who are moved and shaken. We were terrified to move but also afraid to be shaken. This cycle also became a part of our standard ritual. When the time came that we couldn't actively change anything else, we had no choice but to search for new bodies to be with.

You might ask, "Are these different bodies really all that different?" Actually, that is pretty much the same question my friend Brave Tree Lü posed. I once took his cab, and, recognizing me in the rearview mirror, he shouted out and stopped the car. He turned around and we began to catch up on old times. He said that a long time ago he had heard that I had become a famous writer, and he felt proud that he knew me. Afterward, he kept repeating that he had accomplished nothing and was filled with regret. However, after many years of wandering, making a living by all kinds of odd jobs, he had made friends with people from all walks of life and taken in a lot of life's lessons. This was much more useful than studying for any kind of degree. For example, he told me there was a member of the Legislative Yuan who was just getting ready to hire him as an assistant, and he said if in the future he took the road to politics, who knew where that might lead him. Finally he asked if I was married. I shook my head no. He instantly smiled. "With your background, you've probably got more chicks than you can handle. Each piece of ass is different, ain't that right?"

When my sister, fear written all over her face, asked me if she would have a kid as screwed up as her, I was instantly reminded of a whole series of women, all with completely different features. Some of these chicks were tall, some were short, some were fat and greasy while others were thin and bony, some of them had a faint mustache above their upper lip, some of them always had cuts on their legs from shaving, others constantly had the fragrance of malt sugar candy on their breath, some of them would often have cold sweat dripping down their sides from their armpits. It is as if these material differences are the only fragmentary memories of them I have left. Supposing I were willing to take some time to diligently recollect, I could take the special characteristics of those bodies and match them up with their owners with 100 percent accuracy. But I would prefer to think of them all as having at least one intrinsic characteristic in common with my sister—none of them wanted to have a child who was like them.

"Do you think you'll ever want a child that resembles you?" my sister went on to ask.

"Like me?" I asked, shuddering.

And then I thought back to when I was still a child. Holding my hand, Grandma walked me to Dr. Zhong's clinic in the *juancun* alley to have my shots. With the thermometer in my mouth, I stood on that long wooden chair staring at poster after poster of beautiful women dressed in kimonos in the medicine advertisements. I heard the voice of Dr. Zhong consoling my sobbing grandmother, and a moment later I pulled the thermometer out of my mouth, looked around, and quickly planted a kiss on the lips of one of those beautiful poster girls.

Eighteen years later, I shook my head and went on to answer my sister's question. "If he's like me, he'll never grow up."

If I had died during the time I was a tiny feverish ant, I probably never would have become a guy who only knew how to carry out redundant ceremonies of the flesh. Or maybe a part of me really did perish in the flames of my high fever, and the part left only knew how to seek out shells of flesh of the same nature as my own—shells of flesh that don't even like themselves.

聆聽與訴說

Listening Intently and Telling Stories

My sister and I once stood behind two glass windows in a stationery store secretly watching (and listening to) our father deliver a lecture. I was so absorbed in listening that I almost forgot it was my father. You know, when someone is talking to one or two people it is always different from when they're speaking to a whole crowd of people—and when my father spoke before an audience it was indeed enchanting. He became gentle and humorous, more sincere and modest than he was at any other time. I don't suspect that he was pretending, I just think that with a whole audience listening intently it is much easier for the speaker to lean toward virtue and moral righteousness. "I came pretty damn close to being moved by him," my sister whispered as a gleam sparkled from the corner of her eye.

Within our little three-generation family, listening intently and even being moved were both common, unremarkable matters. During family gatherings, Grandpa would often give lectures in which he used life experiences to corroborate the truths written in the Bible. The date of his lecture would always be set one month in advance. Grandma would notify my parents by telephone, and sometimes she would even exhort my sister and me, "Don't forget to remind your mom and dad." In order for the whole family to fully appreciate the wisdom of the Bible and be appropriately moved by Grandpa's life experience, Grandma would always hit the kitchen after the speech. She would whip up a table full of magnificent vegetable and meat dishes, enough to stuff the entire family. We never admitted it, but Grandma's cooking was the only reason we attended the lectures. If Grandpa had found out, he would have had a heart attack.

And just what was it that Grandpa was lecturing about? Even after all those years, I can barely remember. All I can recall is Grandma's cooking, which was always unforgettable. Actually, because of this, I developed a strange disorder: any time I heard an animated harangue, my stomach would begin to grumble and growl as if there were a small snake wildly slithering around inside. As the slithering intensified, my waist and back would sometimes even go numb, and then a notion that moves one's flesh incessantly would clearly appear in my mind—I was hungry. I'm not exaggerating at all: any time I saw the commentary on the evening news, analysis of a ball game, or roundtable political debates, or heard the lecture of some writer who was preparing to shave his head and become a monk, my stomach would rumble with hunger. My sister knew about my disorder—she had the same problem. Just as my sister was getting close to being touched by Dad's lecture, I was thinking of one of Grandma's dim sum specialties: Fried Rose Petal Paste. She was thinking of Grandma's Lotus Cakes.

How come Grandma never wrote a cookbook? My sister and I have been puzzled by this question ever since childhood. Perhaps the answer has something to do with the fact that Grandma is illiterate. This, however, cannot completely explain away the regret Mom, Dad, and even my sister and I felt that Grandma never passed on her cooking skills to us. The valiant attempt on the part of my sister and me to make a record of Grandma's cooking with a V-8 video camera and a notebook ended in failure.

That dish of Fried Rose Petal Paste was a typical example. The first image of the run-down *juancun* that I recorded on tape was of the wooden poles, bamboo fence posts, and asbestos shingles that together composed the torrid kitchen. It was at that second that my sister's narration erupted: "Grandma's Cookbook, Chapter 1, Fried Rose Petal Paste."

Covering her face with her hands, Grandma said smilingly, "Cut it out, it's time to cook."

"Excuse me, Grandma, what are the ingredients used in Fried Rose Petal Paste? And what about the amounts for each ingredient?"

The camera shook terribly as the shot panned closer to the kitchen, but you could still make out the handful of eggs, bowl of wheat flour, pot half-filled with water, and porcelain plate covered with a pile of powder shaped like a small mountain (I later learned that the powder was cooking starch) on the Japanese-style wooden counter. In Grandma's hands were a can of white powder and a bag of sesame seeds. She bashfully turned her back to the camera, saying, "This is the stuff right here!" As she spoke, she put down the can of sugar and bag of sesame seeds and grabbed an empty bowl with her free hand. *Crack, crack, crack* into the bowl went three eggs, and she used a set of chopsticks to scramble them, adding in the wheat flour. She ladled in two (maybe three) spoonfuls of water while the other hand added a pinch of cooking starch, and then continued to mix the ingredients at lightning speed with her chopsticks.

"How about the amounts?" my sister's narration continued from some-where off camera. "How much wheat flour do you add? How much water? And what is that?"

"Dried cooking starch," Grandma answered as she slid an empty wok onto the gas stove. After heating it up for a second, she suddenly threw in that bowl of egg-wheat flour paste and inverting her mixing spoon, used the handle to scramble the mixture.

My camera lens chaotically shook back and forth as I tried to avoid the lampblack emitted from the stovetop. Amid the hazy smoke all I saw was Grandma scooping up what appeared to be a lump of lard from another porcelain dish and holding it above the wok, letting the melting lard drib-ble in over the heat. She then fished the cooked paste out of the wok and slid the whole thing onto a porcelain plate.

"After it cools down you slice it and then fry it. As you fry it you cool it off by adding the syrup. Add some sesame seeds and rose petals and you're done." Only then did Grandma turn to directly face the camera. "What's there worth taping here?"

"But you still haven't told us how much of each ingredient you used," my sister objected loudly.

"If there are a lot of people you cook a bit extra, when you've got less people, you cook less. Just as long as you don't waste any food you'll be fine." Facing the camera, Grandma exposed her gold front tooth—this was her conclusion.

During the recording of chapter 8 or 9 of "Grandma's Cookbook," the V-8 video camera expired. With a puzzled tone, the repairman I hired asked, "What the hell did you do to your video camera to make it look like a kitchen ventilator fan?"

My kid sister, however, began to feel an overwhelming sorrow for Grandma. "She has absolutely no idea just what she is doing!" my sister exclaimed. What she meant was that Grandma did not understand just how magnificent a feat it was to be able to prepare three meals a day (in all, she prepared over 43,000 meals over the years) in that ragged, worn-down kitchen.

The reason most women my grandmother's age never became famous chefs was not that their cooking wasn't up to par, but that they never had the opportunity to describe what they were cooking and how they did it. They had lost the ability to tell stories.

"That isn't how you are supposed to use it." That is what the technician who was repairing the V-8 camera said to the absent-minded duo, my sister and me. That was on a weekend afternoon during the late autumn or early winter of 1991—at the time I was an instructor at an officer school and my sister had just begun her junior year in high school. On several occasions afterward we would remember that we had a V-8 video camera that we still hadn't picked up. It was stuck in the warehouse of the repair department of some electronics store, probably covered with dust—or maybe a considerate repairman had wrapped it in a plastic bag. Then again, by now they had probably resold it. Anyway, no matter what the case, my sister and I would always simply say, "I'll go when I have time." Just like we used to say about "going to visit Grandma." For the majority of the time, we were telling stories while listening intently to our own voices. It was as if by doing this we were able to complete or live out something.

What kept my sister and me from going to pick up the video camera was the person in our family who also frequently played the role of the intent listener: my mother.

As the curtain lowered on my father's painting exhibition, the night before he delivered his speech of appreciation, Mom finally broke down—beforehand there wasn't even the slightest forewarning. At the time, she was alone in her room beside a small lamp, going through the thousands of articles she herself had cut out, pasted together, and bound for Dad. My sister burst into my study (which used to be my father's study) to tell me that the V-8 didn't work. To my sister and me, this was an incident of the most serious nature. Originally we had had everything all worked out: we were going to wait until the concluding day of Dad's painting exhibition to begin carrying out our plan. First we would lie low, hiding out in the stationery store across from the gallery; then when the time came we would rush out, pass through the glossy, mirrorlike hallway, and then push our way through the crowd at the gallery. After that, my kid sister would walk up to the podium and, taking advantage of my father's state of happy astonishment, she would grab hold of the microphone and unleash a shocking denunciation. In front of the audience, we wanted to show how his artistic attainments in the realm of painting were no less genius than his talent for torturing our mother. My sister even planned to "tell him something that would haunt him for the rest of his life." And me, I would be standing quietly off to one side recording everything on my V-8 video camera.

But it suddenly broke. The power button didn't work, so all you saw through the viewer was complete darkness and none of the indicator lights lit up. We tried two different batteries but it was to no avail.

Then, me carrying the V-8 with both hands, we knocked open Mom's bedroom door. In the darkness of the room, Mom's eyes sparkled in the ray of light that came in. My sister murmured, "Why is it so dark in here?" As she spoke, she switched on the ceiling light. My mother's robust body was spread out on the bed, partially leaning against the headboard, with a towel covering her stomach and thighs. Over one hundred albums containing cutouts of Dad's articles littered the bed and covered her towel—this was a scene we had grown quite accustomed to. We even knew that after Dad was promoted to a "deputy position" and no longer wrote journalistic articles, Mom still quietly and carefully carried out her job of cutting and pasting, just like always. She collected any article that she felt *should* have been written by Dad and pasted them in that leather-bound album with bronze gilded characters. Some of the articles were editorials from different papers, short stories and novels by famous writers, essays introducing new breakthroughs in medical science, reports of major traffic accidents and natural disasters, and a whole bunch of movie advertisements. My little sister even discovered an autobiographical essay by the wife of the last president of the Soviet Union, Raisa Gorbachev.

At first, Mom just asked with indifference, "Now what do you want? I'm busy."

It was exactly at that moment that she discovered the V-8 video camera in my hands. Immediately her face turned white. Her hands began to tremble and she pushed away the albums and covered her face with the towel. Timidly, her voice shaking, she said, "Don't tape me! Stop recording! I don't want to be recorded!" As she spoke, she grabbed one of the albums and held it before her face, adding another layer to separate her from the camera.

"We are just looking for a screwdriver," my sister said. "Just looking for a screwdriver."

"Stop recording!" my mother screamed, resolutely shaking her towel-covered head behind the scrapbook.

"Mom, we're not recording. The camera is broken," I said.

"I'm sick, don't videotape me. I'm really sick—if you don't believe me ask your pop. You can't tape me."

She meant to say "pop" but what actually came out was "poop." Many, many years before, my sister and I used to call Dad "Poop." Grandma was against us calling him that—she thought that "Poop" sounded too much like dog poop. In front of my parents I always called him Poop and I never felt that there was anything scornful or sarcastic about it. Even though my father was indeed quite dog-shitlike in character, for my mother it was as if he were the only soul in the world that she could rely upon. After Dad had Mom sign the divorce papers, it is quite possible that he sighed when he ran into his friends and explained to them how he had raised my sister and me to adulthood and now all his responsibilities were fulfilled. But actually he chose the perfect time to abandon the family—because it was just around this time that Mom began to utilize the phrase, "If you don't believe me, ask your father," any time she ran into trouble.

Right now I don't want to tell you just how my father designed my mother's illness—but since I've already mentioned it, I can only give you the simplest of explanations. This is because while "listening intently," I painfully discovered how terrifying an ability "storytelling" can be. It can make the true nature of events clear or hazy, stronger or weaker; it can make them right or make them wrong.

This is the reason my sister came so close to being moved by my father's speech. A glimmer emerged from the corner of her eye and she held my hand. At the time I wasn't holding the V-8 camera. It didn't work. It broke down on the same day as my mother.

The Awakening of Laughter

Just like any other girl, my kid sister went through a phase during which she loved to laugh. When I think back to that time, I cannot explain with complete confidence just why she was giggling, but she truly did use that laugh to confront the entire world. That's right, there are a handful of things in the world that are genuinely funny, like the fat man falling down in a comedy show, an idiot getting knocked upside the head by a wooden revolving ladder, or oranges or balls falling out of the chest of a male transvestite. Or have you heard jokes like the one about the explorer who stuck a pineapple up his ass? How about the one about the guy with the coarse, husky voice who had his wiener bitten off by a shark? Sometimes political news or a television miniseries based on a love story is also enough to make you laugh so hard that you even surprise yourself. But what I want to talk about has nothing to do with any of this.

As for my sister, any event happening in the world at the time was enough to arouse her laughter: a stranger who took an extra glance as he passed her on the street, an adult who asked her how old she was or where she went to school, the poster of a pop idol hanging up on a huge bulletin board, a light breeze from out of nowhere that lifted the edge of her blouse, or the extremely corny music that you often hear in an elevator or restaurant. Who knows what experiences she was reminded of by these insignificant events, but somehow she would always find a way to laugh about them. For the two years she wore braces and the few months after she had them removed, she would laugh with her lips closed or conceal her giggles behind her hands; afterward she would still laugh, except then her teeth were exposed.

I always felt that her laughter was mysterious, filled with an element of bashfulness and insecurity; you could even say that laughter was, for her, a kind of fragile weapon. By then it had been quite some time since Dad had brought up Freud. He had also left behind *The Book of Changes*, Lao Tzu, and the miracles of acupuncture, all of which he wouldn't shut up about for quite some time, in order to embark on what would be a fairly extensive journey through cartography. He dug up and collected massive quantities of maps of different types, sizes, scales, regions, uses, and versions, and he demanded that the whole family join him in his delirious fantasy of a magnificent voyage. One evening in the living room, he unveiled what was said to be an extremely rare and precious map of the New Guinea Island territories. That was the first time that my sister and I (probably my mother as well) learned that upon this planet there existed such a thing as Dobuans. My father provided quite an explanation of the customs, habits, and intricacies of life for the Dobuan people. But all I remember is that when he got to the part about the Dobuans' marriage practices, Mom's face suddenly lost its color. One of the details of marriage for the Dobuan people is that if the husband dies or the couple divorces, the children are not only forbidden to consume any food produced in the father's village but also prohibited from even setting foot in the father's village again. If the mother dies, the same rule applies. When Mom heard this part she quietly sighed and stood up. Slapping her hips, which had already begun to grow plump, she lowered her head and walked toward the kitchen. I heard her opening the refrigerator and frantically gulping down a glass of distilled water. My kid sister suddenly burst out laughing. Covering her mouth, she laughed so hard that she keeled over. Although she tried to hold it in, from the space between her teeth she blurted out, "It is really strange. What is he going on about this stuff for?"

From that day onward, I began to pay attention to laughter and the unhappiness that it so often marks.

Unhappy laughter and other related behavior was the determining factor in my discovery that my kid sister was gradually changing. Unhappy yet not necessarily sad or painful; to say sad or painful would be going overboard, for although young girls like my sister are already willing to take on the burdens of life, they do not necessarily have the strength to do so. And so laughter becomes a key that they can use to search for all of the complications, contradictions, and conflicts in life. They laugh, and during the brief moment when people see that smiling face, they always mistake the laughter for a sign of happiness; but that split second of laughter is actually used to ponder the meaning of what lies outside the realm of happiness.

Just like always, my sister was using that awkward smile of hers to confront an awkward situation; I made the acquaintance of Little Chess at some roller-skating rink or disco (anyway, it was one of those places with a revolving mirror ball and laser lights). The line I used to pick up Little Chess was quite simple: "Your smile is just like my little sister's." God only knows what girl doesn't have a smile like my sister's.

Little Chess really wasn't completely indifferent to me mentioning my kid sister—even though I never felt I went as far as she complained, "all day talking about my sister this, my sister that." One day, without giving a second thought to her senile grandfather and his housekeeper, who were both right downstairs, or to the fact that the door wasn't even locked, she screamed, "Your sister, your sister! Why don't you go fuck your sister!" She buttoned up her shirt, hopped off the bed, and turned the doorknob, leaving my naked, exposed body to blankly face a long hallway. From the veranda window on the right side of the hall, a cool mountain draft slithered in. Before the empty room on the left stood a dark and lustrous wooden door. Out of nowhere, I had the illusion that the whole world was watching me. However, I didn't cover myself up or try to hide; instead, I stood up, placed my hands on my hips, and heaved a deep sigh. Once again, my girlfriend Little Chess yelled out, "Go fuck your sister!"

How old was my sister that year, twelve or fourteen? As my naked body welcomed the cool damp breeze off Yangming Mountain that bore a hint of sweetness, I wondered what my kid sister was doing. If she had the ability to travel through space and see me standing there like that, what would her reaction be? Laughter? You bet, she would definitely laugh.

That day, Little Chess and I screwed like mad—we kept at it until the next morning when, on the brink of exhaustion, she began to sadly cry. Her lips repeatedly mumbled, "You can't love your sister, you just can't fall in love with your sister!" She said it a hundred times, maybe a thousand, or then again perhaps even more, and then we both fell into a deep slumber. After we woke up I almost told her about my theory of how "jealousy is the best way to spice up any relationship," but I stopped myself. That was because I didn't want her to know too much about my own sexual awakening. At the time I was still young (although even today, all these years later, I have yet to grow old), but well before I had begun to grow up I had already realized just how difficult it was to extricate oneself from selfish sexual desire to control and possess a single woman. I didn't want those chicks I dated to learn even a little bit of the methodology involved in the self-examination of the origins of sexual desire. Once they discover that their infatuation with some male's body is a possible result of their own intellectual fragility, they will become cold and distant. So let them be jealous, let them go crazy, let them be even more unhappy than unhappy. Take advantage of that moment when all they have is that awkward smile to confront an awkward situation to terminate their pondering. Let them fall into a deep, heavy sleep.

Could this be my sole desire after having been left with but a shell of mortal flesh? Without you even realizing it, Little Chess and those other chicks will awaken and flash you a winsome smile. In the daylight that followed that long, wild, passionate night, I opened my eyes to see her smiling; she didn't look anything like my little sister. Little Chess continued to button up her shirt—she'd button it and unbutton it, unbutton it and button it back up—and she told me, "One day I will leave you and you will never even know why."

When was it that my sister's smile began to have that enchantingly sweet power? Perhaps I will never know. The autumn I enlisted in the military, my sister was already a sophomore art student at a technical high school. She was obsessed with aerobics and health food, she had begun to drink a bit of alcohol and she carried a lighter and pack of cigarettes around wherever she went. She came to visit me where I was stationed and we sat in the shade under an enormous drooping fig tree. She told me that she had begun to study sculpture, she had met a boyfriend, Dad finally admitted the secret affair he had been having with a woman artist for more than twelve years, and Mom had abandoned the hopeless diet plan she had stuck to for the last few years. And then my sister shook her head, exposing that winsome smile. "You men are despicable," she said.

That day, besides reporting on the latest family gossip, she also brought up a young female teacher named Xu Hua. It was this teacher who once lent my sister more than a few books on feminism that not only opened her eyes to the world, but also awakened my sister's "other self," which had been sound asleep within her body. That "self" told my sister (my sister later told me): Man's invention of the multitude of differing mythologies is a result of their jealousy of their fathers having possession of their mothers. In these myths, the hero slays an evildoer or monster and saves the kingdom. The saved kingdom is also another symbol for a kind of father. After the hero rescues the kingdom, the readers (naturally that includes the inventors of these myths) feel that they have repaid the debt owed to their fathers for raising them. Thus with their consciences perfectly clear and their actions justified, they sever all relations with their fathers. The other meaning of ending relations with their fathers is that they can feel justified when, on a spiritual level, they possess their mothers.

I told her, "That is Freud's stale and rotten tune from eighty years ago."

"And eighty years later, men are still turning the same stale and rotten tricks," she said. "Men are really despicable! Their whole lives they have to play around with a whole bunch of women just because they can't screw their own mother."

"And what about your boyfriend? Is he despicable too?"

"Of course," my sister laughingly replied. During the remaining time in the day's visiting hours, my sister helped me brush up on several aspects of Freudian theory that I had come in contact with during college and graduate school. The main point of our discussion didn't go much further than how the primary characters in male-centric hero stories make use of religious, political, and national disputes to create war, and through these wars they reinforce the heroic status of the male. This status enslaves not only the evil and inferior defeated males but also all women. As for her boyfriend, she just pointed out, "Unlike men, who never want to let women know anything, I let him know he is despicable. Moreover, I let him know that I know he is despicable."

All I knew, on the other hand, was that my time for receiving visitors had been ruined. For the majority of the time, I listened with broken attention to those names and terminology that seemed at once so close and yet so far away, and at the appropriate times I nodded my head or mumbled an "uh-huh" to let her know I was listening. Actually, another part of me was thinking of Mom, Dad, Grandma, and Grandpa the whole time.

I never had the ability to go head-to-head with Freud on anything. I've had a prejudice against him ever since Dad took my kid sister as a specimen for observation, imprinting on me the old devil's theories on the anal and oral periods. Any guy with a name as strange as Freud (*Folluoyide*) can't be a very respectable character. After that, whenever my parents' discussions or even arguments about the Electra and Oedipus complexes unexpectedly made their way into my ears, it was like a permanent brand. For a long, long time I was living in constant fear that hidden somewhere in my body was a strange monster. At any time this beast could tear open my flesh, jump out, swallow my father alive, and rape my mother. And it would do this over and over again. Each time my parents appeared in my field of vision, it was as if that strange beast appeared for a split second. The question is not whether or not the beast actually exists, but rather whether or not you know it exists.

This kind of brainwashing can leave you unable to make judgments; it can lead you to suspect your own father as the sole reason you have the desire to possess your own mother. For twelve years, my father surreptitiously screwed a woman artist, and when I started to hate him because of this, was it really because I myself wanted to have my mother? If I were to put my hatred aside for a moment and think of things from his perspective, just what was it that possessed him to torture my mother like that? Was it also the result of an Oedipal chain reaction? The reason for my inability to answer these questions was not my rejection of Freud, but rather that I never understood my father, mother, or anyone else. Now then, could my lack of understanding also be a result of the strange beast sent by Freud that is hidden in my body? The night after my sister came to visit, I dreamed of her riding on a statue of a strange monster. She smoked with a posture that was quite odd, puffing broken, misty clouds of smoke into the air. Then I realized that she was actually straddling me. What were we doing? Don't ask—I don't believe that I could have such a dream. But my sister indeed said, "Let's go!" Just as the distant wake-up call was pressing near, from within the mosquito net I murmured, "Actually, you can fall in love with your sister."

Is a man just in the state of regaining consciousness willing to admit or confess that he has sexual desire for a blood relative? I unhappily pondered the question. Even though there was no one around, just thinking of that fragmented dream and the sentence that I muttered while still half-asleep was enough to make me shake all over. It was as if I were attempting to shake off some evil spirit that was attached to my body. My facial features squeezed together for a second as if I had been electrocuted. Afterward, this expression scattered and dissolved; all that was left of my grimace were the two slightly upturned edges of the mouth. It looked like a smile, the smile of my sister, which disappeared so very long ago.

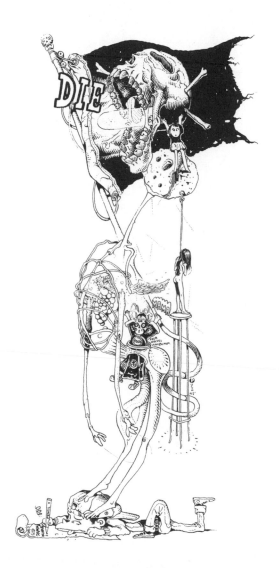

Chronicle of Death

The only sculpture that my sister completed and preserved was a metal figure two feet long, a foot wide, and just over a foot tall. Right now it is on my desk before me. Carved in the head of the statue are a few unevenly shaped cavities—I imagine that they are eyes, ears, a nose, and a mouth. The neck is very thin and made up of crisscrossing strands that resemble fibrous roots of a fig tree or the frame of a lantern (you might say it looks like trees in a forest or something that has been partially hollowed out). The shoulder, chest, and waist area is like a long vine of drooping grapes of different sizes. The largest bunch is near the lower abdomen and after that there are two piles shaped like the lock of a handbag, which I named the butt. Both legs are extended horizontally; the left leg is extended straight out to the left while the right leg is bent forward at the knee. These two legs are the sole element of realism in the whole sculpture. It was also only on the basis of the legs that we could identify the work as "a sculpture." Its name is *The Living Me*. The day I completed my military service, my sister presented me with this living element of herself. You could say it was a gift.

"Is this bronze sculpture of you?" I asked.

She shook her head: "Part of it is bronze, but only one part. What is inside"—she tapped her finger on the grape-shaped part—"definitely isn't."

"What is that part made from?"

"How can I put it?" She began to smile. "Anyway, it's really complicated, so I forgot."

Later that day, in a loud, crowded restaurant specializing in Jiangxi and Zhejiang cuisine, she told me that she was pregnant. Her words were constantly being drowned out and interrupted by the resonant voice of the bald guy at the next table. The bald guy was teaching the other guests at his table how to properly sing the line "I'm called Little Fan" in *The Fourth Son Visits His Mother* with just the right crackling tone.

Grandpa also loves to sing this opera, *The Fourth Son Visits His Mother*; probably everyone from his generation loves to sing it. In this respect he and my father have absolutely no way of communicating. Once, while I was in the courtyard of the run-down *juancun* where Grandpa lived, I watched Grandpa and a whole bunch of other grandpas singing *The Fourth Son Visits His Mother*. I asked my dad who this fourth son was. My father said that it was probably the same fourth son from the Zhenping comic strips, right? Grandpa continued to bow his two-stringed Chinese violin as he twisted his head and yelled at Dad, "That's a bunch of damn bullshit!" When they got to the end of the next section, Grandpa pointed to the grandpa playing the role of the fourth son and said, "His name is Yang Yanhui, and he was the fourth born so they call him Yang the Fourth. His father and all five or six of his brothers were slaughtered in a battle. Only he escaped to the Kingdom of Fan, where in order to survive he changed his name and took the princess from the Kingdom of Liao as his wife. Many years later, Yang the Fourth still direly missed his long-lost mother, so he secretly left the palace and rode horseback several nights to the border region to see his mother once again."

I remember that being a tragic tale; Yang the Fourth was a chain-smoker with a crimson nose that resembled a wax apple. He was drinking strong tea and spitting in the small garden. He was a pitiful grandpa.

A few years later, that Yang the Fourth, while on a Taiwan-bound aircraft leaving America, asked the stewardess for two pillows and two blankets, then went to sleep and never woke up. Grandpa took my sister and me to his funeral. At the funeral, people sang the holy verses and gave sermons. Even though I dozed off once or twice, I will never forget one thing: Yang the Fourth laid out in that black metallic casket. The coffin was covered with ivory-colored satin and bursting with fresh flowers; Yang was wearing a slightly wrinkled gray and black Western suit. People who had come to pay their respects crowded around, walking in circles around his casket. Holding my little sister in one arm and grasping his cane in the other, Grandpa walked extremely slowly. I walked much more quickly. I did two laps around the coffin and discovered that the face of the deceased was much redder than that of the average person. I also realized that that crimson nose of his that had always resembled a wax apple had turned a pale white. This experience was my first encounter with the face of death. It enabled me to tell stories.

Spicing things up a bit, I once retold this story to my elementary-school classmates. I told them that Grandpa Yang the Fourth killed himself. Suicide—how very mysterious and mystical.

My classmates grilled me on how I knew it was a suicide. This skepticism, however, couldn't stop me; I just told them that Grandpa Yang stuffed a suicide note in his pillowcase. The note stated that he would rather die than face the lack of filial piety displayed by his son and daughter-in-law after they emigrated to America. What proved more difficult was explaining the technical details of the suicide. And so I created a 100 percent fictitious ending for Grandpa Yang the Fourth. When he was in mainland China he had had many brothers, but during a battle in the Kingdom of Liao they were all killed, and he was the sole survivor. In order to get by, he changed his name and married a woman from the Kingdom of Liao. Because he was doing underground political work, most of his actions had to be carried out in secret. One example was his study of the "magic art of assassination by will" during a time when the Liao natives were distracted. What is the "magic art of assassination by will"? It is using the power of one's spirit to make another person kick the bucket.

To learn this art you must first learn to meditate; then you must whole-heartedly concentrate on one person, his features, voice, actions, every-thing. Once you have him perfectly clear in your mind, all you need to do is bite down on your teeth and that faraway person will die of bronchial rupture. The Grandpa Yang in my story used this method to take out every person from the Kingdom of Liao who came too close to him, and in the end he escaped back to Taiwan. But because he used his magic to kill his wife, his son hated him and emigrated to America. From then on, his son never again spoke one word to his father. The story's conclusion is, of course, on board a plane. Our Grandpa Yang asked the stewardess for two pillows and two blankets. He placed one pillow behind his head, held the other in his arms, and wrapped his entire body in the two blan-kets (this was to avoid harming other innocent passengers). Grandpa Yang began to reflect upon his past, and the moment he understood his whole life better than he could ever have hoped to, he bit down on his teeth, bringing his life to a close.

Many, many years later, my classmate Huang Anbang still remembered that story. During one of our class reunions he presented each person with his business card (stating that he was the assistant manager of an insur-ance company), and a retelling of the tale of the "magic art of assassina-tion by will." He said I was a natural writer who could create stories a per-son could never forget. Take him, for example: every time he takes a plane, he cannot help but suspect that the character next to him wrapped up in a blanket is in the midst of carrying out a suicide. He stirred up all my old memories of Grandpa Yang, but he had an ulterior motive. Besides praising how moving my stories were, I suspect he was hoping his old classmates would admire him for flying all over the world in 747s.

After that class reunion, with drunken, bleary eyes, I went with a chick whose name was something like Jasmine back to her apartment on the twentieth floor of some luxury high-rise. Her apartment was thick with the mixed scent of air freshener, aromatic oil, essential oil, and perfume. This Jasmine, or whatever her name was, said that she had sat next to me in elementary school. At the time she had burnt brown hair, crooked teeth, and incomparably pathetic grades, yet she claimed to have had a secret crush on me. I don't remember any of that stuff. All I know is that after she grew up she was beautiful and alluring, probably the mistress of some rich businessman. She didn't work, yet had an apartment full of name-brand clothing and jewelry as well as several hundred club cards and credit cards. She threw those cards in the air and, as they fell to the ground like scattered snowflakes, she said, "Actually, I lead a very difficult life." After that she took off all her clothes and draped a soft fur coat, made from what looked like marten, over her body. Standing in the light of the flashing neon sign, which was coming in from the window, she asked me, almost pleading, "Write a story for me, my story, okay? Then I will be able to die in peace."

Her story is pretty much the same as everyone else in the world's story. The main character experiences something and afterward is unable to recover or return to the way things were, like Yang the Fourth reuniting with his long-lost mother, or that Jasmine girl attending an elementary-school reunion. These allow the main character to discover that living is but the accumulation of a series of death experiences: we experience a day of life just to realize that we are unable to return to yesterday's life. When the character realizes this, he feels terribly sad, because the reality of life is precisely the reality of death. Even sadder is the fact that in reality, he or she was never any kind of a main character. They never lived; moreover, they always pass away so insignificantly. And so all that is left is that final wish: "Write a story for me, okay?"

I never took this Jasmine chick's petty, vulgar story and put it down on paper—because of which, during one of her visits when I was in the military, my sister accused me of being a "literary profiteer." That is because I took advantage of my name as a writer to bang that Jasmine chick a good couple of times but never fulfilled my promise to write her story. My sister felt my actions were unjust; she said I was even worse than the rich businessman who provided Jasmine with an apartment, a marten fur, and a whole bunch of credit cards. After my sister's lengthy and voluble condemnation, it was a long time before I was willing to mention my romances to her again, even though I could refute her by saying that sex has its own impetus, objective, and value. But I could not deny that from the beginning, each time I went to that small apartment on the twentieth floor, my objective wasn't this Jasmine's pathetic story—it was her fragrantly perfumed body. And so I can't help but admit that the accusation of being a "profiteer," in an extremely humorous way, is actually right on the money.

Would my kid sister use the same severe language to criticize that little bastard who disappeared after getting her pregnant? Right now, if I lean a bit forward and reach out my hand, I can touch that statue *The Living Me*. Even now I still don't know whether or not my sister was pregnant when she was working on this sculpture. Was she already in love? Or did she already foresee that she would have to experience a death within her? Right now, as I speak, I am using a standard completely out of line with orthodox artistic criteria to read my sister's sculpture. I think what I read from it is "the meaning of my sister's life." Did my sister realize that she was a person with a blurred identity, and is that why she dug out small cavities all over its face? Did my sister feel the suffocating stress of life, and is that why she let the figure have a neck bursting open with holes? Did she feel that the female corporeal body was a string of plump and juicy fruit, a malignant growth that continued to spread, or a combination of both? Is this why she decided to give her sculpture an armless body, lacking the ability to either seize or hug? Then what was the meaning of the pelvis and hips that looked like a closed handbag lock? Could it mean that the organ that gives birth to life is not easily opened? Has the device that deep down contains unlimited maternal potential already been sealed? Then why did she still get pregnant?

The Living Me is a living mystery; the sole part with an explanation is the figure's legs. The legs are an element of pure realism: in their proportion, contour, skin texture, and lines, they are without doubt a perfect simulation of my sister's legs. Why is it that this was the only place where my sister substantively and delicately copied a portion of her true self?

"Only when I walk and walk and walk and walk and walk do I know that I am alive," my sister once told me.

The day she told me that was before I had left the army, and I had just gotten back from Xitou where I had broken up with some chick. When I arrived back in Taipei I got the news that Mom and Dad were getting a divorce. Shoulder to shoulder, my sister and I aimlessly strolled along the city limits—perhaps we were trying to return to a part of our subconscious past? We walked back to the tattered *juancun* where Grandma and Grandpa lived. Pushing open the always-unlocked courtyard gate, I pointed to the fifty-square-foot red-brick area in the corner of the garden and whispered to my sister, "That is where Grandpa always plays his Chinese violin and sings opera."

Once Grandpa was deep asleep, Grandma started to play her Mahjong Mate video game. As she hit the buttons to show the tiles and take new ones, she told us all the latest neighborhood gossip; the latest news was always about death. There was always some grandpa who slipped in the bathroom and passed away, or some grandma who, after putting off her final date with lung cancer for many years, finally couldn't delay the meeting any longer. After she told us about some mother who passed away in a car accident just outside the neighborhood, Grandma turned off her Gameboy and announced that she was cooking noodles for us. She even muttered, "You never know how much time you have left. I'd better eat while I still can!"

Late that night, my sister suddenly asked me, "Did you ever wonder how you will die?"

How could I not? I'm a writer. Are not writers that peculiar breed of animal that spends all its time taking the unpredictability of death (and subsequent resurrection) and putting it down on paper? I delicately slurped a strand of noodle into my mouth, careful not to bite it in two, while I eyed the other half that was still struggling to come to the broth's surface from beneath the vegetables. Honestly speaking, I hate talking about death over noodles.

"Have you ever imagined that your continued existence will mean death for another?" She used her chopsticks to twist her noodles apart, rendering them into short, stubby pieces that looked like a bunch of insects.

I didn't answer her question; instead I just warned her not to play with her food. As I continued to stuff my noodles down, my mind started to wander. My thoughts wandered past Grandpa talking in his sleep and the mosquito net, past the fragrant pittosporums that were growing in the garden, past the several rows of closely packed black tiles that covered the roof, and past several blocks to a small apartment on the twentieth floor of some modern high-rise. Probably inside this apartment we would find a woman called something like Jasmine who always feels she has a difficult life. She hopes that someday she will be able to appear in a novel where she can live with more dignity, live more like a main character, and then she can peacefully die. I finished my bowl of noodles, let out a belch, heard my grandfather call out someone's name, picked up my sister's bowl of noodles, and began to slurp it down. I thought that perhaps I could have this Jasmine character kill herself in my next novel. I could arrange a noble motive for her suicide in the story.

That's right. After putting away two bowls of noodles I realized that I had gotten to an age where I could come up with all kinds of excuses to keep on living. At the same time, I could better find a meaning in death, unlike when I was in elementary school and all I knew how to do was tell tall tales of the arts of assassination by will and suicide by will. Perhaps toward the conclusion of the work I could have this Jasmine come upon some sudden enlightening realization. For example, after living a life of pettiness and degradation, having served as mistress for over a dozen men, she realizes that suicide is a challenge directed at the heart of the supreme power. If we use the words of my grandfather, a devout Christian, God bestows life upon us; thus, suicide is a crime no different from showing contempt for or insulting God. In my novel I could designate this Jasmine to usurp this power from the controller of life, God. Her suicide symbolizes her extrication from His power, for suicide is outside the realm of even His control. This Jasmine leaps from a twenty-story building and, after plummeting past several flashing neon signs, lands on the ground—I could even arrange for her to land on the red-brick corner of a courtyard where a crowd of people are singing *The Fourth Son Visits His Mother*. The noble motive for this suicide is to overturn the sacredness of the root of life.

The day I accompanied my sister to have her abortion, I told her that she wasn't doing anything wrong; all she was doing was taking away a small child's right to hate and detest his or her parents, and that was it. I tried to use a dialectical argument to explain to her that existing, surviving, and living out a full life are all of the utmost difficulty and pain. It is precisely because of the misery of life that with life there must also come a ha-tred for its source. Then I turned to her and told her the whole story about how, before she was born, Dad confined me to the run-down *juan-cun* until I recovered from pneumonia. Looking back, I told her, "That was the first time I discovered that I had hatred within me. Moreover, the ob-ject of my hatred was Dad—and now I realize that I had every right to hate him!"

"You must have fucking hated me back then," my sister said as she wiped the tears from the corners of her eyes. She then grabbed my wrist and continued with a forced smile, "I must be hateful. I've always been nothing but a despicable *wang ba dan*, haven't I?"

I shook my head and asked in reply, "Do you remember you once asked me about someone else dying in order for you to continue living?"

She didn't remember. It is so easy for her to forget those casual details that later influence others. I'm the same (I had completely forgotten about that story I made up about Grandpa Yang, yet it always haunted at least one person whenever he was on board a plane). Afterward I patted the back of her hand, saying, "What we have been doing from the beginning, and always are doing, is *leading to the death of another.*"

I don't just mean Grandpa Yang, that Jasmine girl, and the innumerable number of characters who died in my stories and novels—they are not the only ones. Neither is that real-life fetus that lived in its mother's womb for only three months. But as long as there are people, their existence will nec-essarily be a part of a secret order that will result in the ending of other lives. I went on vaguely explaining this to my sister, though it is quite prob-able that I myself didn't even believe it. I just wanted to help my sister be rid of the evil guilt associated with destroying a tiny life, which I was afraid would gnaw away at her for the rest of her life.

"Oh, I remember!" My sister's eyes suddenly lit up. "I asked you that day we were at Grandma's place. It was because Grandma mentioned some mother who got run over by a car."

"That's right," I said. My sister asked if I knew the reason she had posed that question. I said I didn't know. My sister said she was thinking about our mother.

Twenty-eight years ago, my mother witnessed a terrible bus accident. Squeezed in the bus were ninety-one children and adults. When the accident happened, my mom was beside the road just a few yards away, taking photographs. For the last twenty-odd years she has always felt that she had something to do with that accident. Not only did she witness death, but something within even drove her to take several dozen photos documenting it. After the incident, she gradually, peacefully, gently, and softly fell apart. During this time she had the illusion several hundred, several thousand times that my sister and I were both dead spirits of the accident victims.

116

Could this be who we are? The moment the face of death approaches, the ability to tell stories is born. This ability forces the living to repent from deep inside, confess that the existence of life is a kind of reliance on a supreme power. Precisely because of the devoutness and sincerity of our confession, the ladder to religion and God is long surpassed and we have the opportunity to shed our reluctance to part with life. We also only then understand that life is actually the accumulation of a series of death experiences, and it is also only then that we dare own up to the fact that we all have the mysterious and mystical ability to commit suicide.

終結瘋狂

Ending in Insanity

I still have a perfect impression of the first time my sister came face-to-face with the perplexity of genetics. Grandma was holding her hand and they were walking three, maybe five, steps ahead of me. We were walking past the row of stores near the edge of the run-down *juancun* on our way to have some sesame paste. On the way, Grandma explained to my sister: this is a soy milk shop, they sell scallion pancakes and deep-fried twisted dough sticks; this is a hardware store, and they sell brooms, dustpans, and window screens. Over here is a barber shop, they sell heads—of course, they can't really sell heads because then the person would have to die—so they have to settle for selling clumps of hair. This over here is . . .

"This is the place where your big brother's life was saved." Grandma stopped and pointed across the street to the building that doubled as Dr. Zhong's clinic and pharmacy. "That doctor is actually a veterinarian, but he is nevertheless a brilliant physician." Afterward Grandma shook her head as if she had recalled some fond memory. Letting out a sigh, she went into all the details about Dr. Zhong. She told us his wife was a Japanese with skin that was white and tender, and their daughters had the same ivory, delicate skin as their mother. She went on and on until she almost forgot that we had already passed the sesame-paste store.

"A dragon begets a dragon and a phoenix begets a phoenix," Grandma said. "The son of a mouse also learns to dig holes—"

I cut her off. "Aren't we going to eat sesame paste?"

Then my sister butted in to ask, "Then—can the daughter of a mouse also dig holes?"

As to whether or not we will be able to carry on anything that our ancestors began, I think we are all more than a bit curious. From my observations of this three-generation family, I can offer some modest discussion and analysis. The day my sister was born, Grandpa slipped and knocked out a front tooth. From then on, Grandpa would often unknowingly pout his upper lip downward in an attempt to cover up that leftover front tooth which, without the support of a partner to keep it straight, began to unscrupulously poke outward. This little habit of Grandpa's was something he didn't learn until later in life, so it had nothing to do with genetics. However, during the final day of Dad's painting exhibition, I saw Dad's face (to be more precise, Dad's mouth) do the exact same thing. The network of nerves in the ten square centimeters around both my grandfather's and my father's mouths must have been almost identical. The brain delivered a message to the nervous system saying, "Cover up the front tooth, cover up the front tooth," causing the skin in the upper lip area, which we commonly refer to as the philtrum, to nervously pucker over the bottom, just like a kissing fish.

When my father's kissing-fish painting exhibition came to a close, it was a magnificent sight; in the bottom corner of the majority of his works was a red ribbon, which meant that Dad had done a pretty good job of making connections around town. Dad was standing before painting number 80 with a glass of champagne or vitamin soda (it was some kind of bubbly drink) in his hand, toasting all his admirers who came to flatter him. That old mistress of his, the woman painter, was all smiles as she stood behind a table or counter wearing a thin, jet-black shirt with embroidered flowers, a short black skirt, and a set of raven fishnet stockings. She was scanning the gallery in an attempt to figure out which chump might purchase the next painting. My sister and I were standing in a stationery shop across the way, separated by two glass doors. From time to time we would exchange a glance trying to determine the most suitable time for us to make our entrance into the gallery. We waited for a really long while, during which time I suddenly realized that my father could also pucker his upper lip like a kissing fish—this instantly brought heredity to mind.

Can facial expressions be inherited? Can actions be inherited? What about tone of voice, manner of speaking, and attitude—can they also be inherited? Or how about mood? Let's take the example of happiness. Is it possible that happiness is the result of heredity? Also sadness—could sadness be the product of some gene different from the happiness gene? If those divination experts, fortune-tellers, and astrologers are able to provide right-on-the-money forecasts for the unknowable and unpredictable future of humanity, it is as if everything in the universe has been predetermined from the beginning. If this is the case, then I'm afraid the indignant resentment and coldness displayed by my sister and me at the gallery that day was already decided well before the great primordial explosion that created the world. So I can also tell you that the will for revenge is like this: it is already inherited before any incident calling for revenge occurs or any person deserving of revenge is even born. Before I tell you about this vengeful incident, let me say that any opinion I raise will not mean much; but if you definitely want to formulate your conclusion, it is perhaps best that I go back to talking about heredity.

For example, in my grandparents' relationship you can find traces of the way my father used all types of knowledge to explore, understand, and torture my mother. When Grandpa declared Grandma a heretic and a Pharisee, my little sister was probably still in my mom's womb developing her hands, feet, and comparatively large but useless brain. I was still suffering from my never-ending high fever and Grandpa was constantly worrying that the veterinarian was going to do something that would turn my feverish brain into that of a pig or some other animal. With a Bible in one hand and his reading glasses in the other, Grandpa blocked the doorway with his body. He sternly scolded Grandma as he tried to stop her: "Not only do you not go to church, repent your sins, or do anything good for society, but now you want to take the kid to that veterinarian! Do you realize that he married a Japanese? What's so great about marrying a Japanese?"

Grandma pushed me back; then she herself took a step back and roared, "Are you going to let us go or not?"

She probably already knew that Grandpa wasn't going to let us through, so right then and there she lifted her leg and kicked Grandpa in the shin. As soon as Grandpa teetered over his Bible fell, his glasses smashed to the ground, and a gap appeared in the doorway. Grandma turned around, grabbed hold of me, and with one motion picked me up on her shoulder and dashed out the door into the alleyway. I could hear Grandpa screaming from inside: "Heretic! You heretic! Pharisee!"

After my fever went down, my heretic grandmother started praying and attending church. For Grandma, believing in Christ was probably not much different from going to the temple to burn incense or thanking Buddha for answering her prayers. She also didn't necessarily mind going to those church activities where a whole bunch of people would gather together to sing the sacred verses and exchange everyday life experiences and ideas. I don't dare guess whether or not she was a devout believer, but even though her conversion was the result of my miraculous recovery, she shouldn't have had to put up with Grandpa's brazen accusations—even if Grandpa used only veiled implications to make them.

It happened on a spring Sunday morning. Grandpa was at the podium delivering a testimony; he was sermonizing on the twenty-fifth chapter of the Book of Sirach. He recited aloud a chapter from the holy book: " 'Any wound, but not a wound of the heart! Any wickedness, but not the wickedness of a woman! Any suffering, but not suffering from those who hate! And any vengeance, but not the vengeance of enemies! There is no venom worse than a snake's venom, and no anger worse than a woman's wrath.' " The second he got to this point I saw him cast a sidelong glance at Grandma. I followed his line of sight down to Grandma, who didn't seem to look in the least bit offended. She just sat there absorbed and completely docile, nodding her head with her extremely amiable smile. It was as if she firmly believed every word Grandpa said.

I will never forget that image of Grandma. She was not only willing to be insulted, but also completely oblivious to the vindictiveness of the insult being directed at her. If I remember correctly, it was from that point on that I ceased any type of true prayer, and never again did I piously call out the name of God or Jesus Christ Our Lord. This is because I firmly believe that the words of God and Jesus Christ, as stated in the Bible, can be cut up into tiny slices, just like pork; then you add a bit of anger or maliciousness for seasoning and you can use them on any innocent old lady like Grandma.

My grandparents' shouting match of a marriage has lasted half a century, and it will no doubt continue to endure. Perhaps the reason for this is complicated, or maybe it is simple; then again, it might just be the result of something I don't understand. As I gradually grew older, I still could not forget Grandpa's absurd and severe mocking of Grandma. At the same time I also began to develop the distinction between selfishness and razor-sharp jealousy of an adult male. On one occasion I raised the issue with Grandpa in private. I asked, "In the Bible it says, 'There is no venom worse than a snake's venom, and nothing worse than an angry woman.' Just what chapter and section is that quote taken from?"

"'. . . and no anger worse than a woman's wrath.'" Grandpa started by correcting me and then, without even taking a moment to think about it, answered: "Chapter 25 of the Book of Sirach, somewhere around section 17 or 18."

I went back and reread the passage in question and, studying it carefully, discovered that it was truly brimming with boundless meaning. In pointing out the evils of woman, besides licentiousness the passage naturally cites jealousy of other women, excess talk of the lips, as well as. . . . When I got to this point I couldn't help but conjecture: the instant Grandpa deviously insulted Grandma in front of that crowd of people all those years ago, weren't his lips doing a little excess talking? Wasn't he jealous of that Dr. Zhong? Was this not the case? It was precisely because he had no outlet for his tangled array of insane and evil ideas that he was left with no choice but to tear apart and dismember those words from the Bible like he was slicing pork. He then fried up his meat recipe in a skillet called revenge and served it to the woman who was both his imaginary lover and his enemy.

I don't want to deceive you, so let me admit, I have done the same thing. Since I began writing, I have also learned the art of slicing pork. I take people's experiences, words, my own impressions, illusions, and those tidbits of knowledge that appear to be brimming with wisdom and scramble them together. Then I chop and fry, presenting a dish brimming with hidden anger and malice. It is a meat dish: a Holy Communion saturated in jealousy. There is no need for me to say that my cooking skill was inherited from my grandfather. Actually its origin is much earlier; you could even trace it back to the beginning of the universe.

The direct cause for my life occurred on a certain day in the middle of August, 1965. It was on that day that sexual desire, impassioned by a lust for knowledge, inspired a multitude of sperm to ejaculate into my mother's body. And thus I inherited the unbroken chain of two families and more than eight generations of carnivorous flesh and blood. More than ten years later, my mother became a vegetarian and my parents' marriage began to lose its taste. He already had another sexual partner, plus he could no longer enjoy his favorite meat dishes at home, and so he had no choice but to start torturing Mom.

I've never known just how he thought this scheme up. It is probable that before I caught on to him he had been at it for quite some time. But I must admit one thing: Dad really knew how to take advantage of his vast knowledge to keep the pleasure in his marriage going, at least for himself. At the time I was already in middle school; my kid sister was still playing it easy in kindergarten. I had my own radio with a set of two speakers, each as big as a lunchbox; people called it a bookshelf boom box. Just before the incident occurred, my sister took my speaker cable and another bunch of multicolored cords and wrapped them all up into what looked like a wool ball, then drew a pair of chopsticks in and out. Of course I realized that she was imitating Grandma knitting, but I slapped that four- or five-year-old Grandma anyway. She burst out crying, wailing so loud that she shook the aluminum door and windows. But you know, if both parents are home and the kids are fighting and there is absolutely no reaction after three minutes of shrieking by the youngest child, you know that in the house there is an even greater evil being perpetrated. It was my kid sister who first hushed up and, while still shuddering with quiet sobs, began to concentrate her attention on intently listening. I noticed it immediately after her; coming from outside the room, there was wave after wave of talking that sounded like heavy rain tapping on the window on a summer afternoon. My intuition told me that it was a secret, a secret like an incantation.

I softly unlocked the door so their voices would come through a bit clearer.

"Is it the case or not?" my father demanded several times. I opened the crack in the door a bit wider. I gazed down along the wall to see Dad's silhouette in the corner of the short hallway. He was slightly stooped over with his head facing right, and the living-room floor lamp emitted a golden ring of light that illuminated the distinct edges of his profile. He was looking at Mom. The outline of Mom's body was black, with only the left side of her expressionless face exposed. Between my father's intermittent words, I could hear the sound of her sobbing. Then my sister suddenly called out from behind me: "Ma—" No one paid any attention to her. I turned and signaled for her to be quiet by placing my index finger over my lips, but she apparently thought this was some sort of game. "Mom! Big brother—is peeping," she said.

The person truly doing the peeping was my father. His was so absorbed in his peeping that he didn't even hear my sister's shouts. He continued to interrogate Mom: "Why do you want to deny it? What good is denying it? And even if you admit it, what is the big deal? Sooner or later you have to face the facts! Is it the case or not?"

"I'm not," my mother softly answered as the shadow of her head violently shook.

"Denying it won't change the objective reality, so why do you want to deny it? Come on, tell me the answer and then we can move on." My father extended his arm and grabbed hold of Mom's hand, then one word at a time he asked: "Why—do—you—want—to—deny—it?"

"I'm . . ."

"All I'm asking is why—do—you—want—to—resist?"

"I . . ."

"Speak! Why do you want to resist?"

"I'm . . . afraid!"

"That's it, you're afraid! Fear!" Dad patted Mom on the shoulder and gently said, "Okay, we'll stop here for today. We will continue next week."

At that moment I shot my head up to check out the calendar hanging on the back of the door. It was Thursday, my father's regular day off. From then on, every Thursday I would always keep one ear open for his movements. This went on for seven weeks, until my mother finally admitted what my father wanted her to confess: that she had a serious mental problem.

For many years later, up until the day that my sister and I stood in the stationery shop, we had been planning our scheme, waiting for the proper time to carry it out. As our scheme was just getting off the ground, Mom was probably just entering into her artificially induced sleep. That morning when my sister and I left the sanatorium a stiff nurse with a facial tic told us, "From now on your mother will eat, sleep, and have her shots and medicine all at the proper times—that way it will be easier to keep her from imagining things." If what that nurse said was correct, at that moment my mother had just taken a package of medicine containing red-white capsules and a light blue tablet and was now deep into her afternoon dream. Even now, I still cannot help but believe that our father, taking advantage of Mom's inability to resist, spared no effort in talking her into insanity.

It was then that my sister nodded her chin, signaling that something was up. I turned my head and, through two glass doors, I saw my father explaining work number 80 in the exhibition to some distinguished guest in a three-piece suit. The raven-clothed woman artist held her original position, but her actions—her actions underwent some changes that gave my sister and me a feeling of both shock and familiarity. She was wiping the surface of that table or counter with a thin piece of tissue. After she finished, her high-heeled shoes carried her around the crowd of people to the corner of the gallery, where she threw her piece of tissue into the garbage. Then, smiling and greeting people along the way, she went back to where she was, pulled out another piece of tissue, and went back to wiping that countertop.

At this moment my sister's face went blank (mine probably did as well), and we both verified one thing. This woman artist was doing something exactly the same as our mother. I'm not referring to that minor, almost unnoticeable cleaning disorder—I'm referring to the fact that she was tempting my father to drive her into insanity.

Is it possible that madness is hereditary? The majority of the normal people I have come in contact with would all probably attribute insanity to one's ancestors. During their weekly Thursday heart-to-heart sessions, my father, on several dozen occasions, also told my mother, "Think for a second about your condition, not just about your own past experience, but think about your parents, grandparents, and great-grandparents. Could your cleaning disorder be hereditary?"

Mom's normal reaction was to shake her head. I later estimated that she actually enjoyed sitting there quietly shaking her head with tears streaming down her face. It was a form of encouragement that could inspire my father to continue exploring, understanding, and torturing her. Mom inspired Dad enough for him to affirm that here was indeed a human soul that needed treatment, needed salvation, needed HIM.

"Do you want some more time to think it over? You don't want to rush to deny anything—of course, you also don't want to admit anything too quickly either." That is what my father would say further on into the game. By then he had gone bananas over the *Book of Changes*, Lao Tzu, and acupuncture, and he also used these tools to increase Mom's dependence on him, on his endless caring, and on his words. My father explained the classics to her, gave her acupuncture treatment, and later showed her all kinds of maps and took her on an imaginary tour of the world. And then he asked her, "Do you feel any better?"

Mom would smile, sigh, shake her head, and go back to wiping the table and chairs, washing clothes, and mopping the floor. She would wash clean anything in her sight that could be cleaned.

By the time the woman artist threw away her third piece of tissue, my father was already giving his speech. He first thanked the senior administrator at his newspaper and all those who love and support the art of painting, and then he thanked the woman artist. My sister and I quickly walked over to the entrance of the stationery store and pushed open the glass door. With two giant steps, we flew down the hallway, pulled open the glass gallery door, and appeared unexpectedly in front of our father, who was in the middle of his speech. He smiled happily, and with a completely predictable gesture raised his arm to welcome my sister, who was making her way to the front of the gallery.

"Of course, I also want to thank my children. I'm truly ecstatic that they were able to make it. My son, perhaps you all know, is a young writer. My daughter, she is an aspiring sculptor. Honestly speaking, I'm quite proud. Could it be that it's in our family's genes?"

Amid the applause and laughter, my sister grabbed hold of the microphone and showed off that winsome smile. "Thank you, Dad," she said. "I think this a rare opportunity, and I'd like to take this moment to introduce my own work."

Dad once again took the lead, being the first to applaud, and this time even the woman artist began to liven up a bit and started to clap. She couldn't applaud too loudly, however, because she still had a piece of tissue in her hand.

"The name of my piece is *I Just Aborted a Child*. The reason for this work is twofold. First, I'm not that certain just who the child's father is; and second, I'm not too comfortable with my own genes. My mother is insane—just today she was admitted to a sanatorium. I suspect that a genetic background like this can't be all that good. Thank you!"

My sister was laughing throughout her speech. Her laughter left the hundred-plus elegantly dressed public figures in attendance at a loss to determine whether her speech was real or a joke. Only my father, standing beside my sister, only he was left stupefied, with his eyes emitting a dull confused luster. However, his long-held power of controlling the dialogue did not instantly fall apart—at least he remembered to take the microphone back. Then, holding the microphone like an obsessed singer, he pathetically muttered three useless but terribly honest words: "Are you crazy?"

Is my sister insane? All I know is that as she waved to the sea of people in the audience, she exclaimed, "It's all in the genes!"

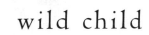

A Drifting Preface

On the streets I met a gang leader who told me: "The longer you drift the more you will learn. What you learn affects the kind of person you end up turning into." That gang leader once had a wish. He wanted to weasel his way into a position where he could take care of things at a harbor port; that way, every day he could help take in all kinds of gang brothers, and of course, he would have to see some off as well. But in the end, because his weaseling didn't cut it, he never made it to any port; rather he became the one that the others take in. Only later did I realize that that is what it is like trying to make it in the streets—either you end up docking at some filthy port, or you forever float, drifting around some unknown place like a ghostly apparition.

Big Head Spring

Junkyard Notice

All that is left in this world are gang leaders, good-for-nothings, and dead people. Teenagers are already a thing of the past.

FRIENDS

Later, I made many friends. Among them are a few whom I will never see again: Zeng Ahzhi is just one. One of his eyes was bigger than the other; the white part of that eye was also notably larger—he usually used this eye to see ghosts, then later he would tell us what he saw. Like the time when he saw Tarō at the junkyard behind the sheet-iron bathroom door, he told us, "Tarō said he was really cold." None of us saw any of this, but we all remembered that Tarō used to always be afraid of the cold. Wearing that ridiculously strange paper hat, he escaped from the slaughterhouse, and the night he first met us, he kept saying, "It's so cold! So cold!" That is also what Tarō said the afternoon he died. Much, much later, there would also come a time when I would never again lay eyes on Hoop and Apricot—they're probably still locked up in a tiny room within that huge hotel being straddled by a bunch of fat, fishy-smelling men. Just as Hoop and Apricot are screaming, a horde of bats flies out through the hole in the window screen and then flies back in. But this already has nothing to do with me; even supposing that I should later meet another woman as terrified of cockroaches, spiders, bats, and Horsefly as those two, there is no way I'm having anything to do with them. Perhaps I'll still run into Horsefly, and maybe I'll even put two bullets in his stomach—but that would just be for fun. After getting shot in the stomach, Horsefly would spring to his feet with a forward somersault and say, "Fuck! Is that all you got?" That would really be kind of funny to see. But besides this, I would be willing to bet that if you were to run into Horsefly, Little Five, and Ah Dibo, you wouldn't be laughing. Little Five can break a beer bottle with a pocketknife, and Ah Dibo has the habit of riding around in stolen RZR motorcycles in search of police cars to go head-on with. They rarely leave Horsefly's side; even when they are sent out to buy cigarettes, betel nuts, or Prince Instant Noodles, you can sense that their imposing, dark shadows somehow remain with him. One time Old Bull stepped on Ah Dibo's shadow. "Did you step on my shadow?" asked Ah Dibo. Old Bull lowered his head to glance at his shoes and said, "I've got it! Those tea leaves . . ." Ah Dibo, throwing one fist forward, knocked Old Bull straight down, just like a bowling pin. Ever since then, Old Bull would always manage to think of some event or person at the most improper of times. Little Horse said that his brain was fried, completely fucked, and I think he's right. But I'm always reminiscing about Old Bull. Besides Little Horse and Little Xinjiang, I think Old Bull is my best friend—my third-best friend. If you were to ask me who my first-best friend is, I would say Little Horse; that's because Uncle Xu is too old, he only counts as an elder, not as a real friend. Annie is also a bit too old, plus she's a girl. That time in the truck, Little Horse asked me, "By the time we're twenty, how old will Annie be?"

"Thirty," I responded.

"By then she'll already be an old lady. Do you think you'll still want to do her?"

"Probably."

"Really?"

"Uh huh."

"Now I understand."

But twenty was so very far away. Just thinking about it makes me want to cry.

THE BEGINNING

Everything began with the sudden disappearance of my father. This same kind of thing had happened in my dreams when I was a small child. In one dream, my mom, wearing a short, green-and-black checkered skirt, called me out from my first-grade class. She had done herself up, so her lips were a bright red. In the hallway she picked me up and declared ecstatically, "Your dad's missing! Let's go!"

I can't remember what happened next in the dream. All I know is that it was one happy dream, so happy that I wasn't even myself. Even Mom turned into someone else—that's how happy it was. Later when I thought of that dream, I would always wonder where that short, green-and-black checkered skirt came from. As far as I can remember, Mom never once wore a skirt like that. This incident led me to develop a strong interest in where these things called "dreams" come from. A few times I asked Mom, "Did you ever wear a short, green-and-black checkered skirt?" If my mom's answer wasn't: "I hate green," it would be: "You asked me that before." The reason I could never remember whether I had asked her this question or not was that she never explained just where that dream, that oh so happy dream, came from.

But then one day my dad really did disappear. That afternoon I was in the principal's office, forced to stand in the corner as a form of punishment. Mr. He, whom we all referred to as "Mr. Hippo," knocked the top of my head like he was beating a drum and said, "A piece of work like you, even if you wiggled your way into some gang, you'd still be nothing but a petty thief! You get my point?" Then he hit me another three times in the same spot, which was already really sore. He probably wanted to get in a few more cheap shots, but the phone rang. He answered it, yawned, and then suddenly his eyes shot over to me. He sucked in his fat gut, adjusted his tie, and said loudly, "Mr. Hou, what a coincidence! We were just about to call you. Hou Shichun is here with me. Do you know what he's done? . . . Hello? Uh, I said, do you know what he's gone and done? . . . It is very loud where you are, I can't hear that—that's right—I can't hear that clearly. . . . What? Hello? . . . Yes, of course it's all right. Hold on one moment." Mr. Hippo handed me the phone, saying, "Your father has something important that he wants to talk to you about. When you finish, I want to talk to him."

"Hello?"

"Hello? Big Head?" It was my dad all right. But the noise was really loud and I could hear two old women discussing renting wedding gowns in the background. One woman was saying that the gown with the veil was too expensive, while the other was babbling that the gown looked too vulgar without it. The first woman argued that it was ridiculous to pay an extra 2,000 NT* for the veil, while the second maintained that that they had better see what Sue thought, after all Sue was the one getting married, not her. The second woman also felt that Sue would like the one with the veil because it looked more like the kind worn by Audrey Hepburn. The first woman then asked who Audrey Hepburn was.

* New Taiwan Dollar. The current exchange rate is approximately US$1.00 to NT30.00. The word "dollars" hereafter refers to NT.

It was during the occasional breaks in their rambling that I heard my father say, "I have to go somewhere far, far away. Hello?—I'll be gone for a while."

If you have watched soap operas before, then you know that as soon as an adult tells a child that somebody has to go far, far away, it means that this somebody is going to die. As my father told me this, I thought, can't you wait a while before you die? This incident of the super-loser Mr. Hippo falsely accusing me of burning the class geography exams hadn't even been resolved yet! But after that my father didn't say a word; it was just like after you put in your last coin and the machine suddenly shuts down and only the words **GAME OVER** appear on the screen. Afterward all I heard through the receiver was the sound of those two women continuing their argument. Mr. Hippo took the phone from me to listen and cursed, "What the hell is this?" He then knocked me upside the head again. "Great," he said. "Your own father doesn't even give a damn about you! Just—great!"

It was at this moment that I violently rammed my head into Mr. Hippo's stomach. He was still holding on to the receiver, which he hadn't had time to hang up, so when Mr. Hippo went down, the teacup, pencil holder, coffee cup, blue and red folders, and a steaming hot lunchbox, which got caught up in the phone cord, all landed on top of him. His back crushed the wooden newspaper rack, and perhaps the newspaper rack busted something else, but I didn't pay any attention because my head was really aching. I wondered if I had knocked my head on Mr. Hippo's tie clip.

This was my last moment in that pathetic middle school. As I scrambled out of the principal's office, I announced to Mr. Hippo, who was sprawled out on the floor with a piece of roast pork on his chest: "I'm not the one who burned the exams! So fuck your mother!"

As for who burned the exams, how they did it, and why, I knew absolutely nothing. All I knew was that after this, that pathetic middle school would never want me back; moreover, I didn't want that damn school either. I left my backpack at school, with my Chinese, English, math, geography, and science textbooks, plus my gym clothes, inside. Sitting on my desk was my lunchbox, and inside were probably the dumplings my grandma had made. And in my desk drawer were three Batman stickers, a set of toy handcuffs, and an old shell that had been vacated by a hermit crab—the top of the shell was sharp and pointy just like a clump of shit.

For pretty much the better half of the afternoon, I just aimlessly wandered around those super-boring streets near my school, endlessly pondering just what else I had left behind. And then some stories began to flash through my mind. I saw Mr. Hippo barging into my classroom with that piece of roast pork still stuck to his chest. He told all the students in the class to stand up and line up beside their desks. Then he went over and confiscated my backpack, lunchbox, and everything in my desk drawer. As Mr. Hippo turned around, I even saw my classmate Huang Munan give him the finger—I hoped he wouldn't get caught. I also saw Dai Wanqing, Li Ahji, and Chen Xiaohao giggling to themselves like a bunch of cute little kids. And then it began to rain.

The rain was really out of control—you could say it was just as violent as our teacher's pointer. I was drenched from head to toe; even my socks were soaked. The area between my toes and the bottom of my socks was even steeping in swishy swashy rainwater. Coughing, I began to run home: cough, cough, cough, swish swash swish, cough, cough, swish swash swish, cough, cough, swish swash swish.

What happened next, you can blame on the rain. If it hadn't been for that rainstorm, or even if it had only been a little drizzle, I would have never run all the way home. If I hadn't sprinted directly home, I never would have gotten that damn phone call. If I hadn't received that phone call, I naturally wouldn't have said all those nasty things over the phone. If I'd never opened my big mouth on the telephone, in all probability, my life would be very different.

I had just taken off my pants and the rest of my clothes—which were soaked so thoroughly that they were as heavy as a cotton blanket—and was drinking a bowl of the mung-bean soup my uncle had left over from the day before. The soup had already begun to go sour. I choked for a second and began to cough again. Then the phone rang.

"Hello? Are either of Hou Shichun's parents home?" It was Mr. Hippo. "This is Mr. He from Minzu Middle School."

". . . . . ."

"Hello, whom am I speaking with?"

". . . . . ."

"Hello?"

"I'm the uncle." My throat was hoarse anyway.

"Who?"

"I'm Hou Shichun's uncle," I said in an even lower tone.

"Oh, hello, hello! Excuse me, but has Hou Shichun come home yet?"

"He's at school."

"Well, let me tell you what happened! This morning in the principal's office we had a bit of an incident . . ." Mr. Hippo then went on to repeat the whole story about the geography exams and how this afternoon in the principal's office I "refused to submit to discipline and hit a teacher." These incidents were of a most serious nature, too serious, and he hoped that my parents could come down to the school at their earliest possible convenience to deal with them.

"That's not possible," I said.

"What? I can't hear you that clearly."

"Hou Shichun's father has passed away. We are extremely busy, call back in another two days."

I hung up the phone.

By the time it stopped raining, I had already changed into a set of dry clothes. I put on a Chicago Bulls T-shirt, on the front of which was the number 23—of course you know who that is. Not long afterward I began to be referred to as "Bull-man," "that little Bull-boy," "Bull," "Bull-tail," and other related names, and it was all owing to this T-shirt. Besides that shirt, I also wore an old pair of my uncle's ripped blue jeans and a pair of brand-new sneakers. Auntie Jade Fragrance brought those shoes to me all the way from America, but printed on the label was MADE IN KOREA. They may not have been anything to show off, but at least they were better than Chen Guoqing's pair of MADE IN CZECH sneakers, which were really lame—really hopeless. I also put on a jacket, although it was so light and thin that it was like wearing nothing. Later Annie's cigarette burned several holes in this jacket, but I didn't care. This outfit stayed with me for a long time. Usually only when it poured would I stand outside in the open—in places like the shipyard—and let the rainwater wash the clothes clean. A few times I lowered my head to see reddish-brown blood mixing with the rainwater near my feet, but by then I had already become numb to the sight of blood.

After I changed clothes, I stood for a while on the balcony. No, it probably wasn't just a while, I actually stood there for quite some time. The whole time I was thinking that in just a moment my mother would come home. She would drive past the front door and park the car in the apartment's basement garage. Just as she turned the corner and pressed the garage-door opener, she would be at a certain angle that would allow me to catch a glimpse of most of her face. Each time her expression was that of a diligent child in class. She would veer to the right, then turn to the left, occasionally licking her lips or teasing the ends of her hair—I really, truly loved her expression as she parked the car.

So it was a shame that before I had a chance to witness her return, Grandma arrived. She would always get out of a cab in the lane below and, carrying a bag of steamed stuffed buns, dumplings, noodles with fried bean sauce, or other stuff that people in ancient times used to eat, walk up to our apartment entrance. It would take her forever to open the main door, take the elevator up, and then open our apartment door. As she staggered in she'd already be complaining: "Exhausted! I'm dead on my feet!" If she caught sight of me she would say, "What's all this about divorce?! All they are doing is driving us parents crazy and upsetting you kids!" If she saw my mother she'd say, "The stuffed buns are fresh out of the steamer!" Only once or twice did she happen to bump into my father, who had come home to pick something up or do some errands. On those occasions she said nothing.

Even when my father asked her, "How have you been?" she completely ignored him.

On this super-lousy day I took advantage of the time Grandma was
riding the elevator up to slip out via the emergency stairs. I ran down six
flights and just as I got to the downstairs entrance I could swear that I
heard Grandma calling out, "I'm exhausted! Dead on my feet!" I suppose
it had to have been my imagination, right?

I stood in the lane, not knowing where I was going to go or how long
I would be away. This was the beginning. Later I realized that no matter
what it is, once there is a beginning, the ending will never come, never.

While out in the streets I could genuinely sense what day of the week it was; moreover, the day in my mind would always be completely different from the day printed on the calendar. The first time I left my family and school was on a Monday—not only did the calendar say it was Monday, but even my class schedule, which read ENG, ENG, CHIN, CHIN, MATH, MATH, GYM, told me it was Monday. As I walked the streets, all I had was thirty-four NT in my pocket, the roads were soaked, and every couple feet I would step in a puddle reflecting the glare of the streetlight on its surface. The whole time I felt that it was a Saturday—which is because every day after that was like a Sunday. Later, whenever I would think back to that day, I would always remember the sound of my new gym shoes trampling the shadows of the streetlights reflected in the puddles. I would recall the fresh scent rising off the streets after the downpour had rinsed away all of the dirt and grime. It felt like a Saturday.

I walked down more than a dozen, or perhaps it was several dozen, broad and narrow roads, and each time I came to an intersection I went whichever way there was a green light—there was always at least one green light. In the beginning I thought I was walking in circles, but the circles seemed to get larger and larger until I barely recognized the streets and main roads. Something else was strange: before I knew it, even the people I saw on the street looked very different from the kind I was accustomed to seeing. I'll just continue walking on like this, I thought, and who knows, perhaps if I diligently forge ahead I'll eventually run into an alien.

Finally I came to a gambling parlor called Bingo Wonderland. I went in and watched people playing Super 8. I watched for over a half hour and not a single machine had paid out, so everybody was really starting to get irritated. There was one guy with a perm that made him look like a poodle, and he said to me, "What the fuck are you looking at? Get lost!"

I took a few steps toward the door and saw an empty slot machine beside me—excellent. Once I sat down and put in twenty dollars, that poodle left me alone. I only had two coins to lose, but for some reason I kept winning. Only after I won seven thousand dollars did I lose a little bit, but then my winnings jumped to nine thousand. And then a strange, ghostlike voice from behind me made its way to my ears: "Pull the lever once more and you'll really be down on your luck."

I spun around and what I saw almost made me fall off my barstool. The character talking to me was a little punk—this kid couldn't have been much older than me. He had one big eye and one little eye—the larger one looked like a bottle cap, the little one resembled a nostril. I hastily turned to avoid looking at that face of his, but he continued, saying, "Go cash out. I'll be waiting for you at the entrance."

He lifted the corner of his jacket and, glancing for a second at his waist, I clearly caught sight of a Rambo-style hunting knife hanging on the left side of his belt.

As I picked up my money, the bingo boss craned his neck to look outside for a second and then eyed me. He then suddenly laughed and said in Taiwanese, "Kid, you really don't have a clue how things work around here, do you? There's no need for you to cash in so much. Come on, I'll cut you a break. Take three thousand and two cartons of Marlboros and get lost. Okay, scram!"

The guy with the weird eyes, who was waiting for me outside the automatic door, asked me how much I got. I took out those three large bills. He seemingly didn't think anything was wrong and conveniently took two of the bills for himself. At the same time, he asked me if I smoked. When I said no, he nodded and extended the hand holding the money to take the cigarettes, saying, "Come with me."

I unwillingly followed him. After we had walked a few blocks, it again began to rain—for some reason, though, it didn't seem like he realized it was raining. Only as we were passing through two extremely narrow alleys that reeked of fish did he stop for a moment and say in an extremely faint voice, "It's okay! Get going!" After that, he picked up the pace and continued ahead. It wasn't until several months later that I finally realized he wasn't talking to me.

I don't know if it was because I walked so much that night or what, but I felt like I had been walking for a hundred years. I felt like I could have walked all the way to the moon, or even America, but he was still roughly two or three steps ahead of me, continually moving forward to an even more distant place. His small and lanky frame almost allowed me to forget that he had a set of eyes even more terrifying than a visitor from outer space. We continued walking, and just as I was about to collapse from exhaustion, we finally came to a 7-Eleven. He threw one of the cartons of Marlboros to a fatso sitting on the steps of the 7-Eleven and said, "He never showed up."

The fatso glanced at me for a moment, then looked at the weird-eyed alien.

"I'll take this carton," said Weird Eyes. "Give the other carton to Apricot."

The fatso nodded, then immediately spun around to glare at me. "What the hell you looking at? You fucking punk!"

I then continued to follow the weird-eyed alien into another alley, and it felt like we walked for another hundred years. I don't even remember him stopping, turning around, or saying anything, but then all of a sudden he hit me in the face. It didn't really hurt; my eyes just lit up for a second and my elbows and ass hit the ground. Weird Eyes turned into a dark shadow.

Behind him was a public phone booth and across from the phone booth was a blinking neon sign.

"So how's Horsefly doing?" Weird Eyes asked, as he stepped on my stomach.

"Who?"

"You motherfucker!" The foot that had been pressing upon my stomach moved up to my neck. With one foot on the ground and one on my neck, Weird Eyes carefully squatted down and, once he was balanced, grabbed hold of my right hand. Then, dragging me into the illumination of the neon light, he let out a "Huh?" Right after that, the foot on my neck eased up a bit. He stood up and with one sudden jerk pulled me to my feet. But he didn't stop there; he forcefully slammed me against a hard, damp wall. I didn't dare look him in the face, all I could do was close my eyes—but even then

I could still smell the stench like a cockroach nest that emitted from his hair.

"You don't know Horsefly?"

I shook my head with all my might, but he slammed me harder as if he didn't even want me to shake my head.

"Then how about Ah Dibo?"

"Ah who?"

Only then did Weird Eyes finally begin to ease up on me. But he still used the carton of Marlboros that I had won to hit me on the head—it just happened that he chose the same spot to hit me as Mr. Hippo.

"Then what the hell are you doing in the streets?"

I told him that I had just come to play some video games.

He laughed and shook his head. Then, waving the carton of Marlboros, he said, "Okay, that's it. Get going."

But I stood there without moving a muscle and demanded, "Give me back my money."

"Say what?"

"Give me my money back."

"You have no idea what you're doing!" he screamed, looking as if he still wanted to hit me with the carton of Marlboros. But in my hand was his Rambo knife and the blade was pressing right against his stomach.

This is how I met Zeng Ahzhi. Later he told Old Bull, Little Horse, Little Xinjiang, and the chicks that the very day we met, he came a hair away from getting iced by me. I said that was far from the truth. He asked how it could be far from the truth. I said it could never happen. Then Little Horse said, "That's because you didn't have any experience in the streets."

Only much later did I learn that in the streets, if a guy's got a knife pointed at your belly, he has absolutely no need to say, "Give the money back," let alone say it twice. It is also common knowledge that after someone coughs up two thousand dollars, you don't instantly return their Rambo knife, let alone grab hold of the blade with your bare hand and demand, "You'd better give it to me straight. Why did you make me stop playing that slot machine?"

He returned his knife to the carved leather sheath that was hanging on his belt. "Do you know what day of the week it is?" he asked, his eyes glaring at me. "Do you know who was supposed to come sit at the machine you were at?"

I shook my head, and sensing my ignorance, he also shook his.

It was then that he told me his name was Ahzhi. The name of the boss at Bingo Wonderland was Yan Xiong. It was a Monday, and on the last Monday of every month, the guy in charge of the neighborhood comes to collect the "protection money." That guy's name is Young River. Young River usually shows up sometime between ten and ten-thirty. When he gets there, he sits himself down at that slot machine and waits for it to pay out—that machine *must* pay out. But since I was sitting there, Young River wouldn't have been able to go about his business. Since things went down like this, Yan Xiong would face a most unpleasant fate; if I had still been hanging around when Young River showed up, there is no doubt that I also would have met my maker in a very bad way.

"So then why did you hit me?"

"The fact that Young River hadn't showed up was already strange enough; but then you appeared and started to cause trouble. I thought that Horsefly had sent you."

"Who is Horsefly?"

"Nosy motherfucker! What's with all the questions?" Ahzhi's expression suddenly turned hostile. At the time I thought this Ahzhi character was really one strange fellow. That's because I still hadn't learned that changing one's expression is a method used to buy time. After getting his thoughts together, Ahzhi seemed to warm up a bit. As he started walking back the way we came, he asked me, "Just what clique do you run with anyway?"

"I don't run with anybody," I answered, and just like before I followed Ahzhi. Only this time I had learned my lesson: I didn't follow as close as before. Even if he suddenly spun around and swung a bat at me this time, he wouldn't touch me.

"You in school?"

I thought for a second and responded, "Not right now."

"You got a job?"

"Nope."

Then for a long time, with him in the front and me in the back, we just walked. The wind blowing through the streets was so strong that it made an empty plastic bag dance around, twirling. I thought I heard Ahzhi faintly mumble something strange like, "I beg your pardon." I figured, this guy's got to have a screw loose someplace. Not until we came to a road brightly lit by streetlights did he turn to me and say, "It's hopeless. This is how the streets are, a chaotic mess."

Even though I had no clue what he was talking about, I didn't ask him anything. I suspected that he was the kind of person who didn't take kindly to questions. If this type of guy doesn't want to open his mouth, no matter how hard you try, you can't get shit out of him. But if he wants to tell you, he'll always fill you in.

"So I think it's best you head home. It's better if you're not always hanging out in the streets; otherwise, you'll end up dead and won't even know it. If I see it, it most definitely won't be a pleasant sight. Got it?"

"I don't really understand what you're . . ."

"I said go home! Don't come back out! You understand that? Fuck!"

I said I didn't have a home. Ahzhi said, "Funny, that's what everybody says." I told him my dad ran off after getting over his head in debt and my mom went abroad until the whole thing blows over, so there's no home for me to go back to. Ahzhi then told me, "Don't give me this bullshit, if no one's at your place, we'll move in, you stupid motherfucking dropout-runaway." I told him that if he didn't believe me there was nothing I could do. "Then where do you normally sleep," Ahzhi asked. I said, "I don't know, maybe a hotel. I just moved out today so I haven't figured it out yet." Ahzhi asked if I was willing to help the hotel make money, how come I didn't help my brother make an extra buck? I said okay.

I then took every last cent I had in my pocket and handed it all over to Ahzhi.

Without even looking to see how much was there, Ahzhi stuffed the wad of cash into his pocket; then, with quick steps, he led me back to the 7-Eleven. That nasty fatso from before was still sitting on the front steps by the entrance. As Ahzhi approached him, he called out, "Old Bull." Ahzhi lowered his head and whispered something in his ear. Old Bull nodded, stood up, and beckoned me with his finger. As soon as I walked over to him, he gently pushed me to one side. We walked off shoulder-to-shoulder like two old friends. Ahzhi called out from behind, "You give the smokes to Apricot?"

"Uh huh," Old Bull answered without turning around. "She went back out to the streets."

I didn't know where Old Bull was going to take me, nor did I know if I would have a place to crash for the night. I still had a faint aching pain around my stomach and it felt like something was stuck in my throat. But oh, how I loved their tone and attitude as they spoke those words: "In the streets." I wondered if I had already become one who could make it out in the streets.

Actually, Old Bull wasn't one bit as menacing as I had thought—his ferocity was just a front. However, on the way to the parking lot, there were more than a few times I wished he were a little nastier. That's because he really couldn't keep his mouth shut.

He told me that according to Ahzhi, anyone who could be taken "to the garage" to crash for the night was all right, you know, like a buddy. If, on the other hand, you were to "take someone to the junkyard," that meant that you were going to get rid of him. If you had to "take somebody to the shipping yard," that meant he needed protection but wasn't injured. Those who were injured were taken to Ma Jianren Hospital. At first they said that Ma Jianren was truly despicable. But his son, Little Horse, was really a good guy. Moreover, Ma Jianren's surgical skill was so amazing that in the end everyone forgot just how despicable he was. Besides that, if Ahzhi said they were "going for a midnight snack," it didn't mean they were going for a bite to eat. Old Bull said he couldn't tell me what it meant—if he opened his mouth, he'd end up getting a beating. He got his ass whipped twice; each time it only hurt a little, but the next day he was in so much pain that he couldn't even move. Not only is Ahzhi vicious, Old Bull told me, but he knows a strange kind of martial arts, and besides that he often goes without eating or drinking. Moreover, he can even see ghosts. Once, while he was at the far end of a suspension bridge, he saw Old Bull's elder sister. She told Ahzhi that when her family was transporting her body they forgot to tell her that they had to cross a bridge, and in the end it cost her two years of aimless wandering. Old Bull verified all of this. Then he told me that his sister used to study at a technical school, but one day she suddenly disappeared. When she was found, her body had been burned a smoldering black, just like a piece of leftover campfire wood. The police medical examiner said that before she died she had had the habit of using drugs. Old Bull asked, what fucking drugs were they talking about, his sister didn't even drink Coca-Cola. Only later did Young River tell them that if the cops could prove she was a druggie, they would hardly be under any pressure when dealing with the case. So probably nobody will ever know how Old Bull's sister turned into a piece of charcoal. Old Bull, however, maintained that sooner or later he'd find out what happened. It had been two, almost three years since the incident, and for a period of time, he suspected everyone he saw on the street of being his sister's murderer. He even considered going on a mass killing spree, and who knows, maybe one of his victims would be the guy he was after. But Uncle Xu advised him not to. "On the outside living and dying are of the least importance; revenge is of even less importance than that," Uncle Xu said.

"So what's important then?" This was the first time I had an opportunity to speak.

"There isn't anything that's important," Old Bull said. Barely stopping for air, he continued, "What Uncle Xu said really makes sense, you know? All it takes is four seconds to rip off a car, three seconds for a car stereo. He's only been caught a handful of times. Later—it didn't matter where, it could be Taidong, Hualian, or wherever—anytime a car was stolen, they'd always say he did it. Once they even accused him of stealing three cars at Banqiao and Jiayi at the same time! Do you realize how ridiculous that is? After that, an automobile company hired him to research antitheft locks. They paid him several million NT, but he only worked for them for a year or so before he quit. When giving a reason for leaving, he asked how he could possibly design a lock that he couldn't crack. And so, Uncle Xu took off. He said he really felt bad about taking their money. As if he was truly ripping them off."

These days Uncle Xu runs things at the parking lot. The lot is about the size of two basketball courts. In front is a highway overpass, in back is a bowling alley, and on the two sides are a couple of buildings over ten stories tall. If you stand in the middle of the parking lot and look around, you'll feel like you have fallen into a garbage can. The ticket box where Uncle Xu worked was like a miniature trash can within the larger one. As Uncle Xu scurried out of his box he looked really strange, peering around in all directions almost like a rat. Really, just like a little vermin. And between his nose and upper lip he had whiskers like a rat.

Old Bull told him that Ahzhi had given the okay for me to sleep there. Uncle Xu carefully examined me from head to toe twice over with a set of eyes just barely larger than two red beans before he asked, "Who's he?"

"Ahzhi said he's a Minzu Middle School dropout. What's the big deal if you let him stay a night?"

"Minzu where?" Uncle Xu asked. "What, did you fly here?" From his pocket he pulled out some thin, black object, then after yawning he asked me, "Till what time?"

"What?"

"He asked what time you want to sleep till!" Old Bull rushed to answer.

"Umm . . . anytime," I answered.

"What do you mean 'anytime'?" Uncle Xu didn't even bother to look at me, he just turned and walked in the direction of the bowling alley. Pointing to a Mercedes-**Benz**, he directed me: "Sleep here until six o'clock; they won't come for the car until seven. At seven you can go sleep in that **Volvo**. If you want to sleep until eight, you can crash in that van over there in the back. If you don't want to get up until nine—you know what, kids shouldn't sleep that late. Here, just sleep in the van."

As Uncle Xu opened the van door for me, I heard Old Bull whisper to him, "Ahzhi said that he never showed up."

In the darkness it appeared as though Uncle Xu nodded. He then opened the window in the front for me, saying, "If you want to sleep, sleep. But no playing around inside!"

I knew that when he said "playing around," what he meant was whacking off. When people a bit older, like Uncle Xu, talk about this somewhat embarrassing phenomenon, they always manage to use terminology that doesn't sound quite as embarrassing. This really makes me want to puke. Already, I felt as if everything Uncle Xu said was completely without any logical basis. Like whacking off—he should just have said "whacking off." What's the big deal anyway? I would despise having to whack off in this van. This van smelled of something wretched.

Gazing out the window from behind the cardboard sunshade, I could make out the neon sign hanging outside one of the side buildings. It lit up one word at a time, TRUE LOVE IS ONE MOMENT OF PASSION, then 6F and the name of the hotel lit up together. My guess was that there had to be a whole slew of people getting busy inside. The scene must have been just like what I saw on the porn tape at Chen Xiaohao's apartment: a dark-haired foreigner with a black beard riding a blond foreign girl with huge tits. He took his big sausage and stuck it in the girl's mouth; then he popped it in below; finally he stuck it in her butt. After that, they switched and it was the girl's turn to straddle the guy. After they finished their riding, they'd chat for a bit, go for a stroll, and then it would be time for the black-bearded man to screw a redhead with black nipples. Just like before, he'd take his sausage and stick it here, plug it there. All the while, the blondie with big tits from before, she would be getting it on with a big muscular guy with blond hair. Then after the two pairs were finished screwing, it was the girls' turn. Finally, in the end everybody got busy. Lin Guoqing said he once saw two guys doing it. Chen Xiaohao said that's nothing, he saw a tape where they didn't even use condoms! Everybody thought what Chen Xiaohao saw was the coolest. So I imagined that that was what was probably going on inside TRUE LOVE IS ONE MOMENT OF PASSION. Actually, none of that was a big deal.

So the reason I couldn't sleep had nothing to do with that flashing neon sign blinding my eyes; the reason I couldn't sleep was probably because I had experienced so much in one day. Usually, at times like this, I take all the things I have experienced and recompose them in the same manner that a Transformer goes from robot warrior to car.

Imagine if Mr. Hippo had died from the fall when I rammed him in the gut, then the police would have chased me around for the whole afternoon. I probably would have taken the same route, ending up in these unknown streets. You can never tell—maybe I still would have run into Ahzhi. I would have told him: I just took out a middle-school teacher. He'd most likely respond: Not bad. Then he'd probably have Old Bull take me to the shipping yard. But I'm still clueless as to what exactly the shipping yard is like. It's probably a place with a lot of shipping containers. Who knows, maybe the cops would still track me down. We would hide behind the containers, ducking here, dodging there, escaping only by the skin of our teeth. Then Uncle Xu would come pick up Ahzhi, Old Bull, and me in a stolen police car. As we made our getaway, the cops would still be playing hide and seek behind the shipping containers. The four of us would take the police car down to Bingo Wonderland to check out the scene there. Just as we arrived, Yan Xiong would run out yelling, "You're here just at the right time! Young River went to catch an escaped convict. You guys take his seat!" Then we'd take our seats and play a few rounds of Super 8, play the slots, and then we would go for a spin on the virtual motorcycle. Before we left we'd tell Yan Xiong, "You can keep our winnings, all we want is to have a good time!"

This was my imaginary story for the day. It isn't necessarily that much more entertaining than what really happened—even though what really happened wasn't entertaining. But there was one scene from the story that I really loved, which was when Uncle Xu, Ahzhi, Old Bull, and I stepped out of the police car. The four of us, lined up side by side stretching across the entire alley, strutted forward in slow motion. In the heart of the night, we walked with style.

Next I should probably tell you how, after the sun came up, I woke up aching from head to toe, how I was taken to the casino, how I got squeezed in with a bunch of people who had blood pouring out of their bodies, and had another string of endless bad luck. But first I'll tell you a story. This is a story my dad told me when I was a kid—he told me many stories, and sometimes he'd even tell me two or three in a single day. I don't recall the majority of them, I just remember Dad becoming a bit cross-eyed as he told them. The reason I remember this special tale is that after he finished the story, my dad played a kind of game with me, one we would often play later. Every time I missed my father because he went on a business trip, was working overtime, or was out fucking around with some wild woman, I would play this game by myself. And even though I didn't really play the game, I would always run through the story. This is how it went:

Once upon a time, a long, long time ago, there was a prince who roamed all over the world. All this prince knew was that he was a prince, but he didn't know where his kingdom was, nor did he know what his palace was like or what had happened between his father, the king, and his mother, the queen. And so each time the roaming prince arrived somewhere he would ask the people of that place, "Do you know of a kingdom that has lost a prince?" Normally people would take him for a madman, and never did anyone provide him with an answer to his question. And so the prince had no choice but to continue his vagrant life. Then one day he came upon a smart man. After the smart man heard the prince's question, he came back with another question: "What kind of prince did they lose?" The prince replied, "One just like me." The smart man said, "What kind are you?" The prince replied, "The one I am right now!" The smart man then said, "But when you were lost, you were not the way you are now! Only if you tell me what you were like when you were lost will I be able to determine which kingdom lost a prince like that!" The prince pondered this for a moment and responded, "I remember that I used to be very small, but I can't recall just how small." The smart man then asked again, "I don't want to know how small you were, I just want to know, what were you smaller than?" Once again the prince pondered before replying, "I remember being smaller than a cradle, but I don't remember what the cradle looked like." The smart man laughed and said, "I don't want to know what the cradle looked like; what I do want to know is where the cradle was kept." This time the prince thought for a long while before answering, "I remember the cradle was in a garden, but I can't recall where the garden was." The smart man said, "Very good, very good. But I don't want to know where the garden was, I want to know what was outside the garden." Again, the prince pondered for a long time before he finally responded, "I remember there being a forest beyond the garden, but I can't remember what was within the forest." The smart man said, "I don't want to know what was within the forest, I just want to know what sounds came from the forest." The prince suddenly screamed aloud, "I remember! I remember! The sound that came from the forest was 'Hoo—bong! Hoo—bong!' But I don't remember what animal makes that sound."

The smart man patted the prince on the shoulder and said, "Child, your kingdom is in the north. Your palace is beside the forest. I am certain that your father, the king, and your mother, the queen, often used to let you play in the garden. That means that the sunlight in the garden must be precious and rare." The prince could barely control his excitement and impatiently implored the smart man, "Please tell me more! Tell me more!" The smart man again laughed and said, "But I haven't told you anything! You are the one who has told me all of this!" From then on, when the roaming prince wandered to a new place he wouldn't ask, "Do you know a kingdom that has lost a prince?" Instead, he would say, "I remember a place to the north where the sunlight is rare and precious, where lies a kingdom. There is a garden within the palace walls that is just beside a forest, but I can't remember how to get there." People would then respond to the roaming prince like so: "Is it that palace on the mountaintop?" "Is it the garden made from stone bricks?" Once someone even asked, "Is it the kingdom that was once ruled by a red-bearded king?" The roaming prince's happiness brought him to tears, and he cried out, "Yes! That's it! I remember now! I remember!"

The story, however, did not have a very happy ending. Although the roaming prince never really made it back to his palace and garden, he and so many other people that he met all remembered those events that happened once upon a time, long, long ago. My father later told me the story of the red-bearded king, the story of the great fire in the black forest, and the story of the walking cradle. The conclusion to all those stories was the same. The endings always became hazy, so hazy that you could make up whatever you wanted and it would still be okay. But my dad told me that within this story there was a meaning.

"This isn't a nice story. Tell me another," I demanded.

"What's wrong with it?"

"It's not fun. Tell me a fun one."

"I don't have any fun ones."

"But I want to hear a fun story!"

"Okay, here is what we'll do, we'll play the game of the 'roaming prince' and the 'smart man.'"

Just like the characters in the story, this game was a bit repetitive; the "roaming prince" had to say, "I remember something, but I don't remember something else." Then the "smart man" has to say, "I don't want to know something, I want to know something else." The first time we played this game, Dad was the "roaming prince" and I was the "smart man."

"I remember leaving home when I was a child, but I don't remember where I went."

"So did you end up going back home?"

"That's not how you play! You should say, 'I don't want to know where you went, I want to know something else.' "

"What do I want to know?"

"Anything you want! Whatever you want to know, that's what you ask. Remember, you're the 'smart man'!"

"I want to know if you returned home."

"I remember I returned home, but I don't recall when I went back home."

"I don't want to know when you returned home, I just want to know whether or not your dad spanked you."

"I remember my dad spanking me, but I don't remember what he used to hit me with."

"Did it hurt?"

"That's not how you play!"

"Okay, right, right, right! I don't want to know what your dad used to hit you with, I want to know, umm, I still want to know what your dad used to hit you with."

"I think he used a feather duster." My dad knit his brow and thought for a long time before he finally confirmed, "Yeah, that's right! It was a feather duster!"

I don't think Grandpa did a good job bringing up my dad. Otherwise I wouldn't be in a van that reeked of cigarettes, liquor, betel nuts, sweat, and maybe even piss, saying to myself, "I remember that there were once three people in my family, but I don't remember how many centuries ago that was. I don't want to know how many centuries ago that was, I just want to know if other people's families are like this too."

GAMES

I couldn't move. Even to breathe I had to be especially careful; otherwise, the area around my lungs would really, really hurt. I wanted to open my eyes but I knew that if I did it would be as painful as tearing a piece of flypaper off my eyelids. Of course, as I was experiencing this pain, my brain was also suffering. You have simply no way of stopping this multiplied pain; all you can do is remain still and try not to think of anything, just like a dead man. Now I know why corpses don't move.

But I was even a bit more unfortunate than a dead man. I could still hear. The sound of birds chirping pecked at my eardrums—peck, peck, and then even harder, peck, peck, peck! It was as if the sound of cars rumbling, horns beeping, and from even farther away, machines grumbling, were all collected in a boiling noodle pot; the brimming stew was overflowing the sides and the bubbles were scalding my nerves. And then there was the sound of voices; the people speaking were either standing or sitting right beside me, and every word was like a saw cutting into my bones. But at a time like this you can't even scream out; if you do, your throat will be torn into thin sticky cotton-candy strands.

Although I didn't move, I couldn't shut out the sounds of their voices.

"What if we can't wake him up?"

"We have to."

"He's got a fever."

"How can you know if you haven't even touched him?"

"You never worked in a hospital, so how do you know that I don't know? Don't touch him! It'll hurt like hell!"

"What do you think happened?"

"What else could have happened? Naturally it had to be Zeng Ahzhi. This time he went a little overboard hitting him. Damn!"

"Should we take him to your dad's or what?"

"Are you kidding? Since when can my dad treat this kind of injury?"

"Then what did Uncle Xu say?"

"He said we should see what happens."

"Then pull him out. Put him on the side there."

"So even if he doesn't die, he'll end up getting picked up by some nosy cop and sent to the juvenile detention center? Anyway, we can't move him now. Let's see if he's any better after lunch."

"No matter what, we can't take him with us, can we? It's already too late."

"There's no other choice. Anyway, as long as he doesn't move he won't be in the way."

"Fuck, this bastard's really big. He'll cut down on our speed!"

"Give me the keys, I'll drive." Afterward this voice leaned over close to my ear and whispered, "It's all right. Don't move. Everything will be okay soon."

"Swaa—*bam!*" As the side door slid closed and slammed shut, I felt like I had been blown apart by a bomb. After that, something even worse than the worst bad luck times ten happened: they started up the van and I became a tattered leaf floating atop the waves of the sea. Swaying this way, jolting that way, popping up as we headed east, falling over as we headed west, every time we hit a bump I thought a new bone was breaking.

If I keep carrying on about how much it hurt, how much pain I was in, I could ramble on for two and a half hours, but other than proving how big of a chicken I am, what would be the point of that? However, right now I needn't tell you: after this incident in the van, I was never again afraid of pain. Never again was there a suffering worthy of being called pain. But before I go on about this, let me get back to the story at hand.

So I lay there like a tattered leaf floating atop the waves of the sea, both my eyes and mouth tightly shut. I wasn't pondering anything in particular, yet I was still hopelessly alert. All that went through my mind was one thing: Where am I? I'm in Taipei. I'm at an intersection waiting for a green light. Now I'm making a right turn beside the vegetable market. Now I'm passing by a sea of yulan magnolias. Now I'm heading downhill. Now I'm . . . Now I can sense speed, we're moving smoothly and steadily, yet I can tell that our speed is continually increasing. Now I'm on the highway. Now I'm leaving Taipei. Shit! Now I won't know where I am anymore.

I could hear the sound of someone clearing his throat from the driver's seat; then the same person said in the faintest of voices, "Hey kid, you should be feeling a little more comfortable now. In a little bit you'll feel even better. Be good and don't move. Pretty soon you'll forget about the pain."

"Ahzhi is really one strange bastard," the guy in the passenger seat suddenly cried out. "Fuck, he hits harder each time!" As he spoke it was as if he were jabbing me in the ear with an awl.

"Keep quiet!"

I started to imagine what the guy driving looked like. He was a bit older than I was, probably around seventeen or eighteen. He looked pale and white, just like somebody's mother. And then I began to think about my own mother. When you are in terrible pain and thoroughly uncomfortable, imagining your mother driving a smelly van isn't difficult at all. But of course it is just your imagination.

Right then, my mom should have been at work. She probably already knew what I'd done yesterday, but just like always she would still go to work. On Tuesdays she would always wear a pair of gray pants to the office. The pants were especially light and soft and very resilient; that way she could go straight from the office to her meditation class without wasting time to change clothes. So if I was correct, she should have been at the office wearing a pair of gray pants and talking on the phone.

"Hello? Mr. He? This is Hou Shichun's mother. That's right. Hou Shichun still hasn't returned! He's really making me crazy!"

I don't know what Mr. Hippo's reply would be, but who gives a damn what he says?

"Then do you think I should call the police?" As my mother spoke, I'm sure she was sketching a draft advertisement or scribbling out some document—who knows, maybe she was knitting her brows and shaking her head at somebody else, telling them not to do anything silly while she was on the phone.

As I thought of my mother and this scene, I drifted off to sleep. It was the kind of sleep where one doesn't dream, and throughout my slumber I could occasionally hear the person in the passenger seat mumbling, "It's already been more than an hour, we've only got eighty minutes left . . . there's only sixty minutes left . . . we've only got a half hour. Can we make it?"

Within my darkened world, the van finally came to a stop. They killed the engine and someone rolled down the front window. Instantly, a strong wind, the kind that blows only on the open plains, rushed through the entire van, sweeping away the stench of cigarettes, liquor, betel nuts, perspiration, and piss. That guy who my imagination told me had a mama's face got out of the van and opened both the side doors, but he opened them only a slight crack. Then he pressed up close to me and, with that same faint and gentle voice, told me, "We're going to play a little game."

I have all too much experience with this—whenever a kid slightly older tells a younger kid: "We're going to play a little game," what he means is: "You don't get to play, only we do." In this van game, the rules I had to follow were: close your eyes just like before, don't move and don't make a sound, at least not until the guy driving returns, bringing with him a few people to play the game with me. I was supposed to play dead until they got back—no matter what I might hear, playing dead till the end was the way to go.

"My name's Little Horse," the guy driving introduced himself. "His name is Little Xinjiang;* we'll get to know each other in a minute."

And then they left. The gusting prairie wind, however, swept their two-sentence dialogue back to my ears from far away:

"How's the time?"

"Perfect. They'll be changing shifts at the back door in six minutes. We can still make it."

How long did I wait after that? I estimate it was somewhere between one minute and one hundred years. Gradually, I began to realize that my body no longer ached as much as that morning after I had woken up. I had already lost the strength to keep my eyes pressed shut; I daresay that if I were to open them it probably wouldn't hurt. I could even hear the sound of my stomach squirming—I was hungry. Could it be? I hadn't eaten or drunk anything all day! What do they think I am, some celestial being? It was at that moment I said, "Fuck their damn game!" I then opened my eyes and sat up.

Fuck!

The van was parked at the edge of a cliff. Looking out through the crack in the right door, I saw that if I went any farther than two book bags away, I'd have to say bye-bye. Over the cliff was a straight, steep, precipitous slope, overgrown with wild grass. I opened the door a little wider and saw that the wild grass spread downward and extended forward all the way to the boundless valley below.

In the center of the valley was a green building that resembled a warehouse. The roof of the building was made up of a collection of crooked and slanted red iron sheets. Parked in front of the building were a couple of shiny black limousines. Parked out back were a pair of trucks and a whole bunch of Honda RZRs, Sanyang Wolves, Harley Davidson Choppers, and other motorcycles. Looking carefully, I caught sight of two spots on the slope down where the grass was matted and crooked. Was that where

---

* Xinjiang Uighur Autonomous Region, in northwest China, is populated largely by Uighurs, a predominately Muslim ethnic group, who have distinctly Western features as opposed to Han Chinese.

Little Horse and Little Xinjiang were? Apparently they were really taking this game seriously. I rubbed my eyes and both my eyes and my hands began to hurt and everything within my field of vision went fuzzy. By the time my vision recovered, Little Horse and Little Xinjiang had already slid down the slope and were cutting what looked like a barbed-wire fence.

Following that, the prairie wind carried a string of sounds to me—sounds of people talking through a set of wireless walkie-talkies:

"Breaker, breaker. They've already descended."

Not far from the van—actually he was standing right behind the van—was a muscular guy with a large emerald dragon wrapped around a pine tree tattooed on his back. This sturdy fellow instantly replied through his walkie-talkie: "Copy. Their van is up here."

"Copy. I'll be up momentarily."

"Copy." The tattooed dragon hesitated for a moment. "It looks like they are going to enter through the rear," he said a bit nervously. "Should we proceed according to plan? We should just push their van over the cliff."

"Copy. Do not proceed. Repeat, do not proceed. Do you copy?"

"Copy."

It was only then that I realized I had already slid off the seat and was clinging to greasy, dirty, and foul-smelling upholstery. I saw that in the faraway gorge, tiptoeing like a pair of thieves, Little Horse and Little Xinjiang were sneaking into that large, green building with the red roof. From that angle, I could no longer make out the guy with the dragon tattoo, who was obscured, behind the space between the right rear windows and the back of the seat. But I could still hear the voices coming from his walkie-talkie:

"Breaker, breaker. Have they gone in?"

"They're in. But if things go down like this, won't . . . won't those inside be taken out by them?"

"Copy. You don't need to worry about it."

"Copy."

Then the firecrackerlike sound of a gunshot rang out from the green building; I knew it was a gunshot, and a *real* one at that. The shot wasn't as loud as what you hear on television, but the sound was much sharper. I found myself tightly squeezing my eyes shut.

There were three of four more gunshots. Then from the front of the van, I heard the sound of someone brushing through the long wild grass. The swooshing sound of a person wading through grass continued right up to the side door, when this person was what must have been only one book bag away from me. I opened my eyes to see that the tiny crack between the door and its frame had already been blocked by that person's body; he was wearing a black and blue raincoat, or maybe it was a windbreaker; his clothes emitted the scent of cologne. By this time, he didn't even have to use his walkie-talkie. He had one sentence for the guy with the dragon tattoo behind the van: "Ah Tang! Horsefly sends his apologies."

Before he even finished his sentence, the echo of two more gunshots came in through the van door. Only this time the shots were much louder, and as their noise squeezed in through the crack in the door, the buzzing sound reverberated throughout the van. At almost the same moment I heard that stout, dragon-tattooed fellow's body roll down the cliff—I even heard the unpleasantly messy sound of his body flattening out the prairie grass on its way down. Next, the front door on the right side quickly opened and then slammed shut, making the van floor shudder. I figured this time out, I was really screwed—this cologne-wearing assassin wouldn't toss in a grenade, would he?

Was this a game? For the longest time, with tears streaming from the corners of my eyes, I repeatedly pondered this question.

I climbed back onto the seat, lay down flat like before, and after I wiped the tears dry from the four corners of my eyes, continued to ponder: Was this a game? I began to shudder; my back suddenly turned cold and wet and beads of sweat that crawled like ants across my chest began to emerge from my skin.

Then the van doors rattled open and some chick cried out, "What the fuck! Who the hell is this?"

I opened my eyes to see a woman's upside-down face almost pressing up against my nose. This was Annie, a woman whom I would momentarily come to know and later love for the rest of my life. With one hand, she grabbed me and sat me up straight. "One seat per rump," she said, facing me, "okay?"

"Ahzhi just gave the kid a run-through with his 'super-chops,' so don't be so hard on him," Little Horse said as he started the engine. "Hoop, go lie down in the back, make sure you put your feet up . . ." Before he could finish, another chick, half rolling half crawling, slid over me into the back seat. Her breasts even brushed against my cheek, ice-cold and slimy. I touched my cheek and found my fingers covered with blood.

It was then that two men squeezed in the left door. Their faces, necks, and even their T-shirts and clothing were soaked with half-dried blood. And that's not to mention their hair, which had hardened into messy clumps, as if they had used blood for hair gel or had just crawled out of a manure vat. Neither of them spoke. In the end it was that girl in the back named Hoop who burst out profanely, "Fuck, we really lost face back there! Hell, we might as well have given our money away! Annie, how much did you lose?"

"I didn't count," Annie answered as she lit a cigarette. The van seemingly made a quick U-turn, which caused a few sparkling ashes to fly from the butt of her cigarette and singe my ear. Annie said she was sorry and even gave me a kiss on the ear. After that, Annie started to get on Little Horse's ass about showing up too late and driving like a maniac, blaming him for not giving a damn whether his big sister lived or died.

I glanced at Little Horse and saw that his hair was straight, long, and near the neck was tied into a ponytail. In the rearview mirror all I could see were his eyes, eyebrows, and the bridge of his nose, but I discovered that his features really did resemble somebody's mother's—pale-white, refined, and delicate. My gaze panned to the right where I also saw Little Xinjiang—he really did have the mug of a foreigner, a face almost exactly the same as an American. It was precisely at that moment that he called out in Mandarin with a thick Taiwanese accent—a voice that was at complete odds with his features—"Who the fuck does this belong to?"

Little Xinjiang pulled out a gun from under his seat.

GOOD-FOR-NOTHINGS

Once while I was at my mom's office waiting for her to get off work, she let me stand before the glass windows and gaze at the sights below. I don't remember if her office was on the thirty-fourth floor or the thirty-seventh floor, but in any case, it was really, really high up. Everything in sight became small and distant; houses, roads, cars, pedestrians, no matter what it was, it was as if it had absolutely nothing to do with you. Except for one strange man.

This man stood on the rooftop of the somewhat shorter building across the street. He was wearing a baseball cap and on top of his baseball cap was another baseball cap. But wearing two hats was nothing—most outrageous was the fact that he was wearing several layers of clothes; there must have been somewhere around, what, fifty layers? I counted for him: he was wearing at least three long overcoats, two jackets—plus a third one that was tied around his waist; under the jackets were layer after layer of sweaters and shirts; and then there were his pants. This guy's pants were even more ridiculous than his shirts and jackets. He wore the shorter pants on the outside and the longer ones on the inside, so you could see crystal-clear that he was wearing at least five or six pairs. Near the bottoms of his trouser legs there was a rainbow of different colors.

This guy was sunbathing, trying to catch some of those rays that appear on a Saturday afternoon at high noon just before summer. First he raised his head and tried to sunbathe standing up, then he lowered his head and pulled open the layers of collars around his neck and took in the sun like that for a few more minutes. Like a statue, he didn't move a muscle. When it looked like he had had enough, he lay down with his arms and legs spread out—he looked like a giant version of the character 大 . He even scratched his wiener a few times. When he was finished scratching his penis, he sang a song. At first I didn't know what he was singing; I could only see his hands, feet, and head swaying back and forth, keeping the beat. Watching him for cues, I also started to sway my head in time. Although I couldn't hear a word of his singing, I indeed knew that song. It was a tune we used to sing when we were little:

> On and on we walk, walk, walk,
> Hand in hand we skip.
> On and on we walk, walk, walk,
> Together we go on a field trip!
> The clouds are graceful and the sun is soft,
> The green hills and emerald water, splendid as can be.
> On and on we walk, walk, walk,
> Hand in hand we skip.
> On and on we walk, walk, walk,
> Together we go on a field trip!

"What's that you're singing?" my mom asked, suddenly patting me on the head from behind.

I pointed out that strange, suntanning character to my mother.

"Oh God, another loser!" As she spoke, my mother patted my shoulder. "What's one to do? These days there are more and more of these characters in Taiwan."

"Is he insane?" I asked.

"Well, he's got to have a screw loose somewhere."

"Look at all the clothes he's wearing."

"Let me see . . ." Mom started to laugh. "He's wearing his whole family's wardrobe on his back!"

"He must be really hot."

"Let's go! Time to eat." My mother pulled me by the collar toward the door as she told me, "If you don't study hard and work hard, that's how you'll end up. Got it?"

"Why?" I asked.

"No whys, that's just how it is."

"End up like what?" Don't tell me you end up sunbathing on top of a high-rise wearing fifty layers of clothing, I thought.

"End up a loser," Mom answered.

"Is there something wrong with being a loser?"

"Of course there is." My mother turned around to take another look at that guy sunbathing. She let out a deep sigh, blinked her eyes, and, scratching my hair, said, "Hmm, maybe there's nothing wrong with being a loser. It's just that he'll end up hurting other people. Hurting his family, like his wife and children."

"That guy has kids?"

In the end my mother never told me whether or not that guy had children. She just gave me a hug from behind and walked away. Only when we got to the elevator did she ask me if I wanted a hamburger, fried chicken, or pizza.

I've already forgotten what exactly it was I ate that afternoon, but I remember that the whole time I kept humming that "On and on we walk, walk, walk" song. Moreover, after we got home, I bundled up in several layers of clothes. Then, just as I had once attempted to look up words like "dick," "cunt," and "fuck," I embraced the dictionary and began to look for the meaning of "loser." Unfortunately, all it said in the dictionary was "see good-for-nothing." I already knew what good-for-nothing meant, it was something that was of no use. But a "loser" had to mean something more than just a good-for-nothing. I figured that it had to be a bit more interesting than that. It's a shame that I couldn't find the answer in the dictionary.

The next time I was to hear the term "loser" was in the van, and Annie was the one to speak the word. She turned around to ask me, "What's a little handsome fellow like you hanging around with a bunch of losers like us for?"

Not knowing how to answer her, all I could do was lower my head.

"What do you mean losers? We're a bunch of good-for-nothings!" Hoop called out, correcting her from the back seat. "If we weren't such a pack of motherfucking good-for-nothings, we wouldn't have ended up having the shit kicked out of us back there."

The two guys on my left who looked like they had just pulled themselves out of a manure vat nodded in unison.

It was not until much, much later that I finally realized that when Hoop said "good-for-nothing," what she meant wasn't just something that was of no use. The true meaning of a "good-for-nothing" is something that "is already of no use, yet continues to be used and taken advantage of by other people." But in order to get into this, I'll have to go back and start from the beginning.

Little Horse and Little Xinjiang rescued Annie, Hoop, and two gamblers they didn't even know from the mountain valley casino. After we got off the highway and were back in Taipei, Little Horse pulled over and had those two gamblers get out. As it happened, they coincidentally blurted out "thank you" at exactly the same moment. Just as Little Horse released the emergency brake and stepped on the gas, Hoop suddenly stuck her head out the window and yelled to those two guys: "Don't ever go back there! Next time you won't be so damn lucky!"

"Humph. Don't tell me it wasn't luck." Hoop let out as snort as she continued to those of us inside the van, "Bursting in and rushing out with only a toy gun and an ice pick—if you don't call that luck, then what is it?"

Little Xinjiang picked up the gun from the floor and said, "Then what do you have to say about this real gun?"

"Save it till we get home," Little Horse glanced at his rearview mirror. I could sense that he was looking at me.

As soon as we got "home," I began to feel a bit on edge—"home" was a junkyard not far from Xizhi; Old Bull had told me that the junkyard was where they took people they wanted out of the way. But Little Horse appeared so very amiable, I couldn't imagine him wanting to get rid of me. He asked me if I was still sore, and I told him not at all. He put his hand on my shoulder and led me into a wheel-less, double-decker tour bus, where he handed me a bottle of mineral water and a package of soda crackers. He then told Annie and Hoop to "go upstairs and hit the sack." Annie went right up. Hoop said she had to go to the bathroom first, otherwise her intestines would burst. Little Horse removed a first-aid kit with MA JIANREN HOSPITAL printed on the lid from the glove compartment next to the driver's seat and handed it to Hoop. She held it for a second and then set it right down, saying, "What do I need this for? I've always had terrible luck but I'm not about to die," before she limped off. After that, Little Xinjiang wanted me to have something to eat. I had two sips of water but for some reason had absolutely no appetite for any soda crackers, so I just said no thanks. Then the three of us just sat around staring at each other in silence, you look at me—for quite some time no one uttered a word.

During that time I started drifting back into my wild daydreams. The first thing I began to ponder was whether Ma Jianren's name was written with the characters for "Ma the Healthy and Benevolent" or "Ma the Despicable Man." If Old Bull was correct, this was Little Horse's father's name. I wonder if Little Horse knew that everyone referred to his father as "Ma the Despicable Man." He probably already knew. But I'd be pretty pissed if my friends all called my father "Hou the Despicable Man"— even though he truly is quite despicable. Then I started to wonder if Ma Jianren had any idea just what his son was up to. Didn't he know how to discipline Little Horse? Or maybe Little Horse didn't even give Ma Jianren the time of day. Otherwise, why would he say that the junkyard was his "home"? Did all of them sleep in this tour bus? Were Annie and Hoop girlfriends of Little Horse and Little Xinjiang? It didn't look like it because both Annie and Hoop seemed a bit too old. But if they all lived here together, wasn't that a bit strange? If they didn't "shoot their cannons" at night, then what the hell did they do? Just as I was thinking about "shooting cannons," Little Horse suddenly said:

"My name's Little Horse. This is Little Xinjiang."

"I know, you already told me."

Little Xinjiang, with his American mug, picked up that handgun again and tried to spin it around his finger like they do in the movies, but because the gun was so heavy it only made it halfway around. Little Xinjiang hastily used his other hand to stop it from spinning and asked, "What's wrong with this gun?"

Little Horse waved his hand, seemingly motioning for Little Xinjiang to stop talking. "Weren't we playing a little game just a little while ago?" As I nodded I saw Little Xinjiang put the barrel of the gun under his nose and take a whiff.

"Did you have your eyes closed the whole time?"

I quickly thought back to the events earlier in the day, but for some reason I felt I couldn't articulate what actually happened. Moreover, I had already begun to feel as if I was in a bit of danger, so I just nodded slightly.

"Then, did you hear anything?"

"I thought I heard someone firing a gun."

Little Horse nodded. "What else?"

"Did you know someone threw a gun in the van?" Little Xinjiang began to raise his voice.

"It was probably there to begin with," Little Horse offered.

"That's impossible! This gun was just fired, take a whiff and you'll see."

It was at that moment that Annie called down from "upstairs": "What the hell are you bugging him about? Bring him up here, big sister wants to get to know him."

ANNIE

Annie was the sole person out of all of them who right at the very beginning asked me what my name was. She changed into a small, gray, sleeveless blouse; her plump, bulging breasts were lit up by the ray of sunlight coming in through the window. I was a little embarrassed to stare at her tits, but they were right there in front of me. If I was going to look at Annie, I couldn't avoid looking at them. There was nothing I could do.

Annie had spread a blackish-green mud mask over her face. As she spoke to me, a clump would fall off whenever she wasn't careful; she'd just pick up the clump and spread it back on. After that she even asked me how to write the three characters that make up my name, Hou Shichun. As I told her, she wrote my name out in the air with her finger. Strange, ever since then I've felt as if my name were floating around the small rear compartment of that double-decker tour bus.

"Are you scared?"

I didn't respond to this question. I felt that even if I was, it was no chick's business. No matter how cool or big sister-like a chick was, they still had no business asking this kind of question.

"Even if you don't say, big sister already knows."

"What do you know?"

"You're definitely scared to death."

"No way."

"As soon as a person's scared, this is how they get." As Annie spoke she propped her feet up on the cloth cushions of the purplish red sofa and began wiggling her ten bright red toenails back and forth. She continued, "It's like this: when your fear gets to a certain level, your senses go numb. You can't see, can't hear, can't smell . . ."

"You're really annoying! Just what is it you want?" I started to get angry.

"I don't want anything. Big sister just wants to let you know that there is nothing wrong with being scared. If you can feel fear, that means that you've still got a head on your shoulders." As Annie spoke, she tapped her finger on her temple, knocking loose a clump of inky-green mud.

Nothing else happened that day. Annie tumbled off to sleep. The sun climbed from one window over to the window on the other side, and then before I knew it, disappeared behind the river embankment beside the junkyard. Without even realizing it, I also finished off a package of soda crackers and slurped down that bottle of mineral water. Little Horse and Little Xinjiang never came back up to the second level of the bus. Thinking carefully, I realized that they had disappeared the moment I announced my name. As for that girl Hoop, she showed her face for a second somewhere around noon. Standing on the small dirt mound next to the tour bus, she knocked on the bus window with a rock or something and yelled to Annie, "I'm still bleeding. I'm taking off now." Annie had no intention of getting up; she didn't even look at Hoop. She just heaved a long, deep sigh, waved her hand, and went back to sleep.

That was probably when I began to eat the soda crackers—food meant to be eaten by dogs. I then began to think back to everything that had happened that day; it was a strange, dreamlike day, only this dream was real.

It was a little bit like when you have a terrible dream, a fun dream, or a dream where you fall in love with somebody; after you wake up you want to put all the pieces of the dream together in their proper order. But this is more difficult than dreaming of what you want to dream about, and a hundred times more difficult than dreaming a beautiful dream that later comes true. Right now, my feeling is that I can only remember a few faces, and it's only broken fragments of these faces that I recall—like Ahzhi's alien eyes, Old Bull's chubby cheeks, Little Horse's long hair, and Little Xinjiang's blue eyes. I can't even remember what Uncle Xu looked like. If you were to ask me, "What about Hoop?" all I could do would be to shrug my shoulders and guess that she was probably something like American Indian. As for Annie, with that green mud mask on her face, she could pretty much pass for ET. And then there was that guy with a dragon and a pine tree tattooed on his shoulders and back—I wondered if he had already turned into a dead man. He was the first person in my life that I actually witnessed transform from a living person into a dead one. He was also the person who left the most unforgettable impression on me that day, but even the image of his face I find myself at a loss to recall.

Indeed, someone that I'd never met, with a face that I'd never seen and most likely would never see in the future, was enough to lead me to go on pondering for an eternity. He stood at the edge of the cliff and although it was already spring and the weather had grown cold, he still didn't wear a shirt. Standing there, he just kept repeating: "Copy, copy." And then he took two bullets—if he had been wearing some kind of shirt or jacket, perhaps the shots wouldn't have hurt as much. I wonder what the guy was thinking as he fell to the ground. "Ah! Am I dying?" or "Ah! Horsefly sends his apologies to me!" or "Ah! Why me?"

If it was me, I'd definitely be thinking, "Ah! Why me?" I know, because that was exactly my sentiment later. As I was munching on those soda crackers, snooping around this tour bus—which might as well have been a secret headquarters—trying to get a feel for what was inside, as I went down to look for a bathroom to take a piss, and as I held the towel and bottle of mineral water for Annie while she washed the mud mask off her face, I was continually wrestling with why some guy who only knew how to repeat, "Copy, copy," like a broken record had to die like this.

He was probably a ferocious character to begin with. But honestly speaking, I've never laid eyes on a ferocious character. Okay, let's suppose

he was as fiendish as Mr. Hippo; if Mr. Hippo got shot twice, I'd even feel
sorry for him. Like the time when Mr. Hippo chased after a student trying to climb over the school wall. Apparently he went up the wall after the
kid and, after letting out a wail, jumped down. Mr. Hippo ended up with
two broken ankles. A few days later, he appeared with a cane at the school
gate and, just like before, went about inspecting our school uniforms and
grooming, and randomly going through our book bags. Then one false
step and his cane would go aslant and fall tumbling to the ground. If you
were to pick it up for him, he'd even say, "Thank you!" This image would
make everyone pity him. Even though right after "Thank you" he'd go
right on snooping through your backpack, there was nothing you could
do, you still had to feel sorry for the guy. Not until the day came when
you got used to seeing him with a cane did that feeling of pity finally fade
and disappear.

After she washed away that disgusting mud mask, Annie's face looked
as if it had just come out of the oven, like a freshly shelled hard-boiled
egg; her face was a creamy white, sparkling and glowing in the dark of the
tour bus.

"Huh, how come you're still here?" she asked.

That was weird. If I didn't hang around, who would hold the towel for
her and help her rinse?

Annie shook her head and let out a series of extended catlike or tiger-
like roars. She went down, walked to the front of the bus, and I don't
know if it was the engine or what, but she started something up and suddenly the entire bus lit up.

"Don't you have to go home?" When she came back up, she had her
hair up in a bun with a short, silver, needlelike object sticking out of the
top. "Won't your family be looking for you?"

I didn't pay any attention to her. I just raised my head and saw that in
the two rows of fluorescent lights on the ceiling, one of the bulbs was broken and kept flickering on and off. But that bulb was seemingly very diligent in trying to keep up with the others, and he continued his struggle
for illumination.

"So you want to hang in the streets for a while?"

"No," I muttered under my breath. My reply was probably audible only to myself.

"Then why don't you go look up your friends or classmates? You do have classmates, don't you?"

I stood up and, stretching on my tiptoes, I could reach out and just touch the shell of that light bulb. I tapped it, but just like before it continued to flicker on and off.

"Oh, so sad, a little fellow who doesn't know what he wants to do," she said patronizingly.

"Please don't talk to me in that tone, okay? I'm not a child, got it?" I had my hands on my hips as I spoke to her, thinking I must look suave as hell. This old chick, who had no idea how deep she was in, seemed a bit uncertain how to respond.

She didn't answer me. She sat back down on her chair and from God knows where produced a nail clipper. *Chic-ching* she cut one nail, *chic-ching* she cut another. This was really annoying. Those fingernail clippings soared through the air, and if I wasn't careful they could fly into my eye or perhaps catapult into my name, which was still floating around the bus.

"Well, what about *you*? Don't *you* have to go home?" I couldn't help but finally open my mouth—actually I just couldn't stand the sound of that continual *chic-ching, chic-ching*.

"What home?" Annie threw me a sidelong glance and continued, "This is my home! This place is all mine. These cars are mine, even the toilet, washroom, telephone booth outside are mine. Things are good now, even you belong to me—but I don't want you!"

What a real man fears most is being looked down upon. When the day comes that you start losing respect from one person, the others quickly follow suit. Especially being looked down upon by a chick—that's the worst thing in the world that could happen. When I heard her say she didn't want me, I unthinkingly snapped back, "Well, I don't want to be here either!" and staggered downstairs, flustered.

However, I found myself unable to open the door that had popped open with just a touch when I arrived; I suspected that when Annie went downstairs to start up that damn machine she'd locked us in. I rushed upstairs and raced to the front of the bus, but the door at the bottom of the front staircase was also locked dead tight.

"Little Bull-boy, don't go and lose your temper now." Annie cracked a smile as she continued, "Run out like this, and if you don't end up dead, you'll at least come back with half your limbs missing."

"That's none of your business!"

"Well, fuck you then! Do you think I'm joking?"

That's Annie—you could never tell when she was joking and when she was being serious. She had a set of particularly long and thin eyebrows; like the wings of a bird gliding high in the sky above, they stretched out, extending toward her temples. Whenever she was talking to you, those eyes of hers, just below her winglike eyebrows, would always be staring at you; rarely would they drift off. Later, when I was somewhere else and would think of her, I always felt a bit guilty because I really have a hard time remembering what people look like. I can only recall her eyes and eyebrows; perhaps at the most I could also remember her breasts, but that's it.

And then, with her tits jiggling, she walked toward me, grabbed hold of my hair, and just like a little girl said, "Come on, tell me about yourself, and then I'll tell you about this place."

THE PAST

I used to know this chick who later emigrated with her whole family to Canada. And from that faraway place, which I can't hope to set foot on even in my next life, she wrote me saying, "The past is like mist, I cannot bear to look back." Not long after that, her name appeared in the newspaper, under a headline that read: YOUNG OVERSEAS CHINESE STUDENT UNABLE TO WITHSTAND PRESSURE COMMITS SUICIDE. I always held on to that article, and from time to time, I'd take it out and read it together with the letter she had sent me. Once while I was in the middle of reading them, my grandparents came over. I knew that they had come to discuss a way to prevent the imminent divorce of my parents. This was a pretty boring subject for me so I didn't bother to go out and greet them. But Grandpa, being truly bored to death, came barging into my room and knocked me on the head with one of Grandma's stuffed buns. I don't know if it was that my head was too hard or the stuffed bun was too soft, but the whole thing fell apart. The soup and stuffing inside all spilled out, spraying all over my desk and ruining that chick's letter, my newspaper cutout, and my homework notebook. I cursed Grandpa: "Why don't you just drop dead!" That day the four adults in the house seemingly didn't mention a word about the divorce, they just took turns offering both single and cooperative lectures on how the older I got the more rotten I became—I guess you could say I saved my parents' marriage that day. But when I yelled at Grandpa, it wasn't because I suddenly got angry; actually I was pondering how a young child, alive and kicking one minute, could suddenly die with "the past is like mist, I cannot bear to look back." All the while, those people who look like they have already lived for a long, long time are not only fine and dandy, but seem as if they'll just keep ticking on for an eternity. The longer they live, the more things about the past they have to tell you.

Take Grandpa for instance—each time Mom calls Dad a worthless wretch, or Dad says Mom is too overbearing, his response is always: "Let me tell you a little story from the past for you to think about."

Then Grandpa usually goes on to recount how during the Anti-Japanese War he traveled from one province to another searching for Grandma. At the same time, Grandma was also running from province to province in search of Grandpa. Searching all over, the two of them left their tracks over more than half of mainland China, during which time they witnessed almost every strange person and oddity that you can think of. Grandpa said he once saw a child with three legs—some adults who charged twenty cents for a peek had put him on display. Grandpa went once on his own and went a second time with Grandma. Grandma sat beside him nodding. "It's true." It's bearable to hear this kind of story from the past once, but after you hear it more than twice it gets really irritating. Even more annoying was that if I happened to doze off while sitting beside him listening, they'd even wake me up. Moreover, just what did this kind of a story have to do with Dad being a worthless wretch or Mom being an overbearing tyrant? But you know, stories from the past are all the same—only the storyteller himself feels that the story really has some kind of connection with the present.

But I'm not the kind of person to judge a book by its cover. I know the importance of the past; back when I wanted to get in that chick's pants, I pretended to want to know all about her past. I would ask her things like where she went to elementary school, what cool comic books she had read lately, and whether or not she had any little pets. I probably wanted to tell her about my past as well. But what a shame, I guess I never told her all that much; nor do I remember just what I did tell her. After she died so mysteriously, I couldn't imagine another person who could entice me enough to want to know about their past, or inspire me enough to talk about my own past. I just wrapped up that newspaper article, her letter, my notebook, and what was left of that stuffed bun in an old newspaper and threw the whole thing into the garbage can. I figured this was what she meant by "the past is like mist, I cannot bear to look back"!

When Annie asked me to talk about myself—honestly speaking, I drew a complete blank, I couldn't think of a thing. I might as well have been a blow-up dummy.

First off, I didn't know if I should talk about important stuff or trivial things. For example, I'd been dying to tell anybody who would listen that I wasn't the one who burned the geography exams. And even though I knew who did it, I couldn't reveal their name. For important events, if you can't give the whole story, it's better just to keep your mouth shut. Another important event was the disappearance of my father, but I had no idea what had actually happened, so what was there to talk about? If I think again, perhaps Mom and Dad's divorce was a bit important; then again everybody on the block was getting a divorce, plus the details were no more interesting than the latest soap opera. Each time you think of something, you feel embarrassed to talk about it.

Besides that, there were those things that appeared of the least importance. For example, I studied Tae Kwon Do but as soon as I earned my fourth stripe I broke my big toe doing a side kick and gave it up. Or the fact that I had more than forty dinosaur models—buying them almost put my family in the poorhouse—but when I finally looked them up in a dinosaur book, I discovered that more than twenty of them were dinosaurs that never existed on this planet. Or that ever since I was little, I was trained by my mother to scrub 150 strokes each time I brushed my teeth. If I didn't get in the full 150 strokes or got halfway through and then lost count, it was really a nightmare and I'd have to start over. So I'd often get pissed and wouldn't brush at all. Is this insignificant enough for you? I just didn't know what to say that would be interesting. And so I just zoned out like a blow-up dummy.

"If you don't want to say anything it's okay," Annie said as she gazed at me.

That was one strange situation—or at least it was a situation I had never run into before. When someone stares at you like that, waiting for you to say something, for a while you suspect that she wants to find something out in order to take some kind of action against you. For instance, I was thinking: if I tell her where I live, give her my phone number, and then tell her what happened at school, perhaps she would contact my parents or somebody else to come and take me away. But this only flashed through my mind for a split second. After Annie said, "If you don't want to say anything it's okay," she took off her elastic hairband, spun it around her index finger, and began to stare blankly like a blow-up dummy.

I could sense that she was also thinking about some things from her past, and of those, there definitely were a few instances that left her far from happy. And so, staring at her beret, she slightly knitted her brow. After a second her brow eased up, but then it knitted again. From time to time when she would look at me I would instantly look the other way. Then something strange happened. . . .

From the blinking fluorescent light, from the glass bus window that reflected our shadows, and from the carpet scattered with newspapers, magazines, mineral water bottles, blue jeans, walkie-talkies, cigarette butts, and a pile of other random items, the past came looking for me. These objects seemingly had absolutely no connection with one another, but let me tell you: each came one after another in strict uniform as if they were a well-ordered battalion.

What came to mind first was the time that my mother took me to the supermarket. When we got there, she suddenly remembered that when we left the house she had forgotten to turn off the gas stove, so the water on the stove was still boiling. Mom left me with a young lady giving away free samples of grilled snakehead roe while she rushed home to turn off the gas.

She was gone really way too long and I in turn ate really way too much snakehead roe. Finally I found my way to another cart that was giving away free samples of something else. By the time Mom came back and found me, she looked like a ghost. Her face was covered with a combination of tears and smeared black and red makeup; her mouth uttered a never-ending series of ghostlike groans while her long fingernails dug into my flesh. I don't remember the exact language she used to curse me, but I can still recall her whispering, "Don't you ever, ever tell your father what happened."

The time my father took me to Wulai came up second. Before we had left for Wulai, my father had told me there was a cable car there and a place to go bungee-jumping. He told me that if I had enough guts, there was no way he could restrict me from going jumping—for man to experience the feeling of flying was simply too good to pass up. But in the end, while we were halfway through the line to buy a ticket, Dad discovered that a pickpocket had lifted his leather wallet. Not only was I unable to experience the feeling of flying, but I had to accompany Dad on the endless foot march home. On the way home, Dad whispered, "Don't you dare tell your mother what happened."

My guess is that Dad also kept Mom in the dark about the third incident. That was when Huang Munan, Xie Caijun, and I took advantage of the time we were supposed to be doing off-campus volunteer work to sneak off and catch a movie. That was the first time I saw a romance flick. As we ran back to campus to get there before the roll call, Huang Munan said that there was no way that female lead was a virgin. Xie Caijun said that in real life the male actor was a homosexual. I said nothing. That is because during the movie my father was sitting two rows in front of us, his left arm caressing some chick with her hair up in a pineapple-style bun.

The fourth event—actually it doesn't even count as an event, it was just a picture. In the picture, my dad had really long hair; it was just as long as Chow Yun-fat's when he was younger. His left arm was wrapped around my mother. Mom was wearing a low-cut Western blouse, but because of her super-small breasts it looked like she had put an evening gown with an exposed back on backward. Two lines were written on the other side of the photo: "In this life and the next, always and forever";

then there was Mom's name written in Dad's handwriting, and Dad's name written by Mom.

In the end, however, I didn't tell Annie any of this. If you were to rank what I eventually told her according to the criteria used above, it would probably only come in seventeenth, eighteenth, or nineteenth. But that's exactly how recollecting the past goes, like a game of guess-who-the-leader-is. One thing always pops out first, even though it isn't necessarily the most important one or even the one that occurred first; it just happens to be the first to burst out. As it pops out, it inspires you to talk about it, and then it helps you to connect it with other events from the past. Perhaps the past is the same for everyone, making people feel happy and sad and all kinds of other emotions, but what escapes from your mouth first is always something that your true self can hide behind and never be discovered.

"We've got a teacher at our school called Mr. Hippo. He's got four huge false teeth, you know, just like a hippopotamus. We all call him "River Horse."* Once while he was at the school gate inspecting our backpacks, he sneezed, sending his false teeth flying into one of my classmates' knapsack. . . ."

If I were to think back to how I fell in love with Annie, I would tell you it started the night she listened to me telling stories. That's because before her, there was never anyone else who made me feel like a true storyteller. But later I realized that compared to Annie's, my past didn't mean shit.

---

* "River horse" is a literal translation of *hema*, the two characters that make up the Chinese term for "hippopotamus."

ON THE ROOFTOP

When Annie was twenty-two years old, she learned how to operate a kind of strange heavy-duty crane—she giggled as she said that I must have still been in elementary school playing dodge ball at the time. This type of crane actually can barely even move; most of the time it stays stationary, extending its four massive, super-huge claws that look like crumpled lotus leaves. It picks up motorcycles, limousines, trucks, vans, and even things like bicycles, and one after another spins them around and places them back on the ground. As it puts the vehicles back, someone is waiting there to examine them and record what parts are useful. Then there are a few other guys who remove these parts. Finally there are a bunch of characters whose job is to remove only tires, seats, flannelette or nylon seat covers, and cushions. These jobs don't require any kind of skill—Annie said that if you train one well, even a dog could learn. When nothing was left but an empty shell, she would pick the vehicle back up and drop it into a crushing machine. And then came the best part: she would get out of the crane and walk over to the small control booth behind the sheet-iron outhouse, and from behind a glass window use the four odd-shaped levers to completely flatten the empty steel shell. What a magnificent power!

"We spend most of the time getting rid of cars. It's like giving them their last rites," Annie said. "So you have to maintain a solemn attitude as you're doing it. Think about it: a car on the road has to brave the rain and wind, race around from east to west, working hard its whole life. So when you're disposing of it, you have to be especially careful. You can't say we just crush them and sell them off as a lump of worthless steel."

"So what about the rest of the time?"

"What do you mean, 'rest of the time?' "

"You just said, 'We spend most of the time getting rid of cars . . .' "

"Oh, right." Annie smiled, throwing her head back.

The rest of the time, they got rid of people.

A long time ago, when Annie was still in elementary school playing dodge ball, she lived with her family on Eternal Spring Avenue. It was a two-story building just off the main street. One day, Annie's father said that they should really try to take advantage of the roof. How could they take advantage of it? Annie's father already had a plan; since there were so many of those "whorehouse hair salons" in the neighborhood and the massage girls roaming the area were so numerous that you couldn't even count them all, he wanted to consult them. Annie's mother and grandmother were both against using the house their ancestors had left them to do that kind of dirty business. But of course Annie's father wasn't going to open up a "whorehouse hair salon"—he could never match the business experience of those other joints. So in the end he opened a Buddhist hall of worship. Inside were statues of the three great guardians, the military hero Guan Yu, the Mad Healer Ji Gong, and the Earth Guardian; then there was the most important of them all, the Big Pig Guardian. A few months later they had the incense burning like you wouldn't believe, and they had to put all the cash in a gunnysack. Annie's dad had no choice but to say, "We'll have to give the first and second floors over to worship as well!" This time both Annie's mother and grandmother agreed. And so all eight people in her three-generation family squeezed into the small rooftop attic behind the altar to the Big Pig Guardian.

The bunk bed Annie slept in was up against the particleboard wall; just on the other side of this wall were the butts of those Guardians. Annie secretly drilled a few small holes in the wall so when she had nothing to do she could check out all the different types of people who came and went. Picking up incense sticks, carrying candles, offering fresh fruitcakes, and kowtowing in her direction, they would even reveal their secret desires and dreams with their chanting lips.

Annie said that she had heard at least ten thousand of these dreams, and 99 percent of them were women's dreams. Some people prayed for peace and security, some prayed for health, some prayed that their sons would get into medical school, some prayed their husbands would come around and change their ways, some of them prayed that their lost dog, cat, or turtle would come home soon, and some prayed they would win

the lottery. There were also those who prayed that somebody else would get sick, get into a car accident, come down with an intestinal parasite, or even get blown away in a typhoon.

By the time Annie got to middle school, most of the people who came to the hall wanted to cast lots. Annie said this was much more of an inconvenience because they had to provide an answer on the spot. Those who came to cast lots would stay a lot longer than the others. It was as if almost all of them were stricken with some kind of senility disease, so before they could choose the next number they had to wait until they had some kind of divine inspiration. This inspiration came in the form of the deities either turning the white incense smoke into a perfect circle or making the candle flames flicker a few times, or when they themselves could swear that they witnessed one of the Guardians smile. Annie was often moved by their devout expressions; the more excited the person praying was, the more excited the girl hiding behind the wall became. Annie was always thinking that people have truly too many hopes and desires. And since it is so difficult for these hopes to be realized, people must suffer. This is also precisely why there are so many grotesque and fantastic deities running around—but even all of them are still not enough. What to do? Annie pondered this until her head was splitting, but still couldn't come up with an answer. Then suddenly one day, as she was spying through the hole in the wall on an old lady who came to cast lots, she sensed that the old lady could see her eye. Annie suddenly found herself softly announcing two numbers. With tears of joy the old lady got up from her knees and left while Annie, for the first time in her life, felt the euphoria of sublime release.

However, helping others realize their dreams can be dangerous. Annie said that, just like smoking cigarettes, it could be addictive. Annie did more and more good deeds behind the deities' backs, but sometimes the result of a good deed isn't always auspicious. One night about six months later a gang boss came to her family's Buddhist hall. This gang leader brought two of his gang brothers and told Annie's father that they were going to "check the place out." They went through the two floors and then even took a stroll through the small rooftop add-on where Annie and her family lived. The leader asked Annie, "You sleep here?" Annie nodded. The leader didn't say anything else, he just took his two brothers and left. Two days later a strange fire burned the entire three-story Buddhist hall to the ground. Annie suddenly awakened to find the Big Pig Guardian lying on top of the Mad Healer consumed from head to toe in a layer of blue flames. Before she could realize what was happening, she slipped back into her lethargic slumber. From that night on, she never again laid eyes on her father, mother, grandmother, or her four little brothers and sisters; she never again went back to school. For the next three years, she would be confined to one place.

Annie was stuck in another rooftop addition. "Actually, it was just a big iron cage. Inside was a glass compartment with a roof, and inside of that compartment were that gang leader's mother and me," said Annie. "That gang leader told me: 'From now on, your job is to take care of my mother. She dies, you die, along with your brothers and sisters.' "

That gang boss's mother came down with this strange disease called lupus erythematosus. By the time Annie came on the scene, her illness had already advanced to the stage where the entire shape of her body had changed. Her cheeks looked as if she had a pair of eggs fused onto her cheekbones, and almost all of her hair had fallen out. When it was a bit brighter, Annie could even clearly make out the red spots on the bridge of her nose and cheeks. It looked like two or three butterflies were taking a rest on her face. "Those were the most hideous butterflies I've ever seen!" Annie exclaimed. "There were even gray and coffee-color scales on them, and as soon as the wind blew it appeared as if the butterflies were about to fly off." But that old lady was a really good person, not at all what you'd expect as the mother of a gang leader. Every day, Annie would have to help the old lady go to the bathroom. In the mornings she'd cook the old lady a pot of rice porridge, and every night a bowl of rice to go with the pickled cucumber, pork, dried minnows, soybean oysters, and pig intestines that the gang leader brought home every evening at dusk. The old lady also had to take medicine, which was brought either by the gang leader himself or by one of his brothers. They gave her quinine pills, which were to cure malaria. Supposedly, if the old lady didn't go out in the sun and took her medicine when she was supposed to, she shouldn't die.

Day by day, time went by and before Annie knew it just about a year had passed. Not only did the old lady not die, she even grew a few patches of hair. Sometimes when she felt up to it, she even watched some television or videotapes, listened to the radio, or played a type of poker called "pulling turtles" with Annie. According to that gang leader's calculations, Annie had been shut up on the rooftop for a full year. On the day of her one-year anniversary, the gang leader came, opened up the iron gate, and let Annie come out for a walk. Only then did Annie realize that the place she had lived for the past year was the rooftop of an eight-story commercial building. From the street below you couldn't even see her iron cage. But the rooftops of all the other buildings in the neighborhood—no matter if they were taller or shorter—also had their own illegal additions, each also surrounded by almost identical iron railing. Annie wondered if there were an old lady secretly locked up with a little girl on each of those other rooftops as well—in the same way that she was secretly confined to her cage. That day the gang leader thanked Annie for taking care of his mother and gave her a Walkman and a video-game system to attach to the television. She asked him, "What about my parents and siblings?" The gang leader answered, "Don't ask that kind of question."

And so, unlike most, Annie went to prison first and hit the streets later. The whole time she was locked up, Annie never considered running away, she didn't dare let the thought even cross her mind. Only once, while watching a nightly news report of a police sweep of the "whorehouse hair salons" and "red-light restaurants" on Eternal Spring Avenue did she get a glimpse of home. As the camera panned a row of buildings she saw the tea factory to the left of her house and the stationery store to the right, but the building in the middle was wrong! The building in the center only appeared on the television screen for less than half a second—but she saw it clear as day. Her house had been turned into a brand-new karaoke club with 3-D images of naked Western women carved on the walls beside the entrance. Annie grabbed the remote control and pressed frantically on the button to change the channel, but for some reason the channel wouldn't change. Still she didn't give up and continued pressing until her fingernail began to bleed, but it was no use. Finally all she could do was cry. She cried hysterically, she cried with all her might, as if the sound of her sobbing could carry all the way back to Eternal Spring Avenue. The result was that when the gang leader came home he dragged her down to the eighth floor, beat her up, and "popped her with his cannon." In the middle of the night Annie heard him call out in his sleep, "Annie! Annie!"

"Annie was the name of his ex-wife," Annie told me.

"Isn't Annie your name?" I asked.

"Me?" Annie's round eyes opened wide as she continued. "I was only called that later."

"So what did you used to be called?"

Annie laughed, saying, "My real name died in the fire that that gang leader set."

Early the next morning when the gang boss's two brothers brought Annie back to the roof, it seemed that the old lady already knew what had happened. She told those two gang brothers to tell her son that if he dared lay a hand on her in the future, she would kill herself right in front of his face. But the gang leader still came back—this time after drinking more than his share of alcohol; he stood outside the iron cage and called out to Annie, saying he had something to discuss with her. In the end, though, it was his mother who came out. She told her son, "If you've got what it takes, why don't you take me on?" She then tore off her clothes and with her hands on her hips, cursed him: "Why don't you fuck your mother?!"

For the next spring nobody saw a trace of the gang leader. His two gang brothers took turns bringing food, beverages, daily necessities, the newest household appliances, dolls, perfume, and from God knows where, they even got their hands on an entire set of high school textbooks. One time they came with a message saying that the gang leader was now doing big business importing machinery, he was really doing well. As one was telling us about the boss's business ventures, the other took out a camera to take a couple of pictures of Annie and the old lady for their boss. Later there was a time when another brother said that the gang leader was involved in a housing-development partnership. Upon hearing this, the old lady didn't say a thing; she just took the beverages and saw the guy to the door. She then whispered to Annie, "Don't they get tired of concocting all these stories to deceive us?"

But apparently the gang leader wasn't deceiving anybody. One autumn evening, he came swaying upstairs. Squatting just outside the iron cage, he beckoned Annie over with his finger. Annie approached and as she opened the glass door, the gang leader stuffed in a paper shopping bag and said to her, "Everything inside is for you. If you run into any kind of trouble, ask Xu for help. Xu's business card is in the bag. Sorry to be so much trouble to you these past few years, but please take good care of my mother. Everything should be fine with the brothers, but if by chance something should happen, don't worry about it. I beg of you, please, just take care of Mom."

When he finished his speech, the gang leader stood up, took two steps backward, knelt down on the ground, and called out, "Mom!" He then kowtowed four times in the direction of the rooftop addition. He never got up again after that. Annie and the gang leader's mother opened the iron gate and rushed out, and only after they turned him over did they discover the half-dozen bullet holes in his chest. Each hole was stuffed with a bloody piece of cloth, and when they pulled out the bloody rags, everything you can imagine flowed out. Annie and the old lady wailed in sorrow. Annie was thinking that now there was no way she would ever know what had happened to her family.

Inside that blood-stained shopping bag were a property deed, a few contracts between a few companies and some equipment supplier, an iden- tification card, a driver's license, a bank book, and two chops. Wherever there should have been a picture attached to these documents was a photo of Annie; however, the name signed was that of the gang leader's ex-wife.

Annie stayed in the rooftop penthouse until the summer of the second year, when the gang leader's mother passed away. For the last six months there was already no one who could restrict Annie's movements. However, besides her daily ritual of seeing the doctor off and buying some groceries, she didn't really know where else she could go, or how to get there. As the gang leader's mother was approaching death's door, the doctor said that her erythematosus had already progressed to the "chronic" stage; her abdomen, lymph nodes, heart, and kidneys had all grown butterflies. As the doctor left, the old lady, with tears in her eyes, implored Annie to do one thing for her: she wanted Annie to get rid of her corpse. Annie was to let nobody else see, or know what happened. The old lady didn't even want her body to go to a burial society or funeral home.

"Why?" asked Annie. Later I also asked the same question.

"Alive I have already completely lost face. When I die how can I dare let anyone know? Please, I beg you to take care of this for me."

Annie said that when it came time for her to leave behind that rooftop add-on, she had indeed learned something from the gang leader and his mother: in this world, some people are destined to live like a stray dog, while others are doomed to die like one.

"There are some people who don't want to be a stray dog, but there's seemingly nothing else they can do," said Annie.

"So did you get rid of her?" I asked.

Annie turned to gaze out the window and covered her lips and chin with her hand. She never answered me.

BROTHERS

When Annie told me about her experiences on those two rooftops, we assumed that these were all bygones, pieces of the past that were already over. Actually, we were wrong. The past left behind a series of things that continued to occur; we simply didn't realize it at the time. I even ignorantly told Annie, "Your story is super cool, you could make it into a movie!" Afterward I told her that: there's this kid in my school named Weng Jiaping. Jiaping is always writing stories in class; all the teachers tell him, "Hey, Weng Jiaping! Can't you wait till you grow up to become a novelist?" He wrote a story about a pheasant that caused a great upheaval at Science City, and a full-length novel about how a detective with a frog's head discovered a ancient Incan buried treasure of gold coins beneath an abandoned train station. Our whole class used to pass it around to read. If Annie were to tell her story to Weng Jiaping, he could probably make it into a great novel, and who knows, maybe in the future they'd even turn it into a motion picture.

"Only a little devil like you would think my story was entertaining," said Annie.

"If the part about the gang leader was a little more developed, it would be even more interesting. Hey, didn't that gang leader have a bunch of brothers? What happened to them? Didn't they avenge their boss?"

Annie shook her head.

"If the boss got taken out, the gang brothers should have avenged him!" I protested.

"And since when does that happen?" Annie continued to shake her head, saying, "I think they ended up scattered all over the place. It's unclear what happened to a few of them, then there was another handful who in no time at all got picked up by the cops. And then there's some who'll have to squeeze by somehow; they will probably look for a new boss. It's just like going to work: when a company goes under, don't the employees have to apply elsewhere?"

This was the first time I heard a real-life gang story; pretty stimulating, huh? But I was really disappointed with the actions of the gang leader's brothers. I felt that if they were the guy's brothers then they ought to have taken it upon themselves to avenge his death. The way they turned the boat around as soon as the current changed is not what you'd expect from a true gang brother.

MISTAKES

Besides that, I made a mistake: while listening to Annie's story I became extremely happy. I was so filled with joy that it was as if I were reading a comic book, watching a cartoon, thumbing through a photo album, checking out a movie, or listening to a story about a walking cradle. That's because no matter how great the danger or how deep the suffering in the story, in actuality it has absolutely nothing to do with you. You just sit there nibbling on dried snack peas and sipping your iced black tea. All you care about is: What happened next? What happened next? What happened next?

Right! That's exactly what I asked her: "So what happened next?"

I had asked Annie if she had taken Uncle Xu's business card from the bag and looked him up, but before she could answer there was a pounding on the back door of the tour bus that sounded like a bolt of lightning striking the door. It was also at that moment that I was seemingly suddenly awakened from a deep, heavy dream.

As Little Horse bolted upstairs, the first thing he said was to Annie; he spoke very softly, but I could still him crystal clear:

"Young River got iced!"

"What happened?"

"It's still unclear what happened. They found his corpse this morning floating in the Halcyon Reservoir. By now every cop in Taipei is probably combing the streets." As Little Horse spoke he approached me. When he got before me he squatted down, and I saw that covering his forehead, face, and neck were pearl-size beads of sweat. He heaved a deep sigh before telling me, "Listen, you little devil! This has absolutely nothing to do with you, so don't be afraid. But don't you dare try to deceive us. . . ."

I probably nodded at this point.

"How did that gun end up in the van this morning?"

Fuck! Before Little Horse even finished what he was saying I knew I was fucked. All I did was head-butt Mr. Hippo in the stomach, get soaked in the rain, and run away from home to hear some strange and fantastic tales. I didn't do a thing, I didn't know anybody; at the most all I did was fantasize about walking with style down a dark alley with a bunch of gang brothers. How could they force me to answer questions like this? I bit down on my lip and could feel my nose getting stuffy and itchy as tears began to well up inside me.

"Don't scare him!" Annie pushed Little Horse aside and sat down next to me. Caressing my arm, she said, "Don't be afraid, Little Bull-boy, we've got nothing to be afraid of."

The more she spoke the more I felt things weren't right—after all, she was the one who'd locked me in the bus earlier that afternoon. She had even said that if I didn't come back dead, I'd at least end up with half my limbs missing. My shoulders shaking, I pushed her arm off me, and those damn tears began to roll down my face.

"How about this, since this has nothing to do with him, let's just go together to bring him back home. We'll worry about the gun later."

"No way! If we do that we may very well be doing him more harm than good." Little Horse wiped the sweat from his face and continued, "Maybe he didn't see who put the gun in the car, but how do you know that whoever planted the gun didn't see the kid?"

"I want to go home!" I couldn't take it anymore. Even the snot was about to drip from my nose, but I quickly sucked it back in.

"I really think we should bring him . . ."

Little Horse raised his hand, cutting Annie off. Then slowly, one word at a time, he said, "Uncle Xu saw the gun. He verified that it was Young River's. The incident with Young River and the showdown at the casino are perhaps one and the same. He probably set everything up from the beginning. They knew that you and Hoop were going to try your luck at the casino, so they intentionally pulled a fast one so that you would see, while at the same time they could take out Young River. By the time the uproar broke out at the casino, dragging Little Xinjiang and me inside, the timing was perfect for them to plant the gun on us. And just like that, you, Hoop, Little Xinjiang, and I, and even Uncle Xu and Yan Xiong, get implicated. And then everybody can say bye-bye, *sayonara!*"

Annie didn't say anything, but I could see her lower lip slightly quivering.

"Uncle Xu said that if they really want to quickly get rid of everybody, it's easy. All they have to do is make a call to 911, tell them they have the missing clue to the Young River case, throw out a few names, a couple of addresses and it's **GAME OVER.**"

"Then . . ." I hesitated for a moment. I knew I was about to make a big mistake, but you should know, that's the kind of person I am—I don't like to see people getting set up behind their backs. Actually, it doesn't even matter if the guy getting set up is a good person or some rotten egg, I just don't like to see people getting framed, period.

"Then why did they want to ice one of their own?" I asked.

"What?" Little Horse and Annie cried out in unison.

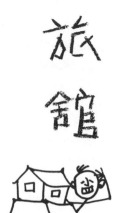

A lot happened after that, but I can omit some of it. Like how Little Horse and Annie discussed where we should go for our next move, and how we should get there. Whether or not we should meet with Uncle Xu. And whether or not the shipping yard was truly safe. I can leave out things like these. After they got halfway through their debate, Annie once again felt that I shouldn't get tangled up in this business and they should just take me home. But Little Horse stood his ground, saying that they first had to verify whether or not that cologne-wearing assassin saw me, otherwise nowhere would be safer than with them. Their discussion lasted around an hour and finally they decided we should hop on a public bus, transfer to another bus that took us all the way out to Sanchong, wind back to Xinzhuang, and probably ended up in some other ridiculous place. But since I fell asleep on the bus I had no idea where we were going. We ended up back on some Taipei street. After we'd been walking for a while it began to rain, and only then did I really wake up. Annie told me, "We're going to a hotel."

All together we stayed in hotels for six nights. Every two days we'd change hotels, so in the end we stayed at three different joints. All three were the kind of dingy places that are made from thin wooden walls, black tile floors, and a sign hanging outside saying THE SO-AND-SO GRAND HOTEL. Actually there was nothing grand about any of them; each was just a tiny hole in the ground. Each time, Little Horse stayed in one room while Annie and I stayed in another. At first I felt uncomfortable about it, but Annie said that she couldn't sleep unless there was a man beside her. I told her that she could sleep with Little Horse. She said that it was terrifying to wake up in the middle of the night and see Little Horse's long hair. I figured she was probably just making some crazy excuse, and what she was really looking for was a chance to jump my bones. Only later did I realize that Little Horse slept during the day and went out with Little Xinjiang at night to take care of whatever business they had to do.

Hotels are among the most boring places in the world. Especially the type that we were staying at. The rugs were always sticky, the blankets were constantly damp, the bedsheets were eternally mapped with yellow and red stains, and the closet and dresser at the foot of the bed would periodically emit the stench of mildew and cockroach eggs. None of the rooms had a refrigerator and the only one that had a television set could pick up sound but no picture. The worst part was that Annie and I had to stay inside almost twenty-four hours a day; later I would even feel that there was more than forty-eight hours in a single day. That's probably because by that time Annie had already told me everything about herself.

Every morning, not long after we woke up, Annie would go out to buy over a dozen newspapers. We would read through them separately, trading sections that we hadn't yet read, checking to see if there were any new developments in the Young River case. After we finished reading the papers, Annie would take out the Walkman that that gang leader had given her to listen to the news. After that we'd call for takeout, eat our lunches, take a nap, listen to the news, and then read through the evening paper. There were two occasions when I was so fucking bored that I even went next door to Little Horse's room to count how many times he snored. When Little Horse stopped snoring, that meant it was about time to order our evening takeout.

"Don't you feel bored?" I asked Annie.

"For a long time now, for a long time I've been used to it."

"Is it really that dangerous outside?"

"You'd better not test the waters."

"Do you often have to hide out like this?"

"Not necessarily."

"Will we have to continue on like this forever?"

"Don't worry, Bull-boy! That's impossible."

"So how much longer then?"

"We'll have to wait and see what Horsefly is thinking."

Who knew what Horsefly was thinking? But no matter what, I was clear on one thing—that was the first time I truly had my heart set on returning to school. What did I care if they sent me directly back to the principal's office to stand in the corner? Even then I'd be willing.

"I want to call my classmate."

"Use your imagination to call."

"I could tell your story to Weng Jiaping."

"And what if Weng Jiaping tells Mr. Hippo, and Mr. Hippo goes and tells the cops?"

". . ."

". . ."

"I really, really hate hotels."

"Me too."

THE PORT

Uncle Xu said that his second career ambition was to open up a hotel; what did he care if it was a drab joint like the ones we stayed in, with only a communal toilet and washroom? His number one goal was to have his own harbor port—but of course this was a dream that he could never realize. Even in his dreams he probably never thought he'd end up running a parking lot. But he wasn't careful and ended up with a couple million NT, rented a plot of land, and all he could do was open up a parking lot—anyway, it's a little like a port. And so this is Uncle Xu's life. The night we switched to the second hotel, Uncle Xu came to visit us. He brought along a whole mess of pickled vegetables and beer just like he was calling on close friends. My guess was that he was just joking when he said he wanted to open a hotel like the one we were staying at. Who would be willing to live with several hundred cockroaches and spiders? In the middle of the night there were even bats that would fly in through the hole in the window screen. The walls and floors would strangely shake as if they had contracted some old person's disease, always teetering and wobbling. It was as if the beer bottles and teacups could fall off the coffee table at any time. And then Uncle Xu, Annie, and Old Bull all laughed aloud.

"There she goes, bringing down the walls again." As Uncle Xu spoke he poured me half a glass of beer. He continued chortling as he told the others, "And so that's why I say the service business is tougher than anything out there." They all broke out in laughter. I chuckled with them, though all the while I had no clue what they were laughing about. But all the same, I liked the feeling of everybody together having a good time. It was a bit like when I was little and used to play house, only this was much more realistic than any game of house.

I couldn't tell you when exactly the earthquakelike trembling in the room ended because I was in the bathroom. As I was squatting over that toilet—which was seemingly doomed to never flush down its contents clean—I had to force myself to think of some happy and beautiful images. For example, Uncle Xu standing beside his very own harbor port. With a smile on his face and his hand waving, he welcomed large and small boats from all over the world. Getting off the ships were both foreigners and nationals; of course my classmates and I were there too. I introduced Huang Munan, Li Ahji, and Chen Xiaohao to Uncle Xu, saying, "This is the gang leader who took care of me while I was out in the streets. He used to run a parking lot, but now he's doing big business at the harbor port, he's doing really well." I would also introduce my classmates to my brothers Little Horse, Little Xinjiang, Old Bull, and Ahzhi. Everybody would be really happy getting to know each other. As soon as my imagination got to this point I heard a sudden scream. I couldn't tell if the sound came from nearby or far away, but one thing was certain—it was a woman's scream. At first I thought it must be Annie, but right afterward I heard the sound of Annie's and the others' giggling coming from the room as if nothing had happened. So I went back to my port. I imagined everybody under a beach umbrella sipping iced black tea and beer, each person wearing a different-style pair of sunglasses. This time Annie was also there, but I didn't make her as old as she really is—I made her just a tad bit older than me. She gazed at me from a short distance away, her love for me written all over her face. I told Huang Munan, "That's my woman."

It was a pity that at that moment someone banged loudly on the bathroom door.

Pounding on the door was a super-hefty giant, who must have been a sumo wrestler or something. Since he was only wearing his underwear, the fishy stench of his body flowed into the air like an exploding volcano. He gave me a malicious glare and I glared right back at him. As he slammed the door back shut, I cursed him: "Fuck!" What was I afraid of? All my friends were just around the corner. Rushing back to my hotel room, I turned my head to look back for a second and bumped into a woman. Originally this woman had been waiting in line behind that bastard sumo wrestler; she probably also had to use the toilet. As she waited there, she was attempting, strand by strand, to arrange her long, messy hair. I muttered my apologies, but she just gave me a wry smile.

Approximately ten minutes later I knew her name: Apricot. The instant she pushed open the door and strutted in, everyone except me stood up and gave her a round of applause and called out her name. Old Bull said, "Here she is, raw and in the flesh!" Uncle Xu said, "Long time no see." Annie said, "You must be exhausted after a show like that." Apricot herself said, "Damn it! The only reason I didn't take any money from that john was because you guys were right here next door! You know, just before when I was screaming and moaning, it was all for you guys!" After that she flashed me a wink as if she were sharing some secret with me.

"This is Little Bull-boy," Uncle Xu introduced me.

"I know, he's one tough cookie." Apricot winked at me again. She then took out a Marlboro, lit it up, and as she continued, a thin, long trail of smoke prepared to exit through the hole in the window screen. "So what's up? I heard that you've run into another little complication."

I think it was about this time that I passed out from all that booze. But later Apricot told me that Uncle Xu put something in my drink. After I heard this I was a bit pissed, but Apricot said it was for my own good. She said that there are some contradictions about making it in the streets—sometimes you want to know everything, and sometimes it's best you don't know so much. Whether I was drunk or drugged actually isn't that important, I just hazily remember Uncle Xu asking Apricot to help him out with something when their voices began to slow down, and between every word was the sound of waves. Later I think Annie approached me and wrapped one hand around my cheek and caressed my hair with the other. The strange thing was that she really was wearing a pair of sunglasses.

At that port where the blaring of the sun causes everyone's vision to go blurry and head to feel dizzy, people from all over the world come and go, and for some reason or another, everyone is happy. On the beach I heard people speaking in slow motion.

"This has nothing to do with whose territory it is! You do your business, and I'll do mine!" a man said.

"That's right! That's how it's always been," a woman replied.

"He's probably after me," another woman said. "You know, Golden Nine's place?"

Everybody was ecstatic, but for some reason I just couldn't locate the people talking. I started to get a bit anxious. There were more and more people at the port, more and more people. But among the crowds there wasn't a soul that I knew; I couldn't find any of my friends. And then my father's voice jumped into my ear: "Big Head! Why aren't you wearing any pants?"

"I *am* wearing pants!" I retorted.

CHANGES

In the end I called Huang Munan after all—Annie and the others had no idea I made the call. It was during the second morning we spent in the third hotel. Annie was out buying the newspapers, Little Horse was asleep in his room, and the hotel manager was on the couch picking out the gook from between his athlete's foot-infested toes when I did it. It was a Sunday and the weather was clear. I collected the loose change Annie had left on the dresser at the foot of the bed and dropped the coins into the public phone in the nearby alley. As I picked and tore at the utilities' and moving companies' advertisements pasted on the alley wall, I listened to Huang Munan's report of what had happened that week at school.

When Huang Munan heard my voice he must have been scared out of his wits, and then he gleefully gave me a wolf howl—that was our basketball team's cheer. He said that everybody in the world plus everybody in the universe was all out looking for me. I said I knew. He said it was really out of control, even the cops were out trying to find me. Once again I coolly told him I knew. He asked where I was, and I told him I was some-place. He said that's good, he said he knew I wouldn't tell him. I said then what the shit are you asking for? He said that he was asking shit from the beginning—what he meant was I was a piece of shit.

But Huang Munan still carefully told me all about what had happened that week at school.

On Tuesday during the flag ceremony, Mr. Hippo announced my "un-fortunate incident" to the entire student body; he included my burning of the exam books and assaulting a teacher as being unforgivable behavior. I retorted to Huang Munan that I wasn't the one who burned the exams. Huang Munan said, "Who cares what you say, anyway? Everybody was re-ally happy for you."

However, the really sticky part came later. . . .

The Department of Education sent a guy to school twice; one of the times my mother went along, and so did the police. And then the rumor started going around school that third-grade student Hou Shichun had been kidnapped. Someone even said that before long my picture would begin to appear on the glass doors at 7-Elevens. "Beside that, Weng Jia-ping has allegedly already begun a new story, it's called something like 'The Final Battle of Big Head Monkey and the Hippo Monster.' More-over, the first chapter already appeared Thursday evening on the Internet!" I told Huang Munan to tell Weng Jiaping not to go overboard, otherwise I'd send someone to teach him a lesson, I'd fix him so good that it would hurt to even blink his eyes.

Huang Munan also told me something funny: when Mr. Hippo went to confiscate my belongings, he got the wrong seat and ended up taking all of Chen Guoqing's stuff. By the time he figured out he got the wrong desk and went back to switch the stuff, Li Ahji had already hidden my Bat-man stickers, toy handcuffs, and shit-shaped crab shell. The funniest part was that when the principal's office sent a notice for Chen Guoqing to pick up his stuff, he rushed down only to find that only one of his super, super-cool gym shoes was left.

"Do you need anything else out there?" That is what Huang asked me after he told me everything that had happened—including the incident of the piano lid slamming down on Mr. Jiao's fingers.

"Nope!" I answered.

"So then what are you doing out there?"

"Nothing much, just hanging."

"Damn! You've really become cool!"

"Not really."

"Did you smoke any amphetamines?"

"Smoke your mother!"

"Did you see any gang leaders?"

"There's been a couple here and there."

" . . . "

" . . . "

"Mr. Jiao's fingers got caught in the piano lid."

"You just told me."

"Oh, okay then. Well . . . well, I guess I'll see you later."

"Bye."

As I hung up the phone, I had a strange feeling that something had changed. I figured that Huang and my other classmates must also have felt that I'd changed, even though, as I knew, from elementary school, when I'd begun to understand things, all the way up until today I'd barely changed at all. However, in the past couple of days something must have happened that made me miss them so, while at the same time leading me to feel that I would never again be as childish as they were. I truly had this kind of a feeling.

The person who pushed the whole incident to the point of no return was my mother. Moreover, the prediction of that classmate of mine who said that my picture would start showing up on the doors of local 7-Elevens unexpectedly became a reality. Only I didn't show up on one of those little missing child posters; my luck was a bit worse—my picture must have been several hundred times larger than those little checkered posters they usually put up.

At first, everything was fine that Sunday. Just after I got back to the room from making my phone call I saw Apricot push open the door and come in with a big bag and a little bag of what looked like breakfast. She told me to go wake up Little Horse, saying that Uncle Xu and the others would be here any minute. I asked why everyone was coming. She thought for a second before responding, "Isn't today Sunday? Doesn't everybody get together on Sundays?" Everybody really did come; even alien eyes Ahzhi showed up. When Ahzhi saw me he raised the edges of his mouth—was that a smile? "Sorry about before!" he said. Finally Annie came back from buying the newspapers and pranced in. She seemingly could care less that the room was suddenly crammed with so many people; she just concentrated on reading the paper and biting her fingernails. I on the other hand was really overjoyed; everybody's head was bobbing with joy; except for Hoop, everybody was there.

"Can we start?" Apricot asked.

"Hoop's not here yet," I cried as I looked at everyone, but in the end no one paid any attention to me.

"Annie!" Uncle Xu called out to Annie, even though his eyes were staring at me. Uncle Xu continued, "Apricot said that bastard Horsefly finally talked; he only said one sentence: 'We'll work it out.' I think everything should be fine. Go take this little Bull-boy home!"

Annie continued reading her newspaper just like before.

Uncle Xu went on, saying to me, "You got a free ride with us for the past couple of days, just feeding you almost put me out. This is where we say 'bye bye.' . . ."

Before I had time to say anything, Annie had already knitted her brow and handed the paper to Uncle Xu. Her finger was pointing to some news article as she said, "We've got a bit of a problem."

Uncle Xu glanced at the newspaper, eyed me for a second, glanced back at the paper, and then shook his head. And so the paper passed from Uncle Xu to Little Horse to Little Xinjiang. Old Bull, who was standing behind Little Xinjiang, cried out when he saw the article, "Damn! Little Bull-dick, your mom is the 'Commercial Queen'!"

That's right! That successful advertisement tycoon they call the "Commercial Queen," Jade Aroma Chen, is my mom. The newspaper headline read: COMMERCIAL QUEEN'S HEART BREAKS THINKING OF LOST SON, CRACKER-JACK HANDS DESIGN POSTER IN HOPE OF SON'S EARLY RETURN. Underneath the headline there were two more lines: EXPRESSING ITS CARE FOR THE YOUTH, THE NEW ERA CULTURAL AND EDUCATIONAL FOUNDATION BEGINS LARGE-SCALE FUND-RAISING PROGRAM. COMMERCIAL QUEEN IMPLORES SOCIETY TO JOIN IN THE SEARCH FOR HOU SHICHUN. Displayed below these two smaller lines was a pair of pictures. The first photo was of my mother and some old man in a suit who had his hair up in a classical-style bun. Together they were holding a poster. It was me on the poster. But did that image of me count as a photo? It was the kind of image made up of tiny black dots; up close it just would have looked like a bunch of black dots, but from far away it looked like me. Just above my black dot face were a few words: ETERNALLY SEARCHING FOR YOU, MY SON! I couldn't read the smaller print, so who gives a damn what else it said. The second picture was of me. I remember the photo being taken on the beach when my dad took me to Spain. That was one super-ugly picture, because just as Dad was about to snap the shot he told me, "Your fly's down!" I looked down to discover it was up the whole time. I angrily glared back at my father and that was the moment he took the shot. And so I ended up looking just like a communist bandit in the picture.

But this was nothing compared to the news, which really blew things out of proportion. The news article read:

> Commercial Queen Jade Aroma Chen is a well-known figure who actively takes part in various activities for the public welfare. Having experienced the misfortune of a failed marriage, she threw herself wholeheartedly into her career and social work, but in the end, who could predict that she would neglect properly disciplining her son? Recently her only son, Hou Shichun, suddenly disappeared without notice, running away from home. Not long before, Hou Shichun was involved in a case of damaging public property on his school campus; moreover, owing to harbored resentment, the accused student went so far as to assault a teacher. As ill fortune has already befallen Mrs. Chen, she has resolved to draw a lesson from her painful experience. Paying no heed to the social convention of "not washing one's dirty laundry in public," Mrs. Chen has bravely stood up. She has taken her own bitter experience as the inspiration and theme in designing a fund-raising activity poster for the New Era Cultural and Educational Foundation, which has long been concerned with problems facing today's adolescents. In the text of the poster, Jade Aroma Chen uses her own experience as a point of departure. Written in the first person, Mrs. Chen's sincere and highly personal message confesses her own heartfelt emotions. She writes: "My child! Your mother is here, your family is here.

The road back is in your heart; give your mother a chance; let us grow together!" The Foundation will assume the responsibility of printing the posters and distributing them to supermarkets, convenience stores, karaoke clubs, and other places frequented by adolescents.

Beneath this report was yet another article. It read:

Since the "Hou Shichun Incident," the Department of Education and the Police Department have been in contact with both the New Era Cultural and Educational Foundation and Mrs. Jade Aroma Chen. Both departments have expressed that the increasingly critical nature of adolescent problems requires a concerted effort of cooperation between the family, schools, and related governmental departments in order to reach a resolution. The incident of a single teenager running away from home, with no news of his whereabouts, is but the "tip of the iceberg." What this incident tells us is that not only in our society but in our very schools there still exists an untouched corner, a corner waiting to be noticed by people of conscience. One reporter asked whether this issue was receiving so much attention solely on account of it being a well-known figure's son who disappeared. The consistent reply from both the Penal Division of the Juvenile Correction Department and the individual in charge of the Municipal Adolescent Correctional Facility was "definitely not." Moreover, the police added that they already had their hands on solid clues and that Young Hou should soon be able to return home.

"It's not so bad," said Uncle Xu. "So far they don't have shit."

"But as soon as the kid goes home, the cops will come knocking on our door," said Little Horse.

"But he can't stay with us forever," said Uncle Xu. "And now we have to take care of things with Horsefly as well."

"And there's more!" Apricot exclaimed as she waved the newspaper. "Sooner or later Horsefly is going to find out about this."

After that everyone stared at me as if they were all thinking of some person or some secret. It was a bit strange—they were all talking about me and seemingly all worried about what would happen to me, yet they all kept ignoring me. All I could do was snatch the paper from Apricot's hands and read through that section my mother had written. I read through twice and the more I read the more I felt it was unlike anything that my mother would normally say. But it was indeed a little bit like an emotional lyric essay—after reading it you had a pins-and-needles feeling deep in your heart. Maybe my mother really did miss me. This is what they mean by "you don't know what you've got until it's gone."

"Little Bull-boy . . ." Annie raised that set of thin, long eyebrows and laughed. "What do you think?"

I glanced at the newspaper and thought to myself: Why don't you just go on eternally searching for me!

SECRETS

Before the Sunday get-together began, Uncle Xu brought me next door to Little Horse's room to talk. At first it was as if he didn't know quite what to say.

"Right now we're drifting, you know?"

I nodded.

"Drifting is like, it's like . . ." Uncle Xu thought for a second, reached his hands into his pockets, and fished around for something. Finally, when he fished out a thin, long skeleton key, it appeared that he himself didn't even know why he had taken it out. He quickly shoved it back into his pocket and said, "It's like this. Uh, there are a lot of things that we can't let other people find out about."

"Like secrets."

"Right—secrets," said Uncle Xu. "So you should know that once we are settled with Horsefly, things on the outside shouldn't be as tense, and then you can return home. What I'm saying is that you don't have to keep drifting with us . . ."

"Why?" I asked.

"Because the longer you drift the more you will learn. What you learn affects the kind of person you end up turning into. And then after a while it gets to the point where you can never turn back. That's because you already know too many things that we can't let others find out . . ."

"Secrets, that's what you were just talking about."

"Right."

"So the reason I can't go home is because I know some secrets."

"Right."

"But if I keep drifting then I'll end up learning too many secrets and I'll never be able to go home."

"You got it." Uncle Xu snickered for a moment and then he suddenly took his smile back, saying, "Like what you saw that day, when Horsefly and the rest of them iced that guy . . ."

"I didn't see anything, I only heard them."

"Okay, so you heard them . . ." Uncle Xu forced himself to show me his teeth. "For the last couple of days Little Horse and the others have been doing a little homework; it turns out that that fellow was iced because he knew too much about something he shouldn't."

I nodded, but deep down I started to get antsy. I couldn't tell if it was on my back or my arms, but I started to get goosebumps.

"Let me give you another example: what happened with Hoop . . ." Uncle Xu thought for a long time, so long that I finally couldn't help but yawn before he continued, "Hoop's case is another headache. Little Horse did some digging around and found out that Hoop has been on Horsefly's side since day one . . ."

"So Hoop betrayed you guys?"

"You can't really say that. Horsefly owns Hoop; if she doesn't help him, Horsefly could take it out on Hoop's family. However, as far as we are concerned, Hoop knows way too much, and that's dangerous. For instance, she's seen you and she knows that you were in the van that day. Now that you and your family are all over the papers, who knows if she'll tell Horsefly, and who knows what Horsefly will do?"

"So are you guys going to ice Hoop?" I asked. I figured that Uncle Xu knew that at least part of what I meant was: "So are you guys going to ice me?"

Uncle Xu said there was no way they would get rid of Hoop. He thought for a long time before he said, "You see—now you know another secret."

There was one thing Uncle Xu was right about: the longer you drift the more you learn. During that single Sunday get-together, I learned almost everything. Like what Uncle Xu told us: Horsefly sent Hoop to bring Annie to the casino in the mountains for a little gambling. But some guy played dirty cards with Annie; moreover, he made sure that Annie caught on to his tricks—that way Annie would make a big scene and call in Little Horse and Little Xinjiang. Of course there was another fellow down on his luck who got dragged in as well—me. With a toy handgun and an ice pick, Little Horse and Little Xinjiang fought their way in, bravely rescuing Annie and Hoop. But the whole thing was a trap from the beginning. Horsefly had everything planned in advance. They iced Uncle Xu's cop friend Young River and then used Young River's gun to off one of the casino brothers. Finally they set up Little Horse and Little Xinjiang by planting the gun on them. Right then all the chips were in Horsefly's hands. For the moment he'd kept a hush on the murder of the casino brother, so thus far all the boys in blue knew about was the dead cop. If they couldn't break the case, at the most all they could conclude was that

Young River killed himself. But if Uncle Xu didn't meet with Horsefly to work things out, Horsefly would let the rumor of the dead casino brother out. If that happened, both the cops and the gangs would add Uncle Xu to their hit lists. Uncle Xu said that he hoped Hoop and Horsefly never saw the news about me in the paper. But Little Horse argued that even if they saw it, that didn't mean they would put "Hou Shichun" and me together. Okay, even if they did recognize me, that didn't mean that Horsefly would see me as a chip that had to be taken out. If he did, not only would he get nothing out of it, but he'd end up blowing Hoop's cover. When Little Horse said this I felt like I'd really lost face; it was as if my life didn't mean squat. All I could say was: "Who could recognize me? That picture is way too ugly!" Everybody laughed aloud. I didn't think it was that funny.

But what was really difficult to figure out was, like what Uncle Xu said, just what Horsefly had up his sleeve, spending so much energy on all this. Maybe he was after Bingo Wonderland, or the land where Annie's junkyard was, or maybe it was something bigger. All of this had to be figured out before any negotiations could begin. And so they turned everything over to "the window" to figure out; before everything was clear they couldn't make any move. When they got to this point, Uncle Xu's pair of red bean-sized eyeballs stared at Little Horse and Little Xinjiang; they quickly lowed their heads.

"A real bunch of heroes, you two!" said Uncle Xu. "All at once you save four people—now wait until the day those other two take the witness stand and say you are murderers. Let's see how heroic you are then!"

Little Horse drooped his head even lower. I figured they must have been pretty damn embarrassed. Every time someone around me caused a stink, I would always feel like I myself was a stinker as well. But for some reason, this time nobody said a word, and the silence made the stink even worse.

"What's 'a window'?" I pulled on Little Horse's sleeve to get his attention and whispered to him.

"It's somebody who delivers a message for a gang boss," Little Horse softly replied.

"So how come the gang bosses don't talk face to face?" I asked him with a whisper. I then noticed that Ahzhi and Old Bull were giggling to themselves.

"It's not convenient."

"So then who's 'the window'?"

Little Horse still looked quite ashamed, but at the same time he couldn't just ignore me, so he forced himself to pout his lower lip in the direction of Apricot.

I patted Apricot on the shoulder and said loudly: "Oh, so you're 'the window'!" This little move proved quite useful; it caused everybody to burst out laughing. That scene of everybody together laughing left a deep impression on me because as far as I can remember it was the very last time.

HAPPINESS

If you were to one day ask me if I'd had any happy days since I hit the streets to drift, I would immediately respond: "Of course!" If you then went on to ask when those happy times were, I would probably have to think about it for a moment before I gave you my answer: "During the last couple of days just before the big negotiation, yeah, probably right around then!"

Everything that happened during that time was pure happiness—to give you an example, it was like when you get into a great big mess and your old man, old lady, and all those other old people in your life, like your teachers, still don't know. But while this trouble you started leaves you with long-lasting memories to savor, you understand that sooner or later you're bound to be discovered, and just thinking about being caught makes you terribly sad. At the same time, it is only during this period that you find it much easier to discover interesting and fun things, happy events, and adorable people. This is perfectly natural; before the ax falls you're always as happy as a pig in shit.

Uncle Xu felt that if Horsefly really intended to "talk things out" then he probably wasn't planning to set us up, so we could relax. I remember that when Annie patted me on the shoulder, we got up and started walking toward the junkyard. As we walked on and on, I kept turning around to stare at Annie. At that moment I felt she was the most beautiful woman in the whole world. I truly wished I could keep walking on with her into eternity.

"So you think living like this is fun?" she asked me.

"So far it seems pretty good."

"More fun than going to school?"

I thought for a moment; tests, homework, standing in the principal's office, Mr. Jiao's voice lessons, and other terrifying images passed through my mind. But when I thought of trading stickers with Huang Munan and Li Ahji, and secretly locking Old Jiang, the school handyman, in the gym, or of when we all dumped the garbage can into the pond that the girls were supposed to be cleaning, I thought that school wasn't so bad after all. So I answered by saying, "School's okay too."

"If my little brother were still alive he would be in high school by now—I wonder if he would end up running off like you and becoming a wild child."

"Who said I'm a wild child?" I immediately protested.

"Don't you know? Actually . . ." Annie shook my shoulders, saying, "You're very different from us. Ahzhi, Old Bull, Little Xinjiang, those of us that have a home can't go back, while the rest of us don't even have a home to go back to in the first place. . . ."

"What about Little Horse? Doesn't Little Horse have a family? Isn't his father Ma Jianren that 'despicable man' who runs that hospital?"

Annie hesitated for a moment. After thinking for a while, she said, "Little Horse will probably explain his situation to you."

"I've got my situation too, you know!" I instantly argued. Deep down I was truly a bit ticked off. How come whenever you're happy and things have just started to go your way, somebody always manages to come along and throw you a curveball? I just don't get it! In school, my teachers would always say, "Don't tell me you're going to be this mediocre and incompetent for the rest of your life!" At home, my mother would always say, "Don't tell me you're going to end up like your father, doing everything stop and go, never finishing a damn thing!" And now that I'd hit the streets, these guys were saying I was actually different from them.

"You shouldn't follow our example and end up as useless as us," Annie said. "Don't you know that after seeing that newspaper article, everybody in the gang envies you?"

"That's enough! I'm the one who envies you!"

"Me? You envy me? What have I got to be envious of?"

"You can operate that heavy-duty crane," I replied.

For a moment, Annie was struck speechless by my reply. It was a long time before she finally burst out in laughter. Her laughter was marked with a happiness that exceeded even my own.

During those happy days I learned how to operate a heavy-duty crane. From that time all the way up to today, I've always felt that learning how to operate that heavy-duty crane, and learning how to control that machine that flattens automobile bodies into small iron cabinets, are the two single greatest accomplishments in my life.

Of course these accomplishments didn't occur overnight; I started from scratch. Whenever you start learning something with the very basics, they always seem completely unrelated to what you're actually trying to learn; the junkyard industry is no different. Annie first taught me how to strip the cars of those things we didn't need; this is something that even a dog can do. However, as we were stripping the cars, Annie threw out a few sentences that made me feel that what we were doing was actually quite interesting. Concentrating on those sentences, I didn't feel so much like a dog. She said, "Some of these objects are completely useless here, but somewhere else they might turn out to be somewhat useful. And then in some other place, they'll prove to be even more useful."

And so each time I strapped on that canvas tool belt and climbed into one of those outwardly atrocious automobiles, I would begin to carefully search—search for those items I felt were utterly useless yet definitely had some use somewhere else. Well, let me tell you, boy, did I find some. In one week I found enough items to fill up half of a convenience store.

Every day I found enough change in the cracks between the car seats to buy one or two bottles of Coca-Cola. And if my luck was good, some days I would even discover one or two earrings set with gems. I always gave the earrings to Annie, who wore them every day; it didn't seem to matter that the right and left earrings didn't match. Most of the perfume bottles that I found in the cars were still half-filled; stacking them up in the sheet-metal outhouse made the place smell almost like the cosmetics section of a department store. I even picked up a couple of books; I think one of them was a weekly journal written by some kid, really weird!* So even a weekly journal can be published and sold! Later, one by one, I tore out the pages to wipe my hands on—that little book was useful after all, it cleaned better than any tissue or paper towel out there!

Usually I would work with Ahzhi and Old Bull. But sometimes Ahzhi would have to go to Uncle Xu's friend's place in the streets to make sure everything was under control, leaving only Old Bull and me. Old Bull didn't know how to keep his mouth shut. This was his shortcoming. But his strong point was that he could take the most complicated job and teach you how to do it in the most clear and simple way. What I feared most was getting halfway through stripping a car and having Ahzhi called away to take care of something. Old Bull would start up, telling me which karaoke bar or restaurant Ahzhi was going to, what kind of a chump the boss there was, and just what kind of guy the big boss who ran things behind the scenes was. Then he would tell me which girls at each place were

* This is a reference to the author's 1993 novel *The Weekly Journal of Young Big Head Spring.* The first in a trilogy written under the pen name "Big Head Spring," the work is a highly satiric and comical vision of Taiwanese society, as seen through the mandatory journal entries of an elementary school student.

easy to get on with and which ones to keep your dick away from. Old Bull always said that he'd never tell me which girls Ahzhi screwed around with, but by the next time Ahzhi got called out to some other club, he would always forget and blurt out the name of the girl from the time before. It's a good thing I'm not as much of a blabbermouth as him; otherwise Ahzhi would have whipped Old Bull's ass a good couple hundred times. Later, I learned a special skill: whenever Old Bull started to repeat his annoying rambling, I wouldn't really listen. Instead, I'd just occasionally let out an "Em," "Ah," or "Oh"—as long as I periodically gave him a little "Ah," he'd be satisfied. I think it was from this point forward that I became more refined. In case you don't know what "refined" means, let me tell you. Being refined takes two people, a speaker and a listener. Refinement is when the speaker has no idea what he is saying, and the listener in turn has no idea what he is listening to.

Anyway, I still had a most fruitful learning experience. At first I used an X-acto knife almost the size of a hand saw to cut off the seat cushions—back then I couldn't even distinguish between plastic and leather lining. Often I'd end up covered in sweat, with tiny oddments of sticky cotton soaked in my sweat all over my face. After I finished with the car the ground would be covered with bits and fragments of things I couldn't even recognize. And then one day Old Bull told me that you had to know how the seat cushions were installed in order to know how to properly strip them. What they installed first you took out last, what they installed last you stripped first; it was all a question of sequence. After that Old Bull taught me how to remove a set of seat belts. "This is called the 'inertia reel,' " he said. The "inertia reel" was the first thing I learned how to recognize when I started working in the junkyard. "This is a 'culvert drill hole,' " he continued. A "culvert drill hole" was the second thing I learned to recognize. I will never forget these two things. It only took Old Bull thirty seconds to strip off the seat belt and hand me the four screws. Looking inside the car, he said, "The guy driving this set of wheels wasn't even wearing his seat belt when he bit the big one!"

"How do you know?"

"The screws in the reel were so loose that you couldn't strap on the seat belt if you tried. The indentation on the left is so deep it must have been caused by a major accident." Old Bull climbed out of the car and went around back to check out the rear. As he brushed the oil and dust from his hands, he said, "Moreover, it was a multiple-car accident. At the time of the accident the car was brand new. This unlucky fellow must have been pretty damn lazy—a brand new car right off the assembly line with a broken seat belt, and he doesn't even bother going back to the dealer to get it fixed. He deserves to die!"

This was really interesting. Later I climbed in and out of God knows how many stripped foreign automobiles, domestic cars, luxury wheels, average run-of-the-mill rigs, cargo trailer motorcycles, and stretch cars, and let me tell you, I could always tell what each car was like before it met its end.

It was actually Ahzhi who was completely indifferent to all this. Once I told him: the owner of this Opel had a dog with long white fur. He answered, "Boring!"

Normally during the daytime, Ahzhi's larger eye would shrink slightly and his small eye would expand a bit, so his face didn't appear as terrifying as usual. I think this was because there were fewer ghosts running around during the day to aggravate his alien eyes. When Ahzhi wasn't communicating with ghosts, the only thing he seemed interested in was machinery. And he never brought up his escapades with women. He just told me not to waste all my time wondering what this or that automobile used to look like. A car was just a car. He said that even an abandoned, demolished car was still a car. Pick any one of these cars, they've all got 13,000 parts, 1,500 of which operate together at the same time. Moreover, each one uses 60 or 70 different types of materials. "You should try to understand how the cars work, and stop fantasizing about where the damn things come from."

Ahzhi is the person who taught me how to truly understand an automobile. He would always be saying that an automobile is something that should never have to break down. A car isn't like rice, vegetables, fruit, or people, which all go bad after a while. The material that a car is made from is extremely resilient; it should last far longer than any person. Each time he stripped off some part, he would always say that the part was still good—it may not have been new, but it was still good. Once after we spent half the day taking apart a 70 or 80 percent new engine, we sat down on the dirt slope to take a breather. That engine was placed on the ground with its bottom axle directly facing us.

"Uncle Xu said that an engine like this revolves 6,000 times in one minute!" Ahzhi said. "Fuck! Imagine how useful it would be if you could grow one of these on your body!"

I thought what he said was really funny, assuming he was going to go on about how much having an engine like that would improve his sex life, but in the end he just heaved a sigh and said, "Machines are much more formidable than us, they never die. A person can't even come close. When we are alive we are already feeble enough, not to mention what happens after we die."

"Can you really see ghosts?"

He nodded.

"Don't you get scared?"

"They are even weaker than you, what the hell is there to be scared of?"

"Did you learn your 'super-chops' martial arts skills from those ghosts?"

"I never set out to learn anything." Ahzhi eyed me for a second and then turned to gaze at that axle, saying, "Humans are extremely feeble and decrepit animals. There's no point in learning anything."

"But I learned a lot from you!" Somewhat excited, I pointed to the engine axle and said, "That's the vibration damper, that's the crank, lubrication oil comes in through those holes over there, over here is the flywheel . . ."

"So what's the use? What part of your body can revolve 6,000 times in one minute?"

That's the kind of guy Ahzhi is. When I was just learning how to operate that crane and picked up a U-shaped BMW, turned it 360 degrees, and set it back down in its original spot, Little Horse, Little Xinjiang, Old Bull, and even Annie all gave me a round of applause. Ahzhi was the only one who didn't clap. But later, after I learned how to operate the compactor and crush automobile frames flat, I could suddenly relate to what Ahzhi was feeling.

"This set of wheels is really wasted this time!" I exclaimed.

"It's just an empty frame," replied Annie. "It was wasted before it even showed up on our doorstep."

I don't know why, but every time I thought back to that last sentence spoken by Annie, I couldn't help but feel that she wasn't talking about cars, but about all of us—especially Tarō.

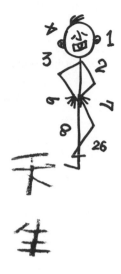

Many of the things in life that make us throw our hands up in frustration are decided at birth. Take Little Xinjiang, for instance; ever since birth he's been a foreigner. Everybody in the world knows that his mom made it with a foreigner before she gave birth to him. The foreigner then disappeared, as did his mother. Then after a few years of being raised by a foreign nun at some convent called the Family of something or other, he looked even more like a foreigner. Later, no matter where he went, all it took was one look at his mug and one earful of his Taiwanese Mandarin, and everyone knew that his mom got bagged by a foreigner and that after she got pregnant, this foreign daddy flew the coop. Some people would ridicule Little Xinjiang, some would pity him, and some were really strange—they went so far as to envy him! But no matter if they felt a sense of ridicule, compassion, or admiration, no one could change the fact that his father's shameless act to his mother was, quite literally, written all over his face. Not only was there nothing he could do to change this, but he also had to face the humiliation of having people constantly notice his less than glorious origins. That's what you call a "birth curse"—it means that from birth he was already cursed to live a pathetic life.

Ahzhi's street-side temple style of "super-chops" martial arts was something else that was completely natural. His ability to see ghosts was also decided from birth. I'm afraid that even the seed for his view that "humans are nothing but a bunch of utterly weak, pathetic, superfluous, and obsolete machines" was also planted at birth. Apricot said that even back when Ahzhi was still in the orphanage he never listened to anybody, never learned a thing, and never obeyed any of the rules. Back then he used to always tell the teacher: there are too many people here, there are too many people there; actually he wasn't talking about people—at least not living people. All of the teachers thought that Ahzhi had a screw loose, but the orphanage didn't have the resources to send him to a doctor. So they just decided not to worry about it and told everyone to try not to pay too much attention to Ahzhi. Apricot said it was a good thing they didn't send for a doctor; there was nothing one could do for him anyway, so it would have just been a waste of money. The orphanage didn't have a lot of money to begin with, so if they'd blown all that cash on a shrink for Ahzhi, Apricot wouldn't have gotten to eat as many apples. But Apricot didn't think of Ahzhi's ability to see ghosts as an illness. She considered Ahzhi's true shortcoming to be his innate ignorance about money.

"Damn! If I were able to communicate with ghosts, I'd really put that skill to use!" Apricot would often pat her thigh and sigh. "I wouldn't have to lift another finger in my life. I'd just open up a store, and make money off people like Old Bull. So you don't know how your big sister died? No problem, I'll find out for you! You don't know where your great-grandfather's inheritance is hidden, is that right? Well, that's no problem, I'll ask around for you! Have you seen that movie called *Ghost*? When the day comes that I can make a big killing and rake in a couple million U.S. dollars, I'll close up shop, go home, and count my money till I die."

Old Bull once said that actually Apricot did make a couple bucks on the side off of Ahzhi's ghosts. Sometimes when she was hard up for cash or business on the streets was in a lull, she'd tell Ahzhi, "Come on, take me out for a bite to eat." That meant she was gonna let Ahzhi get some.

After they finished screwing, Ahzhi would be in a good mood and he'd tell Apricot what street or road had a lonely spirit or wandering ghost. Then Apricot would find a way to track down the family of that lonely spirit or wandering ghost to do some business. Sometimes it happened backward: Apricot would first get commissioned by somebody who wanted her to locate some deceased friend or relative; then she'd go out with Ahzhi for a midnight snack; then the last step would be for Ahzhi to get her in touch with the lonely spirits and wandering ghosts. Anyway, Apricot was "the window," so people were usually more willing to accept whatever she said. I believe that things like being "the window" are also decided at birth.

Old Bull's diarrhea of the mouth was also inborn, as was his knack for easily forgetting. Not only did he always repeat things he'd already said several times, he also often blurted out secrets that he'd previously stressed that he would never let out. My guess is that speaking and forgetting are somehow connected in a way in which they mutually complement each other. The reason Old Bull couldn't keep his mouth shut was that he was always forgetting things. He needed to keep repeating things to himself in order to make the words sink in; that way he wouldn't forget. As for the reason he was always forgetting, of course that stemmed from the fact that he talked too much. In order to keep the world at large safe from his blabbering, he had to forget some portions of what he wanted to say.

From birth, I've always been the kind of person who never finishes what he starts. No matter what it is, I always start off gung ho and want to try my hand at learning it, but once I've almost mastered it, I never fail to lose interest. If you don't believe me, you can look at my report card. I'm almost always getting grades right around 70. If my grade suddenly shoots up to an 80 or 90, that just means that everybody else in class got 100. If I get a 50 or 60 that means that my classmates all got around 90. From birth, I've always been a 70, it has absolutely nothing to do with how much effort I put in. Even the appearance of people who are natural 70s is around 70. When I was little my head was really big; in pictures I always looked like a space alien. If I'd maintained the same head-to-body proportion as when I was little, then it would be hard to say what my appearance would be today—probably just a 10. That of course would've been pretty rare, like that mutant child with three legs. I could've sold tickets and taken myself on an exhibition tour. But as I grew, the proportion between my body and head became more and more normal, normal to the point where it couldn't be any more normal—a 70. And so, just like Little Xinjiang's foreign mug, there was no way to alter my appearance. At least Little Xinjiang could tell people he was from Xinjiang in order to cover up his mongrel, half-breed origins. But I was worse off: no matter where I said I was from, it didn't matter—a 70 is a 70. I had a set of features so average that they couldn't even leave an impression on myself!

Little Horse was a different case. Before I understood the situation with Little Horse and his despicable father, I always thought that he was 100 in every category. He was the kind of person who enticed you to always want to take another look at him. Every time you glanced at him you felt that he had to have the most straight and perfect nose in the world. If you took a second glance, you'd feel that he had the best-shaped ears in the world. Then, just as you were on the verge of being utterly stupefied by his looks, he'd blink his eyes and you'd say that he definitely had the most beautiful blink in the world. That is what you call 100 percent good looks. No matter where he went there were always people who took him for some movie star—however, the day the term "movie star" pops into your head, you'd start to feel like you were insulting this "100 percent."

Once you've got 100 percent good looks, anything you do is naturally also 100 percent. Not only can you play basketball, but you can also be an excellent marksman. Not only can you swim, but you can do the butterfly stroke for 200 meters. You're so good at shooting pool that all it takes is three shots and you're looking at a **clean table**. You can play the violin, master Tae Kwon Do, speak Japanese and English—no matter what it is, you do it better than anyone else. So, do you think you've got what it takes to be a 100 percent person? Because that's exactly what Little Horse is. Moreover, what's really amazing is that he never lets others feel that there is anything so great about his being a 100 percent guy.

The day Hoop came to see us with that big bag of tea leaves, Annie was at the auto store settling the accounts, Ahzhi was at Bingo Wonderland taking care of business, and Little Xinjiang was down at Uncle Xu's

place. Little Horse, Old Bull, and I were the only people left at the junkyard. As soon as Hoop showed up, I ran outside to find something to keep
me busy—another one of my inherent defects is that I despise people who
play tricks on you behind your back. I didn't care about the fact that
Horsefly had Hoop in the palm of his hand, or that Hoop was acting
completely in spite of herself, I just despised the way she treated us as
friends, just like before. Shooting the breeze as if nothing had happened.
It was really an injustice—she even intentionally brought up that guy who
played dirty cards at the casino. It was as if she felt like she could cover
up her despicable actions with a few gleeful cries.

Was Old Bull thinking the same thing? After a few minutes, he ran out
of the tour bus carrying that big bag of tea leaves; he said he was going
to bring the leaves to a cool and shady place. I could sense that he was trying to give Hoop some face. But it was Little Horse who gave Hoop the
most face of all of us. He stayed with her, chatting, even offering her some
mineral water, all the way until Annie returned.

"What the hell are you doing waiting on her hand and foot?" I asked
unhappily.

"Don't be like that, actually she's quite pitiful," said Little Horse.
"Horsefly's people are always threatening her father to scare her, forcing
her to do this and that. She has to do what they say. She doesn't have any
other friends. . . ."

"If she's a 'friend,' how come she sets up her friends?"

"Shouldn't friends forgive friends?"

I thought over what he said for a long time, but it wasn't the kind of
thing a person like me can figure out. All I could do was go on like before
in my dissatisfied tone: "Damn, you even get 100 in personal relations!"

"What?"

"I said you even get 100 in the personal relations department."

"I don't get it." He then shrugged his shoulders and left.

At the time I though he was pretending to be modest, but later I learned
that Little Horse truly didn't know what being 100 percent meant—that
also was decided from birth. In Little Horse's head, numbers had absolutely
no meaning.

Lately I've been spending a lot of time thinking about what it is like when a certain thing has absolutely no meaning in a person's mind. Like, just what form do numbers take in Little Horse's brain? Normal people—including myself, a guy whose mathematics grades are usually much more pathetic than most—would never come up with a formula where after 1 comes 2, after 2 comes 3, the number after the number after 3 is 5, and before 5 comes 4. If you don't line up numbers together, add them up, or subtract them, then you're not dealing with numbers. For example, I find it impossible to imagine a lone 26 just standing around, if it didn't come from two 10s and a 6 added together, 30 minus 4, or 25 added together with a . . . In short, if it hadn't had some kind of relationship with some other numbers, that 26 wouldn't be there in the first place. But Little Horse is really pitiful: for him every number is just standing there isolated and alone. The night Little Xinjiang told me this as we were at the shipping yard taking care of Tarō, I didn't have a clue what he was saying, nor did I believe him.

"If you were to write a 2, and then write a 3 . . ." Little Xinjiang wet the point of his ice pick in the rainwater dripping from the ceiling and drew the numbers 2 and 3 on the ground. "All he knows is that they look different, the 3 has got an extra tail." Little Xinjiang continued. "But he has absolutely no idea that 2 is 1 more than 3. Now do you understand?"

"I still don't get it."

"I didn't understand in the beginning either," Little Xinjiang said.

In the beginning Little Xinjiang took a knife wound in the butt and Uncle Xu brought him to Ma Jianren Hospital. During Little Xinjiang's stay, Little Horse would come to the sickroom every day to empty the garbage can. One day Little Xinjiang asked him how old he was. Little Horse thought for a long while before responding, "I don't remember." What kind of person doesn't know his own age? Little Xinjiang asked, "Then what year were you born?" Once again Little Horse thought for a moment before telling him the year. It was a good thing that the knife wound in Little Xinjiang's ass was deep. That way he had an opportunity to hang in the hospital with Little Horse long enough to figure out that Little Horse had absolutely no conception of numbers. In his mind they would always appear all alone for a second and then disappear. He was able to recognize the numbers 0 through 9, and he also memorized the order of a couple numbers, but to him they were just like the North Pole polar bear and the South Pole penguin, destined never to cross paths. There was even less chance that in Little Horse's brain these numbers would have any order, frequency, size, or calculation relationships. Putting it like this, Little Horse wasn't the only pitiful one—those lonely numbers trapped in his head also become quite pitiable. I'm serious! Think about it, you've got a 26 standing there that can't see the 25 and 27 beside it, nor can they see it. It doesn't even understand the left-hand 2 and right-hand 6 that it's made from! Isn't this pitiful enough?

"So all his life, what did he do about his calculation and mathematics classes?"

"He got a zero, what else could he do? Anyway, for him a zero was no different from a hundred!" As Little Xinjiang spoke he wiped the sweat and rain from Tarō's forehead.

"Damn, that's cool!" I said. "Wouldn't that be the fucking best if it didn't matter if I got a zero or a hundred!"

"If you were Ma Jianren's son, it wouldn't be so cool," Little Xinjiang continued. "Little Horse is Ma Jianren's only son, you know?"

"So? I'm my father's only son too!"

"But would your father hope that his idiot son will one day become a doctor?"

At that moment I diligently tried to recall the image of my father. He seemingly never had any expectations for what I would be in the future. Then again, I'm afraid that he never even gave any thought to what he himself was going to be in the future.

On a Tuesday or Wednesday afternoon just before the end of my second term of second grade, two guys stopped me at the school gate on my way home. They wanted me to deliver a letter to my mother. The main point of the letter was that my father had lost at mah-jongg and owed several million NT. Actually by then my parents had been divorced for a long time; it had also been quite a while since my father had disappeared. Later there was one instance when my father secretly came back to see me. He even took me on his motorcycle to play on a mountain near Xinzhu. When we got there I asked him, "So what do you plan to do?"

"We'll see," he answered.

"Did you pay those people their money back?"

"What's a kid like you worrying about that for?"

"That's really a whole lot of money!"

" . . ."

"You probably have to stay in hiding."

"We'll see."

"Wow! A couple million!"

"When money gets to a certain point, it's all just numbers, but they don't mean anything."

"Anyway, I think you're really pitiful."

"Since when can a son say his old man's pitiful?"

I wonder what my father would think if, standing at the entrance of a 7-Eleven at that far, far-away place, he happened to catch sight of that picture of me made up of tiny black dots? He'd probably think: Damn! My son has run off just like me! Or maybe he'd think: Damn! How did Big Head's head get so damn big? It's big enough to scare the shit out of somebody! Or perhaps after he read through my mother's emotional essay, he'd nod his head—just like each time my mom showed him a new product slogan he'd nod his head and ask, "Okay, so what should we order tonight for dinner?" Or then again, maybe my father wouldn't even notice the poster hanging on the large glass window at the entrance of that 7-Eleven, he'd just stroll in and say to the girl inside, "One pack of Sevens."

By now my big head was taped to the storefront window of every 7-Eleven in Taiwan; this was really a bit irritating. Especially when we stood across the street or were sitting in the car waiting for the light to change—all over the place you could see that big head of mine. Annie said, "So how does it feel? Not bad to be a celebrity, huh?" Little Horse said, "When you look at it up close you can barely tell it's him." Apricot said, "If you blow up anybody's picture that big, they end up looking like a movie star." Little Xinjiang's reaction was to steal a poster and give it to me as a present. Old Bull didn't say a word—that day he was running around in circles like a stray dog, turning everything upside down. Each time he bumped into somebody he would ask, "Did you see that big bag of tea leaves that Hoop brought over?" He even used a hand gesture to show us just how big it was; it was indeed one big tea bag.

Actually the one looking for that package of tea leaves was Uncle Xu. Uncle Xu said that Hoop wasn't the kind of person who would think of buying tea leaves for anybody, let alone a package as large as half a bag of cement. After that Uncle Xu told us, "It might be 'Presidential Tea.'"

Those who have never made it out in the streets will have no idea what the hell "Presidential Tea" is. Back in the days when we were living in hotels, our country elected a president. Everybody was really happy about this, as was the president.[*] So in order to reward the people, the president said: "Everybody's been through a lot, please have some tea, please have some tea." And so some of the more important celebrities all over Taiwan received a gift of Presidential Tea. Moreover, recently the word on the street was that Horsefly had over five hundred kilos of this Presidential Tea. That's even more than Big Brother Luo[**] of the infamous gang the Heavenly Alliance received. Even though Big Brother Luo had a seat on the Legislative Yuan, he only got two hundred and fifty kilos! And because receiving Presidential Tea was so glorious, everyone on the street was keeping their eyes open to see who'd get their hands on a couple of kilos. Those with relatively more kilos of Presidential Tea could pretty much pass as "celebrities."

But Uncle Xu said that if Horsefly really gave us Presidential Tea then something serious was going down. That's because it was Hoop who brought the tea and not Apricot. A gift like that may look like a great face-saving gesture, but if, instead of coming from the regular "window," it

---

[*] A reference to the 1996 presidential election held in the R.O.C. on Taiwan, which was won by incumbent Lee Teng-hui (Li Denghui).

[**] Big Brother Luo or Luo Fuzhu was a figure once referred to as the spiritual leader of the Heavenly Alliance (*Tiandao meng*), one of the largest organized crime syndicates in Taiwan. He later turned to politics and gained a seat on the Legislative Yuan.

came from someone you perhaps no longer trusted, it wasn't a gift at all—it was a warning. It was like saying, "I fucked you behind your back and you found out. But I'm not afraid of you finding out, in fact I'm the one who let you find out in the first place. Moreover, I want to let you know that I'm going to continue to fuck you."

There was a downpour that night. Old Bull combed the junkyard with a flashlight in the pouring rain, saying that he wasn't going to sleep until he found that bag of tea. Ahzhi spent the night out circling the big streets and small alleys; every few minutes he'd phone us and ask, "Apricot back yet?" Apricot had already been missing for two days. Ahzhi said that even if she was dead they should have found her by then. Little Horse was sitting in the driver's seat of the tour bus playing with a red paper plane. As soon as the plane left his hand it smashed into the windshield, its nose completely flattening. None of us bothered giving Little Horse any bull-shit—that paper airplane was made from the official letter that came stating he was to begin his term of obligatory military service.

I don't know what row of the bus Uncle Xu was slumped over in, but after a while I heard him heave a deep sigh. As soon as he sighed, I felt embarrassed to continue *crunch, crunch* munching away on that package of dried snack peas.

"Annie! Do you know what?" I have no idea when Uncle Xu began to suddenly speak—from the compartment where we were sitting, it appeared as if those rows of deserted seats were speaking. Immediately after that Uncle Xu's head popped up from behind one of the seats to gaze at us. Uncle Xu said, "Right now there's no place on the streets for us; there's only room out there for those damn 'celebrities.' "

Annie didn't say a word.

"If only Golden Nine had iced Horsefly with those two bullets . . ."

"Who knows, supposing he had, then it might have been Golden Nine sending you tea instead of Horsefly." As Annie spoke she turned to the window, which reflected the image of her face. Rainwater brushed down by the bucketful over the mirror image in the window.

I quickly stuffed a couple dried snack peas into my mouth and asked Annie, "Who is Golden Nine?"

"He's the gang leader who locked me up in that rooftop jail!"

That was the last major face-to face duel in the streets. Uncle Xu said that Golden Nine aimed at Horsefly's stomach and fired two shots. As soon as Horsefly took the first shot he sprang to his feet with a forward somersault and said, "Fuck! Is that all you got?" But before Horsefly even finished his sentence, the second shot fired, also right into his stomach. Once again, Horsefly sprang to his feet with a forward somersault: "Fuck! You got any more?" Golden Nine's hand went limp and the gun fell to the ground. After that Golden Nine took nine consecutive shots to the chest.

"Bullshit!" I laughed aloud, my hand loosened up, and the dried snack peas fell all over the floor. "Where'd you get a story like this? It's just too ridiculous!" However, right at that moment that image truly appeared right before my eyes: one gang boss aiming at another boss's stomach and firing two shots. The stomach of the gang boss who got hit shrank inward and then he sprang to his feet, doing two somersaults in midair.

Uncle Xu had long slipped back into his seat. And the sound of laughter combined with the sighing from before came to me from the rows of seemingly deserted seats. "Don't you like listening to stories about gang leaders? This is what the life of a gang boss is all about!"

"Since when has anyone heard of such a ludicrous final showdown as that? I don't believe a word of it!" But I still asked, "So what happened next?"

"After that Horsefly became the only big boss left on the streets." It was as if those rows of empty seats continued the conversation:

Horsefly has got two right-hand men who are always by his side; their names are Little Five and Ah Dibo. Little Five can break a beer bottle with a pocketknife, so whenever he orders beer somewhere, he never needs a bottle opener. Ah Dibo is the king when it comes to street racing; what he loves most is going out on the highway in his stolen RZR looking for cops to go head on with. But ever since Horsefly became the main boss in the streets, Little Five and Ah Dibo rarely leave his side. Once in a while—but only on extremely rare occasions, when Horsefly wants to collect his money or wants to buy a pack of cigarettes, a box of betel nuts, or a bowl of Prince Instant Noodles, does he send for a helicopter to take Little Five and Ah Dibo on these miscellaneous errands. But even when the two of them aren't by Horsefly's side, they still leave their large, looming shadows with Horsefly—Little Five's shadow is on Horsefly's right, Ah Dibo's is on his left. If anyone isn't careful and steps on one of their shadows, there's nothing that's going to stop that poor soul from taking a ride up shit creek. . . .

It was then that the sound of Old Bull screaming crossed the darkness of night, the pouring rain, the glass window, and the story of the gang boss to reach our ears. That was one extremely, extremely terrified scream.

As we jumped down from the tour bus we saw Old Bull standing at the tail end of the bus; his face looked like a fluorescent light bulb. He just said two words—"A ghost!"—before he toppled over flat like a bowling pin.

Only after Old Bull fell over did I notice that about ten meters away, standing in front of the sheet-iron bathroom door, was a pair of shadows. One was tall while the other was quite short; the taller one yelled out, "Ghost your mother's ass!—Hurry up and help me!" We recognized the voice—it was Little Xinjiang.

The shorter one was wearing a white hat. By the time I got closer, that hat was already soaked and had fallen to the ground—it was made of paper.

THE ADOPTION

I've always wanted to expand Tarō's story, but it's not the kind of thing you can make longer. So I'll first tell you another story—one that naturally comes to mind whenever I think of Tarō.

Once upon a time, near the entrance to our building's underground parking garage, there was a stray white dog. Nobody knew how that dog got there, and no one knew who kept on feeding it. Anyway, it was on this sloped driveway that this dog lived and grew. Everybody got in the habit of calling out to the dog as soon as they saw it: "Little Whitey!" Whenever anyone drove in or out of the garage, as they ascended or descended the slope they would never fail to either honk their horn or, like my mother, swerve from left to right, as if they were afraid Little Whitey would be flattened under their tires.

And then there were those few days—I don't think anyone remembers exactly which days of which month of which year it was, but anyway, it was just for a few short days, that another even smaller stray dog appeared from God knows where. This second stray dog's fur was half light black—but not really gray, and half light gray—but not really white. Hell, even if we knew what color the thing was, there was no way to describe it. And so during those few short days no one knew what to call this tiny stray dog. However, for convenience's sake, I'll refer to him as Little Mutt.

What happened couldn't have been more simple: Little Mutt became the adopted puppy of Little Whitey. During those few days Little Whitey often would sit beside Little Mutt, watching him eat or sleep. As far as I can remember, Little Whitey never once played with Little Mutt. Perhaps that's because Little Mutt was too weak; he couldn't show his teeth, wag his tail, and dance around like other dogs. As for Little Whitey, he was a bit different from before: he would bark a few times at all the cars that came in and out of the parking garage. Sometimes he would even stand in the middle of the driveway, fiercely wagging his tail at all the cars on both sides of the slope.

The conclusion to this story is even simpler. I'm not sure which day it was, but Little Mutt suddenly disappeared—he probably died. Little Whitey stopped barking and went back to his old ways, with no one ever being able to tell just where on the slope he was or what he was doing. And so people driving in and out of the parking garage once again had to be extremely careful.

This is the story of a stray dog adopting another stray dog.

Was Tarō's real name Tarō? We actually didn't know. We called him Tarō because we had to give him some name—so we named him after Peach Tarō, that Japanese boy born from a peach.

The day of the big downpour, when Tarō ducked into the junkyard bathroom with the sheet-iron door, he scared the shit out of Old Bull. From that day onward, Old Bull was really strange. He would always manage to think of some event or some person at the most improper of times. Little Horse said his brain was fried, completely fucked; I think he's right. Maybe there's still hope and one day something will happen that will scare the shit back into him and he'll be okay, you never know.

But Tarō was far worse off than Old Bull. We had no idea how long he had been out in the rain; we only heard him speak a few sentences. One of them was: "It's so cold. So cold!" Another was: "I don't want to go back to the slaughterhouse." And then he said: "Don't want to go to the slaughterhouse." Everybody suspected that he was a child laborer who'd escaped from a slaughterhouse.

The first thing Little Horse, Little Xinjiang, and I did was bring Tarō to Ma Jianren Hospital. The woman on duty at the hospital asked us, "What is his name?" At the time we still hadn't given Tarō a name, so we all just stared at each other in confusion. After that the woman said to Little Horse, "The hospital director said for you not to keep bringing in these derelicts you pick up from God knows where. When you do this you make things really difficult for us." Little Horse rushed into the hospital to find that "despicable man," but he wasn't there. Little Xinjiang said, "Then let's take him to the shipping yard—it's close and it's warmer there." Little Horse said he wanted to stay behind and have a little talk with his old man.

Little Xinjiang and I temporarily adopted Tarō; all together we adopted him for what, twelve hours? And then Tarō died. After Tarō died I told Little Xinjiang the story about Little Whitey and Little Mutt. Little Xinjiang said, "It sounds like Little Whitey was a more able foster parent than us." I replied, "It seems that way."

That afternoon I myself went to work. I placed Tarō's body inside some abandoned car of unknown make and crushed that car into an iron box. Afterward, Little Xinjiang, Old Bull, Annie, and I buried that box behind the sheet-iron outhouse. The air back there wasn't bad—if you took a deep whiff, you could even smell the scent of the cosmetics section of a department store.

By the time Little Horse got back to the junkyard it was already dark out. Standing before Tarō's gravesite, he said that there was something he had to do before he began his military service; he had already made up his mind. We asked him, "Just what is it?" "Can you let us in on it now?" He shook his head.

"He wants to fuck our big sis!" Old Bull joked.

Annie's face instantly lit up with a smile as she replied, "Both Apricot and I would be happy to offer our services."

"You're crazy!" I was a bit unhappy.

This is everything that I remember about what happened with Tarō. It's all true, if I were to go and lengthen the story, you probably wouldn't believe it anyway. From that point onward, every time there was a heavy rain, I liked to stand in a wide open space and let the rainwater soak my body from head to toe—it was also a convenient way to wash my clothes. Each time I did this I couldn't help but think of Tarō's short shadow, and that white hat on his head—you can see that kind of folded paper hat being worn in almost any slaughterhouse. I would then watch as streams of bloody water seeped from the edges of my clothing. Oozing down from the corners of my sleeves and cuffs of my pants, the blood would trickle into a nearby puddle.

THE NEGOTIATION

My account of the negotiation should be even shorter than Tarô's story. That's because all I did was hide behind one of the columns in the lobby of the Lai Lai Sheraton and catch a few glimpses of Horsefly, Little Five, and Ah Dibo as everyone came into the hotel. Moreover, I've already forgotten whether Little Five was accustomed to standing on Horsefly's left or his right. And then which side did Ah Dibo stand on?

Horsefly and his two men walked in a row as they entered the Lai Lai Sheraton, but they didn't walk up the steps in slow motion as I had imagined. Actually, they walked quite briskly, as if they were in a rush; Horsefly even almost slipped—the floor was probably too slick. What's more, they didn't look like they were about to go on any killing spree. In fact, after carefully observing the area from their waists to their torsos, I saw that not only weren't they packing any heat but they weren't even carrying Rambo knives or ice picks!

When they saw Uncle Xu approaching from far away the three of them began to light up with smiles. As Horsefly smiled he extended his right hand in preparation for the coming handshake. While taking the next seven or eight steps, Horsefly bowed slightly forward at the waist and maintained his grinning expression, nodding amiably at the strangers who passed by him! Could he have known them? But not one of them paid any attention to him. Later when I thought back to that day I realized that Horsefly's expression as he smiled and nodded was actually exactly like that of an election candidate hitting the streets to raise votes. After that Little Five and Ah Dibo followed suit. They were both wearing this atrociously putrid cologne. First Horsefly shook hands with Uncle Xu and then Little Five and Ah Dibo greeted Uncle Xu, or maybe it was Ah Dibo who greeted Uncle Xu and then Little Five. After their eight hands had all come in contact with each other, each person extended one of his hands with an open palm in the direction of the hotel bar. After that I just saw four almost identical silhouettes, four almost identical behinds, and eight almost identical legs moving farther away.

This is everything that I saw when the big negotiation went down. It was just the beginning—actually it wasn't even enough to qualify as a beginning! As far as the content of the negotiation goes, all I can do is rely on what Uncle Xu's portable microcassette recorder caught and transcribe it below:

"Come on! Please sit. You also have a seat, have a seat. Everybody take a seat! Relax!"

"After you, please have a seat!"

"No, no, after you, please!"

"It's been a long time, Xu!"

"It sure has."

"Did you get the tea leaves?"

"Yes, yes, I got them. Many thanks, Horsefly."

"Just as long as you got them."

"I got them."

"Golden Nine's wife—that young girl, An, what's her name? An what?"

"Annie."

"Oh right, Annie. How is business going for her? Doing okay?"

"Not bad."

"That's good, as long as she's doing all right. Tell her to keep at it! Oh, how about yourself, doing okay?"

"I'm getting by."

"That's good, good."

". . ."

"About what happened last time—there's no misunderstanding there?"

"No, not at all."

"That's good. That's good, as long as there's no misunderstanding. Oh, that's right, did you get the tea leaves?"

"Yes. Many thanks, Horsefly."

"Just as long as you got them. From now on I'm going to have to ask you to help out a bit more, okay?"

"Uh, sure."

"Come by for tea when you have time."

"I'll be sure to. Thanks, Horsefly."

"Okay then! Uh, I guess I'll be going! Okay, take care. Good-bye."

"Good-bye."

"Bye."

After listening to the entire recording Uncle Xu closed his eyes. Annie pulled the silver hairpin out of her bun, took a look at it, and then put her hair back up. After about five minutes, or maybe a bit longer, Annie appeared extremely reluctant to open her mouth, but in the end she couldn't help saying what was on her mind: "So that's what you call 'working together'?"

"No, that's what you call 'work together or you're fucked.' "

"So what is it you are going to work with him on?"

"Didn't you hear him keep talking about the tea leaves?"

In the end we never actually found that bag of Presidential Tea, but Uncle Xu closed his eyes and said, "It doesn't matter! He'll send more."

Just as arranged, Uncle Xu showed up at two-thirty in the morning of the day Little Horse was to begin his term of military service; moreover, just as Little Horse had requested, he showed up in a transport truck stolen from the shipping yard. Little Horse asked him if he wanted to hop in and go for a spin, but Uncle Xu said he was tied up, he still had a few things to take care of for Horsefly.

"Moreover, I'm going to need a few hands." Uncle Xu let out a yawn, turned to Ahzhi, Old Bull, and Little Xinjiang, and motioned them over with his index finger. "All of you come with me!"

At first everybody ignored Uncle Xu's order, nobody even wiggled a toe, but then Uncle Xu let out another yawn and cursed, "Motherfuckers! Has it been that long since my boot went up your asses? It seems like you already forgot what size shoe I wear!" By then Little Horse had already climbed into the driver's seat of that transport truck and waved me over. Only then did he call out to that trio of sullen, long-faced guys, "It's cool, you guys go ahead. Little Bull-boy's going with me."

Annie rolled down the window in the rear compartment of the tour bus, stuck out her hand, and waved to us.

"So what is it you guys have to do?" I asked Uncle Xu before getting into the truck with Little Horse.

"One of the members of the Legislative Yuan hasn't been a good boy. We're going to lock him up in a dog cage,"* Uncle Xu responded as he rubbed his eyes.

"There he goes again," Ahzhi and Little Xinjiang said simultaneously, with a sigh. They then squatted down on the ground and took turns yawning.

Only Old Bull suddenly turned and sprinted like mad toward the heavy-duty crane. As he ran he shouted, "I've got it. . . ." He went on to say some other stuff, but nobody paid any attention to him. However, all of us knew that he was probably going to run off again.

250

There was nothing Little Horse or I could do about this. He started the engine. The thunderous sound of the truck's engine was like an airplane getting ready for takeoff as it approached the end of the runway. At first I covered my ears, but then after I thought for a second I realized that it was a shame to shut out such an awesome sound! And so I let down my hands and let that unbridled sound, more raw than thunder, a rainstorm, rock 'n' roll music, or the explosive sound of firecrackers on National Day, funnel in through my ears, filling my chest and blood vessels.

We didn't step on the brakes once the whole way; the pavement beneath our wheels was swallowed up by the front of the truck like it was meeting head on with a large, black curtain. The lights that illuminated both sides of the street flew backward one after another—you could say they resembled an army of fireflies or a meteor shower from outer space, but no matter what you called them it would be too late, for in a flash they were gone.

---

* This is a reference to the kidnapping of Legislative Yuan member Liao Xueguang. On August 10, 1996 Liao was kidnapped from his home by four men who, after handcuffing him and taping his eyes and mouth, locked him in a dog cage in a remote area near Linkou.

As the transport truck dashed past the entrance to Ma Jianren Hospital, Little Horse veered sharply to the right and then quickly turned to the left, driving into the opposite lane—we didn't see, nor did we care, if there were any cars coming the other way. We were too focused, our sights set on the three columns outside the entrance to Ma Jianren Hospital, which appeared in our rearview mirror. Do you believe me? Well, if you had been in the truck at the same time, you'd have done exactly the same as us.

And then at that moment, the side of the transport truck met perfectly with the first cement column, sweeping it over. Then came the second column, and the third—they all collapsed. It was a shame we couldn't hear the sound of the front section of the first four floors collapsing; it was drowned out by Little Horse tearing open his throat screaming a string of blasphemous words unlike anything I had ever heard emerge from his mouth: "Fuck you! You despicable dickhead!"

In case God was still asleep, I hope the devil blessed and protected all those derelict losers who were lying in their sick beds when the hospital collapsed! From this second onward, you needn't live another day as losers, nor do you need to spend the energy to become gang bosses, because you're all dead!

After that we discovered that our truck windshield was bathed in splattered blood. Little Horse almost went crazy doing everything he could before he finally turned the windshield wipers on, but no matter what, they couldn't wash away the tracks of blood left on the windshield. Little Horse and I looked at each other and then suddenly burst out laughing. That's because from the beginning those worthless windshield wipers couldn't wipe away shit—the blood came from inside the car, it came spurting out from our own bodies. But Little Horse and I just kept laughing at those stupid windshield wipers—they kept at it so diligently, so uniformly, back and forth, back and forth, but they couldn't wipe away a damn thing. Those stupid windshield wipers were really just too ridiculous.

Moreover, we couldn't stop laughing hysterically like that. When you get to that point you realize—it was that hysterical laughter that was keeping our blood from continuing to gush out, and was keeping our truck moving forward.

"Six thousand revolutions in a minute!" I yelled.

"Six thousand revolutions!" Little Horse, who had absolutely no conception of what a number was, repeated.

After that, did the truck slow down or not? Did it speed up? Or did it finally come to a stop? We couldn't care less. But our conversation was just like it was at any other time, always bouncing back and forth on an unclear glass surface.

"Do you love Annie?"

"Yeah."

"But she's already really old."

"She can't be much older than us."

"By the time we're twenty . . ."

"What do you mean 'we'? You're going into the military today, you're already twenty; but I've still got a good couple years to go!"

"Anyway, you know what I mean. By the time we're twenty how old will Annie be?"

"I guess around thirty."

"How much is thirty?"

"Thirty is . . . it's about the age when her tits will start to sag."

"By then she'll already be an old lady. Do you think you'll still want to do her?"

"Probably?"

"Really?"

"Uh huh."

"Now I understand."

"What do you understand?"

"Numbers."

I glanced at Little Horse and saw that he was still laughing. It was the kind of laugh that lingers on the edges of your lips but never gets stale, like when you're with a bunch of friends gleefully celebrating your birthday. Fuck! I thought. As of today Little Horse is already an adult, but what about me? My twentieth birthday is still so very far away; just thinking about it makes me want to cry.

And supposing that I run into Weng Jiaping in the future, should I tell him all the things that happened? I'm a bit apprehensive because Weng Jiaping is practically an amateur writer; wait until he gets a bit older and he'll become a professional writer. In what ways would he adapt my story to turn it into a book? According to Huang Munan, Weng had already turned me into a Big Headed Monkey and made Mr. Hippo a strange monster. And even though I would still love to read Weng Jiaping's novel, you should know that given the fact that the world is indeed one funny place, I don't think all the things I've experienced are really that entertaining.

Not only that, but supposing that you wrote out every aspect of every event that happened, it would truly be too exhausting. For example, should I let out the names of those kids who burned the geography exams and tell how they got the green safety cabinet open? Supposing I don't talk, everything will be left hanging, and not even the upright official Bao Qingtian will be able to clear my name. But supposing I spill my guts, isn't that too far from the loyal and heroic image that I want to convey? Wouldn't that make all my time in the streets a waste? This is truly just too frustrating a predicament to be in.

Moreover, I was really annoyed at Uncle Xu's decision to join with Horsefly's clique. I always imagined Horsefly to be an extremely vicious and doughty fellow with first-rate marksmanship and martial arts skills. But in reality he looked like a blob, soft and fluffy just like a loaf of Wonder bread; he wouldn't even bounce back to shape if smooshed in on one side. Who would believe that a blob of Wonder bread could just show up and tell Uncle Xu to help out with this, help out with that? He even handed out several thousand NT to Little Xinjiang, Ahzhi, and Old Bull. The first time we locked a member of the Legislative Yuan who couldn't keep his mouth shut up in a dog cage for a few days, Horsefly gave me three thousand bucks. He even stroked my head and said, "Who would guess? You're such a cute little fellow!" Cute? Your dick is cute! For a gang boss to speak like your grandmother is really pretty damn pathetic! It wasn't at all the way a gang leader should behave. An experience like this, for example: supposing I were to tell Weng Jiaping, he'd laugh his ass off at me and who knows, he might even think I made the whole thing up.

There are also a handful of extremely insignificant events that I'm unsure I should talk about. Like that time Apricot disappeared for several days, making everyone anxious and worried. Finally Ahzhi went out to the streets to ask a ghost what he knew about it. That ghost told Ahzhi that he spotted Apricot out near the train station on the street with all the cram schools. Ahzhi then went down to look for her around those cram schools. After poking around for half the day he finally found Apricot in an apartment building that rented exclusively to students from outside Taipei. She was tied to a bed with one foot in death's door. Later he learned that some student who wanted to fuck her brought her to his room. Then two other guys barged in saying the room was theirs; they also wanted to screw her. There was nothing Apricot could do but say, "Okay, but I can't cut you any discounts." They all agreed. But who could guess that after a while yet another guy would show up, saying the room was really his! In the end Apricot didn't make a penny but got fucked by more than thirty little bastards. Afterward she was tied to the bed and scared half dead by a bunch of spiders and cockroaches that were crawling all over the room. Ahzhi was pissed as all hell, so he asked his ghost friends to give him a hand in restoring justice. But, fuck! After getting popped by these thirty evil, little punks, Apricot couldn't even formulate a sentence. How was anyone supposed to know just which kids were the perpetrators? But Ahzhi's ghost friends promised him: just wait until the day before the college entrance exams and they would take a trip to those cram schools and give those bastard turtle eggs something to get excited about. They'd make sure that those little punks failed their exams and wouldn't be qualified to go anywhere besides a pig farm. However, in the end this never happened and the issue was never resolved. And so this story is only an unimportant and very disgusting interlude. I figure that even if I were to mention it, there still wouldn't be anyone who would find it the least bit interesting.

And so, other people don't necessarily want to listen to what you have to say, just as they also don't necessarily hear what you have to say. But people are always interested in what you don't want to talk about or can't talk about, so much so that they always force it out of you.

That's how things are. As soon as you begin to tell people some stories, you're sure to end up in a very bad way by the time the curtain falls. They'll just continue munching on their dried snack peas and sipping their iced black tea as they ask you, "So what happened next? So what happened next?" If not that, they'll say, "No, no, it should be like this! It's much better this way!" Or "No, no, it should be like that! That way is much more interesting!"

And supposing that you don't say a damn thing, supposing that you could forget everything before it even happened, and supposing . . .

FORGETTING

Later—or was it actually before?—I told Annie the story of the roaming prince and the smart man. But I played a trick on her—I changed the prince into a princess. She really liked that story, perhaps because it was so short. After the story I played that game with her. The game was also very short; it ended almost before it began.

"I remember I left home, but I can't recall where I went," said the princess.

"I don't want to know where you went, I just want to know what you learned," exclaimed the smart man.

"I remember I learned how to forget, but I don't remember what I forgot," said Annie.

"I don't want to know what you forgot," I said, "I want to know how you forgot."